BALLAD of KAZIRANGA

DILEEP CHANDAN

Translated from Assamese by

PARBINA RASHID

THORNBIRD

NIYOGI BOOKS

Published by
NIYOGI BOOKS
Block D, Building No. 77,
Okhla Industrial Area, Phase-I,
New Delhi-110 020, INDIA
Tel: 91-11-26816301, 26818960
Email: niyogibooks@gmail.com
Website: www.niyogibooksindia.com

Editor: Manali Das
Design: Shashi Bhushan Prasad
Cover: Misha Oberoi

ISBN: 978-93-85285-88-2
Publication: 2018

Printed at: Niyogi Offset Pvt. Ltd., New Delhi, India

It was evening. The bright moonlight had flooded the dense jungle and its surroundings. The moon, which looked like a huge, round, white plate, floated in the sky. Far away, a village, lit up with the serene moonlight and dotted with mysterious bamboo groves, looked mesmerising. The pucca road that ran through the national park was generally quiet, except for one or two odd cars that ran at breakneck speed, making a hissing sound.

There is a speed limit for vehicles on this highway. However, the speed of the cars goes up as they hit this free road. Many animals trying to cross the road from one range to the other, often get hit because of this.

In fact, many animals die their premature death during the floods when they come out of the forest in hordes looking for some dry landmass. Sometimes, the media creates a hue and cry about it. The forest department employees stop those cars; they even arrest some of the drivers. The local residents and wildlife organisations stop the traffic in protest, but only for a few hours. Slowly, the abnormal situation eases itself out. Normalcy returns. This is how life in Kaziranga has been going on, in a sombre manner.

There were only a few vehicles plying today. Probably because of the government-declared holiday on Lakshmi Puja, the pace of life had halted for a while. Only a few big trucks were moving on the highway. Forget the highway, even the jungle seemed to be quiet. The continuous screeching sound of crickets gave an eerie feel to the surrounding. Far away in the village, some stray dogs were barking. Probably they were hungry or they must have spotted some suspicious characters. They often did so when they saw poachers who sneaked into the jungle in search of rhino horns. Who knows? This year saw the maximum number of rhino killings. Many a time, the forest guards on spotting a bleeding rhino after the horn was severed, tried in vain to save its life. It would eventually die from excessive bleeding.

Kaziranga's history is quite recent, Arunabh recalled. In 1904, Mary Curzon, the wife of Viceroy Lord Curzon, came to Kaziranga to see the world-famous one-horned rhino. Despite spending several days, she could not find a single rhino. Disappointed, she pestered her husband to preserve the one-horned rhino by declaring Kaziranga a reserved forest. After a few months, on 5 June 1905, steps were taken to preserve this 232-square km of forest area as a reserved sanctuary. It is an amazing story. Thanks to his career as a journalist, Arunabh had the opportunity to travel to several dense forests the world over, including the tropical forests in Africa. But his mind kept coming back to Kaziranga, its trees, the animals, the villages and the rain. For him, Kaziranga was unparalleled. Nothing compared to the sunny days and moonlit nights in Kaziranga.

Only a few days ago, Kaziranga was opened to the public. It allowed tourists only for a few months in a year. So, when Amal da asked Arunabh to accompany him on this trip to Kaziranga, he just hopped into his new car and reached Kaziranga. Amal da was his first cousin and lived next door in Guwahati. Amal da seemed to have had enough of his construction career. The famous contractor of Assam, his affair with cement and stones seemed to have hit a low point.

Amal wanted to start something new. Actually, he had made enough money. Of late, he had been getting restless. He couldn't stick to one place for long. He would forcibly take Arunabh to the interiors of Arunachal Pradesh, Mizoram and Nagaland for no other reason than to enjoy nature. Arunabh's sources in those places would often help them in organising those trips.

In the beginning, this looked odd to Arunabh. Did his cousin have a hidden motive? No. It didn't take him long to read his cousin's mind. After all, they grew up together playing on the river bank in Uzan Bazaar.

Actually, Amal da was getting lonely. His wife, on the pretext of educating their two sons, remained mostly in Delhi. Though Amal da frequented Delhi, he couldn't stay away from Guwahati for long. He was attached to his parents, who lived with him. This simple, social guy, even in this ultra-modern, detached city life, couldn't do without his old friends. But most of his friends, neck deep in their family responsibilities, could barely spare time for him. So, a kind of loneliness and sadness filled his life.

Amal da's friend, Hridayananda Saikia, who was a forest officer in Kaziranga, had booked a room in the official lodge, Aranya, for them. They had spent the night there. But this morning, they vacated the lodge and came to Rishi's hut. Rishi, Arunabh's friend, had left Guwahati a couple of months back to stay at Pamua. The village was about three kilometres from the Kohora Range, close to the highway. The village had about

60 families. One of Rishi's distant uncles lived at the far end of the village. After the death of his aunt, his uncle who had no children, left for Haridwar on a pilgrimage. Actually, he wanted to stay back in Haridwar. On his request, Rishi settled down in Pamua, at least temporarily, to look after his uncle's property. Rishi had opened a music school in Golaghat, 20 kilometres from the village. He had quite a fan following there. He took classes thrice a week. On other days, he played the violin and grew vegetables. Sometimes, he played football and carom with the village boys. He also went fishing, and sometimes, loitered in the local market.

The sound of the drumbeats still lingered in the air. The *namghar* was situated in the middle of the village. It had a huge courtyard. Every evening, the villagers sang together in praise of Lord Krishna. One would find mostly the elderly of the village at this place in the evening. But today was an exception. Probably because it was Lakshmi Puja. The daughters and daughters-in-law of each family were busy welcoming Goddess Lakshmi. Nobody wanted to leave anything to chance with the Goddess of Wealth.

This evening, Rishi's house was quiet. He had left for Bokakhat. Amal da and Yashodhar had also gone to visit his friend in a tea garden that shared its boundary with Kaziranga. The manager of the tea garden was Amal da's friend.

This time, Amal da brought Yashodhar with him. Yashodhar was a middle-aged blind man who played the flute on the busy streets of Panbazar. His melodious tune never failed to attract people. He survived on their love and the 10- or 20-rupee notes which they gave him. The owners of the restaurants in that area made sure Yashodhar ate one hearty meal in the evening. At night, he slept on the verandah of the Baptist Church. There was no summer or winter for Yashodhar. The melancholy tunes of old Hindi songs reverberated in the bylanes of the dry city. His ever-smiling face bore a humble expression.

Amal da knew Yashodhar since his childhood. Sometimes, he took Yashodhar home. His parents also enjoyed Yasho's music. If Amal da had to go somewhere for a day or two, he would take Yashodhar along. This time, Amal told him, 'Let's go! Let's play music for the rhinos and elephants,' and brought him here. This was another whim of the eccentric Amal da.

Actually, Amal da wanted to open a resort at Kaziranga. One of his friends owned three bighas of land here. But as he couldn't do much with the plot, he wanted to sell it off to Amal da. The plot also shared its boundary with Pamua village.

Someone rang the cycle bell near the gate. Arunabh, who was sitting in the front yard, trying to shoo away the mosquitoes hovering around him, wondered who it could be at that hour.

'Are you home, Rishi dada?' The voice belonged to a young boy.

Arunabh got up from the bamboo *muda* and walked up to the gate. 'Rishi is not home, Bhaiti. I am his guest, his friend.'

Arunabh, in the darkness, could make out that the boys were feeling a little awkward in front of him. Hesitantly, one of them came forward.

'This is prasad from Lakshmi Puja.' He held out a small packet neatly tied with a *gamosa*.

'All right. I will give it to Rishi. But who do I say it is from?' Arunabh asked.

'Tell him it is from Lakhimi's home.' They both chorused. 'My sister's name is Lakhimi,' one of them explained.

After handing over the bundle to Arunabh, the boys rushed back the way they came. It was a sandy lane which was half lit up with the moonlight and half shadowed by the trees. They kept persistently ringing the bell as they rode.

Arunabh marvelled at how Rishi, a boy who grew up in Guwahati and worked in Mumbai for many years, could leave everything to settle down in a place like Kaziranga. He had no adjustment problems. Though he moved in here just a couple of months back, he was already a popular figure in the village.

But then who was Lakhimi, Arunabh wondered. The boys didn't take their father's or mother's name, but only their sister's name. Was there a romantic angle to their relationship? It will be clear in a day or two, he told himself.

He desperately needed a cup of tea. But there was no gas connection at Rishi's house. Rishi used a kerosene stove instead. And if there was no kerosene, then he used an earthen hearth which was in one corner of his backyard. There was wood piled up next to the hearth. Arunabh didn't feel like pumping the stove for a cup of tea. He was known for his lack of domestic skills. He thought of an alternative. There was this boy who ran a tea stall near the point where the main road of the village met the highway. But today being Lakshmi Puja, the possibility of finding the boy there was slim.

But then he decided to try out his luck rather than sitting there all by himself. God knows when Amal da or Rishi would be back.

Lighting up a cigarette, he secured the door with a piece of bamboo. He slowly walked towards his destination.

It was indeed a beautiful place.

Though he was surrounded by dense forest, Arunabh felt safe as he wandered around in that quiet village. In fact, this jungle, a World Heritage Site, was home to two-thirds of the entire one-horn rhino population of the world. It also had the highest density of tigers compared to all the tiger reserves in the world. In 2006, Kaziranga was declared a tiger reserve. Kaziranga, which completed 100 years as the reserved park, was one of the most attractive national parks in India. No wonder it attracted poachers as well. If the media reports were anything to go by, it was those poachings and the chases between the forest guards and the poachers that were making Kaziranga famous, or rather, infamous.

The road that ran across the village was a wide one. Rishi's house was in one corner of the village, a little isolated. There was a stream that ran behind his house. It originated somewhere in the hills which demarcated the boundary of the village. The sparkling clear water of the stream was used by most of the villagers for their daily needs. There was also a well in the village.

The road was covered with dry leaves. The moonlight meandered through the branches of the tall trees to reach the ground. It was enough to light up the surroundings. Arunabh kept walking slowly, almost like a sick person. He was still half a kilometre away from the highway.

The houses that sparsely dotted the road still bore signs of celebration. There was a lingering fragrance of some flower in the air; maybe sotiyona. It's said if one took in the smell of sotiyona flowers for long, it caused sneezing and cold. But its fragrance was irresistible.

Wild animals raided the village quite frequently. Rishi had warned them about it. From east to west, the jungle stretched 80 kilometres from Kaliabar in Nagaon district to Bokakhat of Golaghat district. North to south, it was only a 13-kilometre stretch. But it had a portion of Sonitpur district and also the disputed boundary of Karbi Anglong district. But did animals bother about man-made boundaries?

Pamua village was established in 1959. Some 23 families of Moriahola, from the southern bank of Brahmaputra, unable to withstand the fury of floods, relocated to this area. Actually, in 1958, those flood victims gathered at the *namghar*. Collecting a rupee from each family, they sent a representation to the local MLA Naren Sharma. The generous MLA felt obliged to help them out. Looking at their valid documents, he allotted this piece of land to them. Gradually, it grew in size and got the status of a village in 1962. There were about 60 families now living in that village. There were quite a few such villages in the middle of Kaziranga. None of them could progress though. There were no civic amenities. They didn't even have land for cultivation, let alone other infrastructure.

The main highway wore a deserted look. Arunabh could see the tea stall. It was visible from far because of the lantern that hung from its bamboo wall. Arunabh started walking towards the rickety stall.

The shopkeeper was winding up. Seeing Arunabh, the short, fat boy politely asked him what he wanted.

The wood had almost burnt out at the hearth.

'Can I have a cup of tea, Bhaiti?'

With a courteous, 'wait for a while, I am making it', the boy stopped what he was doing and started boiling the water. Sitting on the bamboo bench in front of the shop, Arunabh struck a conversation with the boy.

The shopkeeper, Bipul, stayed with his uncle in the village. He originally belonged to Majuli. But two years back, his family lost everything in the flood. First, their paddy fields and then, their village. So, leaving his parents at someone else's house, Bipul came to Pamua to work with his uncle. He did all the household chores and now that his uncle was growing old, he took charge of farming too. In the free time, he sat in the shop to earn some pocket money. He sold tea, biscuits and a few other grocery items.

The boy was short and heavy, but he had a charming face. Bipul placed a piping hot glass of tea in front of him. Arunabh started sipping it. With a finger, he indicated to Bipul that one glass was not enough. He wanted another.

As he was starting his second glass of tea, Amal da's black car screeched to a halt in front of the stall. Parking it at a distance, Amal da stepped out. In the dim light, his face looked sad and worried.

'Arunabh, just ask him if he can make me a cup too.' As he said it, Amal da walked up to the car and opened the passenger door. 'Come out, Yasho!' Amal da sounded almost rude.

Yashodhar was walking unsteadily, holding Amal da's hand. The blind man still had the same fixed smile on his face. The face, however, wore the expression of innocence and bewilderedness.

It was only then that Arunabh noticed the bandage on Yashodhar's head.

'What happened to him, Amal da?' Arunabh was concerned.

'Don't ask. He fell in the drain in Jiaur's bungalow and fractured his head.'

'How on earth…'

'He wanted to walk around without a stick. Didn't listen to me. He said he wanted to smell the freshly plucked tea leaves. As he went out to do that, the idiot fell into the ditch. Jiaur informed the compounder. Thank God he came and bandaged his head. He really has become irresponsible these days.'

Arunabh felt really bad for him. Though Yashodhar was old, his brain worked like a young boy. He would often forget that he was visually challenged. He had dreams. He wanted to do so many things like other people…

Amal da and Yashodhar started sipping tea. Yashodhar made a slurping sound as he drank from his glass.

Bipul finally started closing his shop. Paying for the tea, Arunabh started walking leisurely. There was a slight nip in the air. Autumn was fast approaching. The subtle breeze blew from the west to the east over the vast stretch of Kaziranga. Arunabh took a deep breath. Towns and cities on one hand and this naturally endowed Kaziranga on the other. There was so much of difference…

Arunabh stopped all of a sudden. He trained his ears.

From somewhere, a melodious note came dancing out of a flute and spread around like a young stream flowing through a series of rapids. An Indo-Western fusion tune that had the softness of a symphony, yet was hauntingly piercing. Starting on a low key, it went up on the octane and trembled as it got echoed around. It was a heart-rending note. It was mesmerising. Turning back, he saw Yasho, seated on the bamboo bench in front of Bipul's shop, breathing life into his flute. The smile was still glued to his face, a shy kind of a smile. As if the Little Krishna was playing his flute in the gardens of Vrindaban. The music was absorbed by each element of the jungle around them.

Amal da forgot about the cigarette which he was about to light. He remained stupefied, just starting at Yasho's face. Arunabh walked two steps forward. Even Bipul forgot to close down his shop. The moon, all of a sudden, looked a lot brighter.

Forest officer Hridayananda Saikia was in a terrible hurry. Today's to-do list was a bit too long. Every day was the same for him actually. His working hours started before anyone else in the office and there was no saying when his duty would end. Besides work, there was always some kind of pressure from his friends who were visiting the national park, for bookings, safaris, vehicles and what not. In fact, his friends would even take back some vegetables with them from his kitchen garden when they left. He didn't mind that though. A bachelor, he had no strings attached. All he needed in life was a square meal and a place to sleep. Most of his friends had school-going children. When he saw them visiting Kaziranga with their families during holidays, he would feel lonely for a nano second, but quickly managed to get over those feelings. Who said family meant just people? Wasn't Kaziranga with all its trees, its animals and birds his family? He has been a part of this huge family for so many years now. So, what's there to feel bad about?

His parents were still alive. They lived in Lakhimpur. His two brothers were married and had children. He had a sister who was married off in Dergaon. He loved to visit them and would spend a night or two at their place. He loved to buy goodies for his family members. He regularly sent money to his parents. His life went around Kaziranga and his extended family in the same familiar circle…

Since yesterday, he'd become all the more busy. His close friend, Amal Duara, was visiting Kaziranga. He was not a casual visitor. Amal had some business plans. Amal had rung him up from Guwahati to discuss his plans. He wanted Hriday's advice on his business venture. Hriday couldn't say no to his friend.

They had studied together in Cotton College in Guwahati. They sat on the same bench, shared the same cigarette. There were so many other 'first time' stuff they did together. Whenever he could, he would run to Amal's house in Uzan Bazaar for a hearty meal. At times, Amal even helped him financially.

Yesterday, he met Amal only for a brief period. Amal had not changed all that much. The way he talked, the way he behaved, the way he acted when he was angry and even the way he ate, everything was still the same. The only visible change was his receding hairline. In fact, he was almost bald and now his face constantly wore a sad expression. Even his eyes lost that usual twinkle. It was probably age or maybe the disappointments in life.

The mobile started ringing. Hridayananda had just started shaving. As he ran the razor on his right cheek, he picked up the phone with his left hand. Who could be calling this early? Maybe Amal; to scold him for not meeting him last night. He braced himself for a volley of abuses. Amal was known for his short temper, but it evaporated soon enough. Looking at the tough exterior, no one could judge that he was such a softie inside.

But no. The caller was not Amal. It was a colleague. The buzz was that some minister was going to spring a surprise visit to his office. Media was breaking news about rhino killings in Kaziranga. So much so that it had become an issue for discussion in the Lok Sabha. A few days back, Forests and Environment Minister Jayanthi Natarajan was forced to issue a statement in Delhi regarding this. This year, so far, 65 rhinos died in Kaziranga. Out of that, 20 were killed by poachers, 23 died in flood and 22 died of natural death. The minister had visited Kaziranga to take stock of the situation. The Tarun Gogoi government in Assam had to face the music for not being able to give protection to the rhino population. And the Centre faced criticism from the international community. So, the forest department was on its toes. Those surprise visits by the forest minister became quite a regular routine. That's fine though. In fact, there were other pressing issues to think about. The buzz was that the government was bringing in a small aeroplane called drone to keep vigilance over the rhino population. The central minister had already declared it in the Lok Sabha. The drone was not flown by a pilot. Hridayananda's staff was floating all kind of theories regarding the functioning of the drone. No matter how it worked, its responsibility would eventually come down to them. The entire world was very involved with wildlife protection these days. It was a good sign. If the flora and fauna disappeared, the human race would also disappear along with it. He remembered that in 1988, when 123 rhinos died in Kaziranga, nobody raised such a hue and cry.

His mobile was still ringing. Pressing the receive button, Hridayananda discussed the day's agenda with his colleague as he hurriedly shaved the remaining stubble.

He could see Dijen cooking dal in the kitchen. Dijen worked as a watchman in the neighbouring tea estate. In his free time, he cooked for Hridayananda. This has been the arrangement for the last couple of years. Hridayananda helped him run his household. Hridayananda ate the rice and curry Dijen cooked in the morning before going to office. Several cups of tea and biscuits here and there made him function during the duty hours. Once in a while, he joined his colleagues for a meal at the camp sites. But once he ate a hearty meal in the morning before going to office, he didn't bother much about food. This has been his routine for a long, long time.

After taking a bath and changing into his office clothes, Hridayananda sat on the recliner in the front yard. The morning sun was delicately warm and bright. Dijen threw a fistful of grains in the yard. Immediately, a flock of birds came aiming at the grains. They always did. They felt quite secure inside the boundary of Hridayananda's house. Sometimes, after finishing that fistful, they would surround his recliner and plead with their eyes for another round of morsel. Hridayananda could spot a few migratory birds in the group.

Today, as usual, a couple of kapaus, along with 10 others started dancing as they nibbled at the grains. They made a strange cacophony. Their songs and their innocent behaviour could touch one's heart and soul. It's said Assam had about 960 different species of birds, out which 290 were migratory, flocking in from far-flung countries. Kaziranga alone was home to 478 species, according to a bird census conducted by the forest department in 1999.

A huge, blue bird plonked itself on the branch of a tree that grew inside his premises. It was so big that the branch could barely hold its weight. From his experience, Hridayananda could make out that it was a water bird. The tanks and swamps inside Kaziranga were home to such colourful birds. They painted a beautiful picture against the backdrop of those water bodies. Most visitors were deprived of witnessing such beauties. Only the forest workers were lucky enough to catch a glimpse of such mysterious and breathtaking scenes in the deep of the national park. Especially in the Aarimura, Gathaga, Kathpara and Chalaha ponds, one could often see rare species of birds frolicking in the water. They came from the highest lakes in the Himalayas, China, Japan, Korea and Siberia. There were many species of birds which were getting extinct all over the world. Kaziranga had at least 25 such endangered species.

Dijen placed a small table in front of Hridayananda. After a while, he arrived with a plate of piping hot rice, a bowl of dal, fried fish and green chillies. Hridayananda enjoyed his morning meal while basking in the sun, surrounded by greenery and the playful birds.

Suddenly, the huge, blue bird started making a loud, laughter-like sound, as if trying to catch Hridayananda's attention.

'Hey, what's wrong with you? Go and catch a fish in the pond. You will not enjoy my piping hot rice,' Hridayananda teasingly scolded the bird.

The bird seemed to understand him. Looking quite embarrassed, it flapped its wings and flew away towards the jungle.

Finishing his meal, Hridayananda got up in a military-like fashion. It was almost eight. No more relaxing. Picking up his plate, he ran towards the water tap and hurriedly washed it. He put on his cap before making a dash towards the motorbike. The party was waiting for him at the range. Last night, they heard a few gunshots. The forest security wing started investigating the matter at night itself. They surrounded the area where the sound had come from, but even after three–four hours of investigation, they found nothing. Last week also, they found evidence of poachers close by, but after last night's Bagari Range firing, the forest department was on its toes. Hence the pressure on Hridayananda.

Actually, he couldn't sleep at all. He kept thinking the whole night. If another rhino was killed, he would have to face the music. He would be answerable to the CCF, the director as well as the minister. So what if he has earned the reputation of a dedicated officer?

Though the headquarters were located at Bokakhat, most of the action took place at the Kohora Range. In the official hierarchy, the director was the topmost guy and then the DFO. The DFO was assisted by two ACFs and just one step below were the four officers for the four ranges. Hridayananda was one among them. The headquarters of the Bagari Range were located at the range itself.

Hridayananda started his bike. The jeep was ready at his range office. He would park his bike there and take the jeep to go inside the jungle. The director had issued a strict order to conduct a search operation immediately after he found out about last night's firing.

As soon as he parked his bike, the forest guards came running and jumped into the jeep. Once Hridayananda was seated, Hareswar, the driver, started the jeep immediately. They took the tourist's safari route. After a two-kilometre drive on that road, they would have to enter the jungle from the left side. There was no road whatsoever. They would go by the jeep till they could and after that, start on foot.

The elephant safari and jeep safari for tourists had already started. In fact, the first batch started its safari long before dawn. They stood a better chance of seeing wild animals early in the morning. By 10 in the morning, the elephant safari was over. The jeep safaris had different time schedules.

A forest guard offered him a betel nut and paan. Hridayananda accepted it and put it in his mouth. The first betel nut of the day. A forest guard always kept a few ready for him in a separate container. Everyone knew his weakness for betel nut and paan, and how frequently he needed to indulge.

'Have you all eaten?' Hridayananda asked.

Nobody replied. Except for the sound of the engine, there was no noise at all.

Hridayananda looked back from where he was seated.

One of the guards answered, 'We got up quite late, sir. After the night shift, we slept at around two in the morning. Didn't have the time to cook. So, we just had tea and puffed rice.'

Hridayananda kept quiet. There was nothing that could be said. This was the life of a forest guard in Kaziranga. Away from their families, this is how they lived, braving hunger pangs and tiredness, cold and heat, sometimes even taking a bullet from poachers and dying while protecting the wild animals. This was the condition of a forest guard. They were not provided with adequate clothes and shoes. They were not even equipped with sophisticated arms and ammunitions. There were not even provisions of necessary food supply at the posts.

The jeep came to a sudden halt. Blocking the road stood a huge wild buffalo. It was probably heading towards the grassland which was not far from there. Ignoring the jeep, it stood there for what seemed like an eternity. The only movement was the wagging of its muddy tail to shoo away the hovering insects.

Hareswar was an expert driver. After years of experience in the national park, not only did he know the roads like the back of his hand, but also about animal behaviour. He stopped the engine.

Complete silence. As if the group had stopped breathing.

In such a serene backdrop, the huge buffalo kept standing, as if contemplating its next move. After some time, it stopped moving its tail. Even though it was covered in mud, the animal looked majestic, proudly showcasing its black, shiny pair of horns.

Hridayananda looked at his companions. Their eyes reflected awe and admiration for the beast, although none of them were tourists. Every day, they had such encounters. Yet, every time, it seemed like their first.

After five minutes or so, the buffalo decided to move. With slow, measured steps, it went down the kutcha road and walked into the dense thickets, towards the west. Everyone heaved a sigh of relief.

Hareswar immediately started the jeep. After covering some distance, he maneuvered the vehicle down the road, towards a narrow patch. It was not exactly a road, but rather a track which was made by the footprints of the animals that passed through it. The jeep probably would not move any further. Right. There was a swamp ahead. The jeep came to a halt. And with the swift action, like that of an army in the battlefield, the guards jumped out of the jeep without making a noise and took their positions.

'You all are carrying your guns with you, right?' Hridayananda whispered

'Yes, sir,' they all replied in unison, keeping their decibel low.

The group carried two .315 rifles. In the hour of need, it was a good weapon to tackle the enemy. Or, one could shoot attacking animals for self-defence. They also had three 12-bore double-barrel guns. These were used to scare the animals away. It didn't kill the animals, but made them uncomfortable enough to flee.

Hridayananda gobbled another betel nut and paan before giving the group the go-ahead signal. The mission started in complete silence. They carefully combed every inch of that area. This was the place where gunshots were heard last night. But the mission had to be aborted halfway that night due to dense mist, and of course, it was getting too late.

The seconds ticked into minutes. The guards divided themselves into three units for an effective search. They also went down the water bodies to find out if there was any dead rhino. No, there was none. There was no dead animal, let alone a dead rhino. During their combing operation, the groups came across only a few deers, a couple of hungry jackals and a group of ill-mannered monkeys. Nobody sighted a rhino, dead or alive.

After a thorough search that continued for about two and a half hours, the exhausted guards gathered near the jeep. Hridayananda had given them a time limit.

'Sir, looks like they misfired last night. Probably the poachers have left our range and went to some other area,' said the guard named Haleshwar.

'Maybe you are right! But in all probability you people will not be able to sleep even tonight. Let's return now. We should take a look at the other side of the lake before going back,' Hridayananda said in his no-nonsense tone. Everyone jumped into the jeep.

Hareswar was about to start the jeep, but Hridayananda stopped him with a hand gesture. He suddenly had a hunch. The forest guard group, taking the cue, became alert and picked up their guns.

Hridayananda felt as if someone or something was looking at them from behind the thicket. A pair of eyes with a piercing gaze. Was it really there or was it just his mind playing tricks?

Close by, a heteluka bird sitting on a tall branch of a tree, started making a desperate sound. As if it was trying a give a hint.

Hridayananda took a deep breath. There was a peculiar smell in the air—the smell of the king of the jungle. The source of the smell was somewhere close by. Probably it was feasting on its prey.

There was no time to waste. Asking Hareswar to start the jeep, Hridayananda stuffed another paan into his mouth and switched on his walkie-talkie.

Sitting on the floor of the main house, Lakhimi was separating the leafy part of the greens from the stems. A melodious *bargeet* was playing on the radio, which was kept on a stool close by. The radio was Lakhimi's constant companion. Not that she did not have friends, but then where was the time to go out and meet them? In the evenings, when they met in the village *namghar*, they formed a group and caught up with each other. They exchanged notes on their day-to-day lives.

Lakhimi's house was located right in the middle of Pamua village. Beyond the main house and the courtyard, there was another small house. On the southern side of the premises were the cowshed and a storage room for the paddy.

The cowshed had no walls. The kitchen was a small extension of the main house. The only bedroom in the main house had two beds. One for her brothers and the other for herself. After her mother's death, her father started sleeping on the floor on a makeshift bed.

Lakhimi lost her mother about four years ago. Her mother was the most beautiful woman in Pamua village. A brief spell of fever and then suddenly she left this world, leaving them all by themselves. Lakhimi was to take her matriculation exams that year. But with her mother gone, the responsibility of running the household fell on her young shoulders and there was nothing she could do, except say goodbye to her academic dreams. Her father was forcing her to at least complete her schooling, but she argued against it. What difference would a school degree make in her life? So, she stashed away her books and the school uniform.

She explained to her father that the boys were too young. If she concentrated on her studies, their lives would come to a standstill. Rather, let them study. Once they completed their studies and stood on their feet, would they not take care of their sister? The logic and reality of her statement left Padmeshwar speechless.

Lakhimi was almost done with her chore. Her father had left for office. Her brothers were at school. Everyone ate sticky rice in the morning before leaving home. She was making preparations for lunch. Lakhimi learnt cooking in no time. But feeding the chickens and the ducks, milking the cows and taking them to the field for grazing, washing clothes, sweeping and cleaning the house, and stacking the paddy took away the major part of her day. She was passionate about weaving, an art her mother had taught her before she passed away. Whatever little time she could spare, she liked to spend it on the loom. *Gamosa*, *chaddar*, *endi chaddar*—she was good at all kinds of weaving. Sometimes, young girls and newly married women from the village came to try out their hands at Lakhimi's spinning wheels. Not every house in the village owned a loom. How would they? Most of them were landless. Life was a struggle for survival on a daily basis, trying to make both ends meet. So, weaving good clothes was a luxury most of them could not afford.

Many of them were trying to get out of the village in search of a decent living. Some tried to set up small business ventures. Those enterprising ones made a few bucks during the months when Kaziranga was made open for tourists. But then, nothing was guaranteed.

Pamua was not the only village reeling under the economic burden; from Burapahar to Bokakhat, there were more than a hundred villages. Some of them were established ones with landed people or with a sizable population that were gainfully employed. Only those villages that had come up recently with migrating population were in a pitiable condition. Pamua, surprisingly though not a village of recent origin, was still lagging behind.

Those residents, who had no legal documents of their holdings, lived in constant fear of being evicted by the government. There was some strange news doing the rounds recently. Young boys who went out in search of jobs only brought back home such scary news. They said many Bangladeshi migrants had encroached land in Kaziranga. Not just the Char areas, but also inside the jungle. Lakhimi heard that these people were rampantly killing rhinos for the horn. They were going to create problems for all of them.

But Lakhimi couldn't dwell on such negative thoughts for long. She hated worrying. In fact, the Lakhimis of this part of the world wanted to lead a simple life, without having to worry. But the changing wind in the region was forcing them to anticipate the worst.

Lakhimi went inside the kitchen. It was time to prepare lunch. The watch on the side table in the main house ticked the time as 12.

She was running out of firewood. It was her responsibility to collect firewood for the hearth. Her father, who worked as a peon in the Bokakhat Post Office 20-km away and ran around distributing letters throughout the day, had no time for such mundane things. People knew him as a sincere postman. Everyone was fond of him. People have stopped writing letters, but still he had no respite, except on Sundays.

The firewood Lakhimi put on the clay oven was perhaps moist. The kitchen was filled with smoke. She picked up the kerosene stove with both hands and shook it gently. There was hardly any oil in it. It was difficult procuring kerosene oil. The amount which was sold at the government provisional store was not enough for the month. So, Lakhimi judiciously used the stove and firewood.

Some families in the village had gas stove. God only knows how they managed to get gas cylinders.

Placing the pot on the hearth, she went to wash the rice. Sauted leafy vegetables and the leftover dal would do for lunch. She would put the goroi fish, which her brothers caught, in *khar*. Lakhimi prepared the menu in her mind. Her brothers would be ravenous when they got back from school.

'Lakhimi, are you home?' The voice came from the gate.

Who could it be at this time of the day? But the voice sounded familiar.

Suddenly, an electric current passed through her body. Oh, it was him! Rishi—Rishi Barua from Guwahati. He had been around for a couple of months. Earlier also, he used to visit the village. He had an uncle living in Pamua. In fact, now he was staying in his uncle's house. People said he was going to live there for a long time. They said he was running a music school in

Bokakhat. He was a strange, young guy. The owner of a bearded face, fair complexion and a lean body, Rishi Barua became the most popular figure in the village. He taught the villagers many new things, helped everyone in whatever way he could, right from carrying sick people to the hospital to collecting firewood for cremations. He was someone the youngsters looked up to.

Nevertheless, Rishi was a strange fellow. He cooked his food, grew vegetables and maintained a small garden with beautiful flowers. He also went fishing often, played football, cricket and volleyball with the village boys in the field that belonged to the *namghar*. There were days when he would become a total recluse, talked to no one, played sad tunes on the violin till the wee hours of the morning. But at times, he also played peppy tunes on his huge guitar. A strange character indeed!

Even with the craziness and beard and all, the handsome Rishi sent every village girl's pulse racing. Many fantasised about him. Lakhimi knew it, but she also knew that none of them would be able to express their feelings for him openly. And she? She was no different from the rest. But what was the harm in fantasising?

The major advantage Lakhimi had was that the road that linked Rishi's house with NH 37, which he frequently took, ran just in front of her house. So, she often bumped into him. And Rishi, who was friendly by nature, talked to Lakhimi without any hesitation. Probably her sober and genuine nature must have caught his attention slightly better than the rest of them. Probably!

But how come he was here at such an hour? Wrapping herself up with the *chaddar* and quickly tying her hair into a knot, Lakhimi came out to greet him.

'Lakhimi, are you busy?'

'No…I mean, I was cooking.'

'Oh! Good timing. Now that the hearth is burning, make us some tea, please. I got a few guests from Guwahati,' said Rishi, laughing out loud at his own joke. Rishi had this habit of breaking into splits anytime, anywhere.

Lakhimi threw a quick glance at his three companions. One of them was a middle-aged, sober man. The other guy was of the same age group as Rishi. The third one was probably the blind flute player from Guwahati. Last night, the whole village enjoyed the melodious notes coming out of his flute. Moonlight and melody…

There was a shady corner under the tree in their courtyard. Rishi, like a host, gathered the chairs and *muda*s on the spot and offered them to his guests. Lakhimi placed a wooden table in their midst.

'Lakhimi, this is my friend, Arunabh; he is a journalist. And he is Arunabh's brother, I mean our brother, Amal Duara. And this is Guwahati's famous flute player, Yashodhar. Amal da is planning to open a resort in the plot adjacent to your village. We are coming from there.' Explaining everything to her, Rishi started drinking straight from the water jug which she placed on the table.

Lakhimi was a little worried. Making tea was not an issue. But there was nothing else in the house to offer them. How could she offer only tea to the guests?

Lakhimi rushed to the kitchen and took out the rice flour from the pitcher. She removed the half-cooked rice from the hearth and put a kadai to fry *ghila pitha*. Keeping the teapot on the stove, she started frying the *pitha*s. She could snatch bits and pieces of the conversation that took place under the tree.

She could hear Rishi requesting Yashodhar to sing them a song. Yashodhar tried to scuttle out saying he was having a cold. But Rishi was adamant. It seemed Rishi was actually crazy about music.

Lakhimi was halfway through with her frying, when she heard Yashodhar's soft and nasal tone. He sang with feelings…

> Why did you bring me to this huge world of yours, Guru?
> Why did you burden me with so much pain?
> I do not know you, you do not know me…
> Why did you fill my eyes with complete darkness?
> Why did you bring me to this world of yours, Guru?
> Hey, Guru, my Guru…Guru…

The singing session went on. The tea was brewing. Listening to Yashodhar, Lakhimi felt sad. Why did Yashodhar have to sing such sad songs in the middle of the day? He was talking about his sad life through his song.

As she came out carrying the four cups of tea on a huge plate and the *pitha*s on another, Lakhimi found all three of them stupefied. Only Yashodhar, with his omnipresent smile, tried to feel his surroundings by moving his head.

Lakhimi felt awkward. Was she late in offering them tea? But then that much time was required to make tea and *pitha*. What was wrong?

The sound the plates made as she placed them on the table, brought all three of them back to the present.

'Have tea. There is nothing else in the house. Just plain tea…' Lakhimi said softly, as she wiped her hands in her *chaddar* to hide her nervousness.

'What plain tea? You have made so many *pitha*s in such short notice,' Rishi said in a tone as if he was being forced to say something. She noticed Rishi's friend, the journalist, Arunabh or whatever his name was, staring at her.

A couple of betel nuts fell from the tree, very close to the person who Rishi introduced as Amal da. He was startled and almost jumped out of his seat. He looked up at the tree with suspicion. How could a huge man like him get scared so easily! Lakhimi tried to conceal her laughter. She turned crimson as she looked up and saw a squirrel jump out of the tree after doing the damage.

On the pretext of getting them betel nut and paan, Lakhimi dashed into the house. As she came out with the traditional *bota*, Lakhimi saw the last of her *pitha*s being devoured by her guests. She felt bad. They must have been really hungry. There were no more fried *pitha*s to offer them.

'You made yummy *pitha*s, Sister. So fresh! We don't get to eat such *pitha*s in Guwahati,' Amal da said with a burp as if to prove his point. Lakhimi felt even though his statement was sincere, it had some undercurrent.

'There was nothing else in the house. Do come back again. I will serve you different varieties of *pitha*s,' Lakhimi meant what she said.

Though they came from a big city, they seemed like good people. They got to be good, after all, they were Rishi's guests.

Putting a paan into his mouth, Amal da lit up a cigarette. Arunabh too followed suit, borrowing a stick from Amal da's packet. They sat there for some more time. They discussed some plans and Rishi and Amal da took notes.

'Lakhimi, once the resort is completed, you will have to supervise things. We are going to employ village people for everything, right from the cook to the security men.' Rishi said it on a serious note, looking hopefully at her. Lakhimi felt more awkward. 'Why is he giving me so much importance?' Thousands of thoughts that crossed her mind made her all the more unsure. What was she supposed to answer?

'That's alright! Let it come up first. Rest of the things can be taken care of later,' she was not sure of herself as she said this.

'Oh, no no! Every detail has to be sorted out at this planning stage. Only then we can start the resort by the end of next year. Rishi has told me about you. That's the reason we came to meet you,' Amal da snatched the conversation.

What was she supposed to say? She kept quiet. With her downcast eyes, Lakhimi saw Arunabh still staring at her. She felt terribly uneasy. She had never seen Guwahati. She didn't even know much about the big city. Would this group of people, whom she liked at the first meeting, be able to mix up with the village crowd? Rationalising her thought process, Lakhimi tried to gain control over the situation.

After another round of paan, the group got up to leave. Lakhimi trailed behind them till the gate, to see them off. Crossing over the bamboo poles of the gate, they got into the huge car. Rishi guided Yashodhar to the back seat. Amal da sat in the driving seat.

Even though the car was started, Rishi came back and stood close to her. 'Please don't mind, Lakhimi. We troubled you,' he looked into her eyes with a strange look as he said that softly.

The word 'Rishi' meant the one who denounced the materialistic world for the spiritual one. The man lived up to his name.

'What are you saying? I enjoyed your visit. Bring your guests for lunch one of these days,' Lakhimi tried to sound casual when she could barely conceal her happiness. There was a tug of war between the head and the heart.

Rishi, on the other hand, didn't wait for her reply. Saying what he had to, he dashed off and sat in the car. Leaving behind a trail of exhaust fume, the car sped off.

Even after the car was out of sight, Lakhimi stood there, holding onto the pole of the gate. A feeling of emptiness engulfed her. Those parting words and the image of him looking deep into her eyes kept flashing on her mindscape. There was an emotional upheaval. Along with Rishi's face, there was another face that kept flashing in her mind. The face of her mother. There was some kind of resemblance between the two. Maybe it was the way he talked and conducted himself. This was probably the reason why she felt drawn to Rishi since the first time they met.

With a heavy heart and even heavier steps, she returned to the house. She glanced at the empty chairs laid under the tree. The voice of Yashodhar kept ringing through that emptiness...

> Why did you bring me to this huge world of yours, Guru?
> Why did you burden me with so much pain?

A pigeon somewhere crooned, emphasizing the hollowness of the day. The emptiness of the surroundings matched the emptiness in her heart. She missed her mother terribly. Why did she have to leave them so soon? Who could answer that? Four years have gone by, but there was not a single day when Lakhimi didn't miss her first thing in the morning.

Lakhimi was born in this obscure corner of Kaziranga. She heard that the world was huge. The moon she worshipped during the month of Kati, people had landed on it. Now, the Chinese were planning to set up a village on Mars. She heard her father, who read about it in a newspaper on his trip to the town, narrating it to her brothers. But why on earth, mankind that could conquer such distant planets, not able to eradicate malaria from Kaziranga? Her mother breathed her last because of it. Just two days of fever and she was gone. Not just her mother, but every year, three or four people died of malaria in her village. Medicine didn't help. That's why most people believed it was the hand of the supernatural. With her limited knowledge, she knew that whether ghosts killed people or not was not sure, the monster called malaria definitely did. Malaria killed people throughout Assam. In fact, more than two lakh people died of malaria in India. That was what Rishi had said in front of the congregation at the *namghar* recently. He said that in states such as Orissa and Jharkhand there were more deaths due to malaria than in Assam.

The trend of thoughts brought back the memories of the last few moments of her mother like a flashback. Everyone thought it was simple fever. They had no clue that she was about to leave them forever. But probably her mother had known about it. That was why in the hour of dawn, she had clasped Lakhimi's hands with her own and looked at her with sad eyes. There was no time for her mother to teach her the ways of the world. The whole thing felt so surreal...

Four years had gone by, but Lakhimi did not forget anything; the memory still vivid. Every day, as she lit a diya in front of her mother's picture, she recalled each and every detail. But she never showed her pain, either to her brothers or her father.

The fire in the hearth was dying. Putting a couple of firewood, she started blowing it with a hollow pipe. She did everything mechanically. It lit up finally. The crackle of the fire broke the silence. Somewhere far, suddenly, a group of dogs started barking, bringing Lakhimi back to reality.

A feeling of uneasiness crept upon her.

Dogs don't bark in unison in the middle of the day. Something must have happened or they must have seen something. Many a time, wild animals from the jungle came out on the road. That may be the reason for their anxiety. Some hungry animal or a herd of animals must have come out in search of food.

She didn't have to wait for long to find out what had caused the uproar.

Proving her suspicion right, a group of people from a corner of the village started screaming at the top of their voices, 'Tiger, tiger! Save the goat…chase him…'

Lakhimi took out the big Naga knife from the kitchen.

A thin envelope of mist covered Kaziranga in the evenings. The days were still hot though. Just a brief spell of drizzle and the tourists were forced to take out their woollens. Global warming was making an impact, even in Kaziranga.

When Amal talked to his mother on the phone that evening, he got to know that it was getting cold in Guwahati also. At least, there was no need for the fan any longer. After chatting with his wife and sons over the phone, he got to know that in Delhi, the winter had already set in.

Amal was sitting with his friend, Hridayananda. Arunabh, Rishi and Yasho were also present. The backyard of the house shared its boundary with the jungle of Kaziranga. Dijen, in a separate room near the courtyard which was being used as a kitchen, had already started preparing dinner.

Amal and Arunabh had gone fishing during the day. All they could, however, manage to catch was a few small fishes. So, in the evening, they went to Bokakhat and bought a huge sital fish. Dijen had bought two big desi chickens from the village. It was a feast. Amal had just sealed the land deal with his friend by giving him the initial amount. Now, the deal was final. Hridayananda didn't have much to do, except give them company, and of course, lend them the kitchen and the cook.

The situation in Kaziranga was not too pleasing.

Hridayananda was busy day in and day out, but it was his responsibility to entertain Amal.

Amal was special. He wished he could offer his help with the project. He tried to mediate the land deal and pressurise the owner to lower the price though. However, he felt the money was not an issue with Amal. It did not bother him much. Probably, as a contractor he earned enough. Maybe, he was not even trying to make money through this resort business.

Hridayananda increased the volume of his mobile's ringtone so that he would not miss any important call. Off and on, he kept on checking with the guards through the walkie-talkie. He had informed the DFO about his guests at home, but nevertheless, he kept his walking shoes, hat and the jacket ready so that he could leave in a moment's notice, if the need arose.

They lit a bonfire in the courtyard. It was not cold enough to light a fire, but then what was a feast without a bonfire? Rishi took over the kitchen. Dijen stood dutifully, providing him all the help that was required. Rishi loved to cook. And he loved to feed people.

Amal's companion, Arunabh, was quiet most of the time. In fact, he was busy typing on his laptop. Arunabh had joined a South India-based bimonthly magazine as its North-eastern correspondent. So, there was no daily deadline pressure to file stories. His job was to write analytical pieces on subjects that found flavour with pan-Indian readers. That too, one write-up in 15 days. He was enjoying his new assignment. Even the salary was much higher than his previous one.

In between sipping the whiskey from the glasses kept on the side table, Amal and Hridayananda discussed the important paperwork to be done before starting the resort. Arunabh too enjoyed a peg and fish fry.

Yashodhar was getting bored, left all by himself. He kept yawning. But then he never complained about anything. With the bandage on his head, he looked weird.

'Hey, Surdas! You are sleepy already? Here, have some liquor. It is an expensive whiskey, I mean scotch. And then play the flute for us,' Amal tried pulling Yashodhar's legs.

'Wait, Amal da. Ask him to sing instead. He sang so beautifully the other day. After the singing session, there will be a *jugalbandi* of Rishi's violin and Yasho's flute,' Arunabh suggested.

Hearing that, Yashodhar laughed like an idiot. He felt good that finally they paid him attention. It was evident in his body language. With his hands, he ironed out the creases of the collar of his shirt.

'The bonding between alcohol and music is as old as the history of human civilization. Right from the Vedic time to the courts of kings and emperors to the landlords, everyone belonging to that class preferred alcohol and music. Most people who like music also like alcohol. Here Amal babu, give me a shot of your rejuvenating drink,' Yashodhar gave this soliloquy with a shy look. His white teeth were dazzling, even in the dark. He knew quite a lot about religion and history. He could speak Assamese so beautifully. Where did he learn it?

Amal liked Yashodhar's cravings for alcohol. Except for that he was visually challenged, he was like any other normal man, with normal needs. Let him drink. He will light up the party with his music, Amal thought.

Rishi brought out a plate of fried chicken. The aroma of the chicken was mouth watering. It proved that Rishi was a good cook. He had not touched alcohol yet. All it took Rishi was one peg to get high. Arunabh knew that.

'Hey, Hriday! You have been chasing those poachers since last night. Is there any chance of nabbing them?' Amal asked with a sarcastic tone.

Hridayananda was blissfully chewing a chicken bone. This question was the last thing he expected. He stopped chewing all of a sudden and threw a curious look at Amal's direction.

'What do you think we do day and night? Chop fodder for the horses? Poachers do come. Sometimes, we catch them, sometimes, we kill them. We have to do our job,' Hridayananda replied, slightly irritated.

'But what I don't understand is how come the poachers are here at this time, when poaching is such a burning topic everywhere,' Amal asked again.

'Look, there has been a hue and cry about poachers in the media, in the parliament. Based on that, there will be action plans, but that will take time to be implemented. The poachers know it well. They will strike according to their calculations and we will try to stop them. We will keep trying to either catch them or kill them.'

'Despite all the efforts, Hriday, the killing of rhinos in Kaziranga has gone up this year, like never before. Why?' Amal was persistent.

Hridayananda kept quiet. There was truth in Amal's statement. Compared to the previous years, the poaching of rhinos had gone up. In fact, cruelty of mankind as a whole was on the rise. Assam itself was not untouched by crimes which were considered heinous in a civilised society. Every day, there was some report on crime being committed. Every day, the criminals innovated something shocking. So, how could the world of Kaziranga remain unaffected? Still, whenever crime was committed against innocent animals, it was difficult to digest. Men and animals—they were all similar—made of flesh and blood. But the brain of the human being was the root cause of all destruction.

Hridayananda was lost in his thoughts when the crackle of the fire brought him back to the present. He pushed his chair further from the fire and gulped down the remaining content of his glass.

'Hriday da, how big does a rhino grow? How much does a fully grown rhino weigh?' Arunabh, who was quiet all this while, threw the question at Hridayananda.

Hearing Arunabh's question, Hridayananda felt relieved. He was getting sick of Amal's sarcastic comments. Taking this opportunity to deviate from the serious subject, he poured himself another large peg and said, 'Do you know, Arunabh, going by its size and weight, the rhino is the fourth largest animal in the world? We have rhinos that weigh up to 4,000 kilograms. But most of them fall under the category of 1,600–3,500 kilograms. From head to tail, it measures up to 368 cm–380 cm.

'The height of the rhino is somewhere between 4.82 feet–5.68 feet. The female rhino weighs around 1,600 kilograms. Both male and female rhinos have the horn, which starts growing once it reaches six years of age. The horn measures up to 25 cm, but there are records of 57.2 cm long rhino horns also. It has body hair, but very sparse.'

'Wait a second! How do these giant animals run around?' Arunabh sounded genuinely curious.

'Oh! I will explain that later. Just remember, a rhino can run at the speed of 55 km per hour. So what if it has a giant body? Once in water, it can swim effortlessly. Yes, it has problem seeing things, but its hearing ability and smelling power make up for its weak eyesight.

'A mother takes care of her offspring till it reaches the age of four. It feeds on grass and water planktons. And the most amazing thing, it can make 10 different types of sounds. A rhino has the lifespan of 40 years, but there are evidences of a rhino living up to 47 years too. However, most of them die premature death fighting, rather than dying of old age.'

As Hridayananda completed his long speech on the topic of Indian rhinos, he looked at his audience huddled around the fire. He enjoyed their rapt attention.

Suddenly, Hridayananda's mobile started ringing. He took the call immediately. Listening to his caller, Hridayananda got up and started pacing. The expression on his face changed. Still talking on the phone, he left the group and went out of his house.

'You know, Arunabh, yesterday I was reading an article in a journal that said in India hunting was declared illegal only in 1910. Actually, in the 18th century and the early 19th century, kings and landlords gave hunting the status of a royal game. There was this army guy who shot dead about 200 rhinos in the mid 19th century. There were probably only 12 rhinos left in Kaziranga by 1908. The rhino population started growing only after that. As many as 692 rhinos were killed from 1980 to 1993. And in Laokhua, a small forest in Nagaon district, 41 rhinos were killed in 1983 alone.' Grabbing the opportunity of Hridayananda's absence, Amal plunged into a long lecture, like an expert historian. Actually, having stayed in Kaziranga, Amal was getting curious about the national park and its flora and fauna.

Amal knew Kaziranga was not just about rhinos, but they were definitely the centre of all discussions lately. Kaziranga had become synonymous with rhinos, the pride of Assam. About 70 per cent rhinos of Assam were found in Kaziranga. In fact, the biggest rhino population in the world was concentrated in Kaziranga.

Almost running, Hridayananda came back. He seemed agitated. He took off his hat and was holding it in his right hand. His hair stood up in spikes and his faced turned red.

'Amal, I will take your leave now. You guys have fun. I am being called urgently. The team of forest guards has located some poachers in our range. They are already on their trail. We won't let them get away this time,' though his voice remained calm, the underlying anxiety in Hridayananda's voice didn't go unnoticed by the rest.

Nobody uttered a word. They just stared at Hridayananda's face awkwardly. As if nobody knew how to react to the situation.

'Do you have to leave immediately? I mean can't you have your meal at least?' Amal asked his friend hesitantly. His face wore a bewildered expression.

'Come on, you have no clue about the whole situation. Should I be eating here instead of chasing those poachers? Will they wait for me to finish my meal?' Hridayananda asked in an angry tone as he tied the shoelace sitting on a *muda*.

Amal didn't say anything; he banged his glass on the floor. Yashodhar and Arunabh too kept quiet. Holding the spatula in his hand, Rishi too joined them in their silence.

Seeing their awkwardness, Hridayananda felt bad, but he was helpless.

'Please don't mind, Amal. This happens quite frequently here. In this job, a situation like this is quite expected. You people know how everybody is blaming us for the rhino killings. And now, if I keep sitting here despite knowing about the presence of poachers, I will have to regret it big time. So, please, excuse me. Dijen is around. You all spend the night here. No need to go back to Pamua at this hour,' Hridayananda explained everything with great precision, but there was a sense of urgency in his actions.

Hridayananda reminded them of a good general going into battle. Amal had never seen this avatar of his close friend. How did the docile boy of those college days turn into such a responsible officer?

They followed him with their eyes as he stepped out of the house. In a moment, he was gone.

Amal's mind was busily rewinding the scenes from the past. An intense emotion within him was trying to find an outlet. Suddenly, he got up and grabbed the jacket which was lying on the chair. His body language showed some kind of agitation. 'You people stay here. I am going with him,' saying that, the rolly-polly man ran after Hridayananda.

'Hey, Hriday! Wait for me. I am coming along,' Amal shouted after the departing figure.

Shell-shocked, Yashodhar, Arunabh and Rishi had no chance of uttering a single word.

In the darkness outside, the sound of the car engine died down. Probably, there was an argument between the two. From whatever conversation they could snatch, the three could make that out. After sometime, the engine sprang into life again. And then, the sound of the car roaring. Then, silence...

Exhaling long and hard, Arunabh understood that Amal da too had gone into the jungle. Hridayananda's argument didn't cut any ice with this stubborn man. Once Amal decided to do something, nothing could stop him. Because of his stubbornness, Amal had suffered in life, yet he couldn't improve himself. He was understanding, responsible too. But his stubbornness, his ego made him a difficult person at times. Arunabh had seen this side of Amal da since his childhood. He was an enigma.

The celebratory mood evaporated in seconds. The food was almost ready. Rishi was about to fry rice powder-coated pumpkin pieces, but he lost all interest. Asking Dijen to take care of the frying, he sat in an empty chair and poured himself a peg.

Arunabh shut his laptop. The situation was too tense. Everyone was feeling dejected. Actually, Arunabh too was angry with Amal da for having left like that. There were hundreds of things that could go wrong while chasing a gang of poachers in the deep jungle. Amal had no experience at all. He had no clue how inhuman those poachers could get. God forbid, if something happened to Amal da, how would Arunabh face his uncle and aunt? He could never approve of Amal da's stubbornness. But then, Amal da did what he wanted to do. Now, there was nothing they could do except wait for the two to return. They wouldn't be able to sleep tonight. Probably, it would be a good idea to engage Rishi and Yashodhar in some music.

It started drizzling. In such kind of drizzle, when the water made contact with leaves and grasses, it made an amazing melody. When they started for Hriday da's house, Rishi had kept the guitar and violin in the car. Those were now placed on the floor, leaning on the wall. Arunabh picked up the guitar and handed it to Rishi.

Rishi looked at Arunabh quizzingly.

'Play. Let's have some music,' Arunabh answered his friend with a slight smile. However, Arunabh's voice lacked conviction. Rishi, for a long time kept sitting without responding.

Taking a sip from his glass, Rishi started tuning his guitar. As he started fiddling it with his long fingers, a Western tune soon danced around Hridayananda's bachelor pad and ascended to the sky. The peppy rhythmic beat soon drowned the sorrow that had engulfed the campus not so long ago. It seemed the guitar too was dancing to Rishi's sensitive touch. How fast Rishi could change the scenario!

Sometimes, Rishi's patience level was even shorter than Amal da's. Whenever he felt that he was indulging too much, he would let it end abruptly. He would berate himself for getting carried away.

That's exactly what Rishi did tonight. After playing the peppy tune for a tad too long, he suddenly stopped.

'Oh! I can't play any more. My fingers are hurting. Ask Yasho to sing,' Rishi said, leaning the guitar against the wall. He did not look up at Arunabh and was visibly upset.

Arunabh didn't pay attention to Rishi.

The heady feeling he was currently experiencing was not letting him sit at one place. Insensitive to Rishi's mood swing, Arunabh started whistling. He wanted to be occupied till Amal da came back. So, alcohol and music were a must.

'Hey, Mr Surdas! Everybody is asking for a song. No flute, but song. A song that touches the heart,' Arunabh's voice was unusually loud as he said that slapping Yashodhar's back.

'Ok, Ok. I will sing. But I will sing a *bauul* in original Bengali. Is that fine?' asked Yashodhar.

'Go ahead!' Both agreed.

Yashodhar cleared his throat. To make it smooth, he emptied the entire content of his glass down his throat.

'*Bauul* originated at the same time of Srimanta Shankardev, the great Vaishnavite guru. One of the great gurus of Vaishnavite culture, Nityananda's son, Birbhadra, started these songs called *bauul*. They share close similarity with Sufi songs. Till the end of 19th century, these songs were passed on orally from generation to generation. Later, those songs were written down,' Yashodhar explained without a pause.

Both Rishi and Arunabh were listening to him in admiration.

'Hey, Yasho! I didn't know you were so knowledgeable. Where did you learn such facts?' Arunabh couldn't stop himself.

'He, he. Arunabh babu, I have recently passed my Sangeet Visharad exams. My guru taught me all these things,' Yashodhar replied with a shy smile, his voice barely audible.

'Really? I had no clue. Alright! Sing us a *bauul*. Don't worry, we understand rural Bengali,' Arunabh genuinely requested him. His eyes were full of admiration for the blind man. The night was getting serious once again.

The contours of Yashodhar's face had changed. His expression was that of a bird flying high in the sky. He was beyond the realm of this world. He shook his body and sat straight. In his typical nasal twang, he started singing in pure rural Bengali, the famous *bauul* of Lalon fakir…

> Samay gele sadhan habe na…
> Dil thakte diner sadhan
> Tumi keno karle na?
> Tumi keno aage janle na…

The song came to an end, but delving deep into the meaning of it, Yashodhar kept humming the last stanza, again and again. He couldn't have had enough of it.

The rest of the group was sitting still, holding their breath. Each word of Lalon fakir's *bauul* touched their hearts. It was not a mere song, it was a reality check for people neck deep in the whirlpool of materialistic life. When listened to carefully, the lyrics gave one goosebumps. One felt like delving into the past.

Yashodhar started another one. Language was not a problem, as his voice beautifully presented the words.

Dijen, who had forgotten about his duty listening to Yashodhar, went back to the kitchen in reluctance. The sizzling sound of *tadka* distracted Yashodhar for a second and he apologised for that.

'Wish we had a *dotara*,' Rishi commented as Yashodhar took a pause.

'Not *dotara*, Rishi babu, *ektara*,' Yashodhar corrected him.

An *ektara* is the actual accompanying instrument for such devotional songs. It's, however, difficult to procure one these days. Of course, *dotara* is also used for *bauul* along with *dogar*, an instrument made of earth and goat skin. The *dogar* keeps the beat and rhythm of the song in check. If there is a *khartal*, it adds up to the melody of a *bauul*. The devouts dance along with the music created by the flute, *ghungroo* and the other instruments. Yashodhar went on explaining.

'Hey, Yasho! It's amazing. How do you retain all this information?'

Yashodhar didn't feel it necessary to answer Arunabh's question. He rather proceeded to the fourth *bauul*. His face was serene like that of a yogi. His music had transformed him into another personality.

Shaking off the sadness which had earlier engulfed them, Rishi too sprang into action. He started tuning his guitar. Probably, he wanted to compensate for the lack of an *ektara*.

Exactly at that moment, Dijen came running from the kitchen and stood next to them. He looked agitated. Putting a finger on his lips, he asked them to stop. With the other hand, he gave a light push to Yashodhar asking him to keep quiet.

Looking at his worried face, Arunabh and Rishi stopped their music too. Yashodhar also tried to assess the situation. They all trained their ears to catch the source of the sound which had excited Dijen.

Far away in the jungle, there was the sound of gunshots. Overriding the sound of crickets and the rain, the continuous firing pierced through the jungle. A flock of birds created a cacophony before flying away towards the sky. But nothing deterred those shooters. A war was waged. The peace was lost to the cruel music of gunshots. Bang…bang…

The bicycle made a screeching sound. It was time for Padmeshwar Bora to return home from the post office. His entire day was spent riding that old bicycle from one hamlet to another. Before he knew it, it was evening. The first thing he did when he reached home was take a bath with the hot water Lakhimi kept on the hearth, then sit in front of the *thapona* for the ritualistic worship before taking rest. This had been his routine for years. There was never a break. It's been almost 40 years since he joined the post office as a peon. From being a contractual employee in the branch office of Bokakhat to a permanent staff in the sub-office, his life had been moving in the same circle. There were not too many off days for a peon, but they enjoyed certain facilities. He never suffered from any major ailment during his many years of service.

Leaving home early in the morning after having a hearty meal of rice, he was often offered tea, biscuits, *pitha*, laddoo, and betel nut and paan several times when he visited the families to deliver letters or parcels. Even then, he never had an upset tummy. Sometimes, he caught the seasonal bug and had fever.

That's all. Sometimes, the doctor in Bokakhat gave him some free medicine for blood pressure. That also was not regular. Whenever he visited the doctor's house, he used to collect the medicine. The doctor had asked him several times to take it regularly. When his wife was alive, she used to nag him to have his medicine. After she was gone, he stopped asking the doctor for the medicine. He stopped taking it altogether. There were many other things which he stopped doing in life after she died.

Padmeshwar was carrying a bag full of vegetables in the carrier of his cycle. A family had given him a small gourd, another family a raw papaya. The family in the town gave him two cauliflowers from their kitchen garden. The plastic bag that hung from the cycle handle contained a few kaoi fish which he bought from the Bokakhat market. Padmeshwar preferred meat though. These days broiler chicken was easily available. But his daughter and two sons liked fish better. So, he went to the familiar fishmonger in the weekly Saturday market and bought 300 gm of kaoi fish. His sons loved fishing, but they never caught this big a kaoi. These were from some big pond.

The rear wheel of the cycle felt a little flat. It made his ride unsteady. Holding tightly onto the handle, he applied pressure on the pedals. His legs were still strong. The pair of sandals that the cobbler had made from the rubber of a car tyre gave him a good grip. It was a comfortable pair, good for cycling, good to walk in. Many people advised him to buy a motorcycle. If not a new one, a second-hand one. But Padmeshwar had no intention of buying one. Learning new tricks at this old age! Cycle was good enough for him. His father, grandfather both rode bicycles. They say bicycle came to India 14 years after the Golaghat Post Office was established. Cycling was comfortable, it had health benefits too. Even the thought of riding a motorcycle made him uncomfortable.

The Saturday evening always made him feel good. It meant Sunday was just round the corner. A holiday gave him the chance to pay attention to the household chores, talk to his children, meet people in the village, and of course, get the much-needed rest. He planned to visit the field too. Sundays came and went by so quickly, but still he waited for this weekly off. In the evenings, he cleaned the cycle with oil and readied his companion for the coming week. If he was relaxed enough, sometimes, he would hum along with the tune that played in the radio after munching the *pitha*s and sipping tea which his daughter prepared for him.

Padmeshwar was focused and applied all his strength as he rode the cycle. He wanted to reach home as soon as possible. The village development committee had organised a meeting at the *namghar* that evening. The village head had asked him time and again to be there. There were only three service holders in Pamua village. Among them, he was the most respected, as he was the oldest and held a Central Government post. Padmeshwar barely talked, but when he did, people listened. He was also one of the most financially sound people in the village. After 30 years of service in this sub-post office, he was drawing a salary of ₹16,000 per month and by the standard of Pamua people, it was big.

The bag of letters that Padmeshwar was carrying on his shoulders weighed at least 3 kilogram. Though it was officially not allowed, Padmeshwar did carry some letters home so that he could deliver to the houses that fell on his way to his office. The trend of sending and receiving letters had changed with time.

Now, the sender intimates the receiver beforehand on mobile. So, the receiver would ask Padmeshwar whether that particular letter had arrived or not. It created problems for him. Earlier, he could delay the delivery of a letter for a day or two, but not any more. People kept tab and if was late than expected, they blamed him. And most letters were now registered ones. So, there was no question of it getting lost in transition. In case it got lost, all hell would break loose on the peon.

Padmeshwar recalled when he had just joined the postal service, Khagen Mahanta had sung a song about postmen, which had become very popular. Those days were the days of postcard, inland letters and postal stamps. Those were the happy ol' days! Registered letters that required taking signature from the receiver were rare. There would be four or five money orders to deliver and the rest of the days the peons would be totally free. Those days were over. And people thought after mobile, Internet and email, there would be no work for postmen!

Really? Then how come he was not free from morning till evening? The place of letters and money orders had been taken up by scores of pan cards, cheque books, call letters for job interviews, notices from the DC office, letters from LIC, telephone bills and all types of registered letters. The month of March was particularly hectic for Padmeshwar. Distributing the balance sheets from the banks left him with no time, even for breathing. Taking signature of the receiver took up a major chunk of his working hours. They said the Assam Postal Office stood second only to the Chattisgarh Post Office in terms of volume of work. Last year, the postal department in Assam earned ₹120-crore revenue. He had heard the post master saying that the total distribution from the competitive exams earned the postal department ₹2 crore and another ₹8 crore from distributing the books for the Sarvasiksha Abhiyan. The speed post alone generated ₹6 crore. The Assam postal department had ₹53 lakh savings accounts and ₹12 lakh 50 thousand recurring accounts. In the postal history of Assam, the post office of Golaghat occupied a significant position. He knew that the first postal telephone was installed in Golaghat office during the British Raj in 1876. The Assam postal circle in the North-east province was established in 1873. After the Partition, there were not many circles left in India, but Assam had seven of the remaining. In entire India, there were 20 of them.

Padmeshwar did not care much about the statistics, but he could answer promptly if someone asked for such information. He learnt them by heart.

In happier moments, Padmeshwar shared his knowledge with his children, talking like a school teacher. His children would stare at his face with bewilderment, but with rapt attention. However, most of the facts he himself didn't understand.

It had become dark already and he was still some distance away from home. The highway was deserted. He just had to take a turn from that peepal tree to take the kutcha road leading to his village.

'You are back, Bora? You have shopped quite a lot today!' someone coming from the opposite direction in a bicycle at equal speed shouted. In the semi darkness, Padmeshwar couldn't recognise the person. His eyesight was also not like before. Everything about his body was on the decline. Sometimes, he couldn't even recognise his own shadow—he was shocked. Was life like that?

Pushing the bamboo gate aside, Padmeshwar Bora climbed up the verandah. He rang the bell of his cycle. There was complete silence all around. Probably the children were not home. Lakhimi, after working the whole day, had some free time and went out to catch up with her friends at the *namghar* courtyard. Both the boys were crazy about sports. They often played till they could see in the dark. Their sister would have to bring them home forcibly.

Parking the cycle on the stand, he sat down in the armless wooden chair on the verandah. It was dark. He felt at ease in the darkness. After a hard day's work, he welcomed the silence.

Often, when alone, Padmeshwar remembered his wife. As he did now. Had she been alive, what would she have done for him in such moments? Why did the silly woman go away so soon? He felt a weight on his chest. Silently, he sat in the chair.

Suddenly, a cow making a chocking sound from the shed brought him back to reality. He got up and pushed the door. Lakhimi simply bolted the main door of the house; it opened at his push. The lamp on the floor was giving out dim light. He increased the flame and kept it on the table. Then, he went back to his cycle and got the grocery. The kaoi fish, still alive, made a splashing sound inside the plastic bag.

Padmeshwar didn't lose more time. Changing his clothes in a hurry, he took the fish to the backyard. Spreading a kosu leaf on the verandah, he started filleting the fish. Lakhimi did not like filleting fish with bones. How much she could do? It was time to marry her off. Poor girl, her life was spent taking care of his and the boys' needs. She was doing her duties without any protest. Like her name, she was indeed Goddess Lakshmi.

Completing his task, Padmeshwar kept the fillets in a bowl and covered it with an aluminium plate. He took a quick bath. Perhaps, he had arrived earlier than his usual time. He checked what Lakhimi kept in the kitchen. She had boiled the milk and washed the flatten rice for him. Taking out a metal bowl, he put the rice and milk and a generous amount of jaggery. Seeing the bunch of bananas tied to the pole in the kitchen, he peeled two fat ones and added them to the rice. He was hungry.

After finishing his evening tea, he dressed up neatly and as he was just about to step out of the gate, he saw his children returning. They all were talking at the same time.

'So, you are back. Now sons, go wash yourselves and study. Aai Lakhimi, I have got kaoi fish. I have cleaned them up. Cook as you like, just put a little black pepper. I am off for the village meeting,' saying that, Padmeshwar stopped for a while to let them in. Once they were inside, he drew the bamboo poles and closed it.

It was windy. Darkness. The persistent howling of jackals came from the hillock which bordered the boundary of the village. It seemed as if they were crying. The wind distorted the sound.

Padmeshwar recalled his childhood days which he spent in Moriahola. His mind flashbacked to its lanes, the river bank, the road, the trees and animals, his friends who roamed around naked in those lanes. He could hear that ritualistic drumming sounds that came from the *namghar* of Moriahola. He left that place in 1962. He was a mere child then.

When they couldn't withstand the flood and subsequent soil erosion, 23 families from Moriahola relocated to Kaziranga and formed a tiny hamlet. That tiny hamlet later grew into Pamua village. The day they left Moriahola, Padmeshwar's father put him in the bullock cart along with whatever household goods they were left with. His parents and his widowed aunt walked along the cart. He had no clue where they was heading. In fact, he was happy thinking that they were going for an outing. A few families, with sad faces, bid them silent farewell as they travelled on that winding kutcha road. Later, he got to know that a few families had already migrated to the new place. They had already started constructing huts within the boundary allocated to them by the authority of Kaziranga. They left Moriahola for good.

The way he felt when he stepped inside the two-room, thatched-roof hut in that isolated area was still etched in Padmeshwar's memory. He could feel that there was something terribly wrong, somewhere. He realised that those carefree days of playing by the river were gone forever.

When darkness fell, young Padmeshwar would start howling, urging them to go back home. Once, his aunt carried him in her chest and took him to their nearest neighbour Madan's hut and fed him rice. When he saw Madan sitting there, he shook him up, saying, 'Hey, Madan, aren't you going home?' In fact, he pulled Madan by his arms in his anxiousness to get back home. Padmeshwar didn't remember how the people, who had gathered at the newly cleared courtyard of Madan's hut reacted, but he recalled Madan, who was equally clueless about the going ons then, embracing him and crying. The people who couldn't bear to see two innocent boys cry like that, went away. The womenfolk tried to hide their tears by covering their eyes with their *chaddar*. That was the first memorable scene that unfolded in Kaziranga, their new home.

That child had now turned into a 60-year-old man, but the memory of that mysterious evening, that scene, those unshed tears and those silent cries of the residents of Moriahola village who had lost everything, could still evoke a sharp pain in Padmeshwar's chest. Those memories of him picking wild berries, digging for edible roots, fishing, grazing cows, listening to his grandmother's stories as she cooled him down with a hand-fan during those summer nights, lighting up the *mezi* in Magh Bihu, playing stappu with his friends, taking care of those lost puppies, flying those colourful kites—nothing was lost from the treasure trove which he stored in his heart. In fact, whenever they got a chance, they erupted with full force, chocking him with emotions. How much havoc flood can unleash on people's life!

Does darkness get denser with time?

As Padmeshwar walked on the fallen leaves that lined the potholed road, he felt surreal. Lately, he had started feeling that way. As if he was just a bystander, witnessing his own life go by. There was a stabbing pain in his chest—a pain that was not physical. A bamboo tree by the side of the road made a cracking sound, as if to ask, 'Padmeshwar, are you all right?'

The helpless sound of that old bamboo tree got carried by the wind to the deep jungle of Kaziranga. Padmeshwar stopped for a moment. He felt as if a huge, black monster was devouring him—a monster that even Kaziranga feared.

Padmeshwar was not too far away from the *namghar*. He had to just take a turn, cross the dry drain and he would be there. This *namghar* was younger than him. Each family had contributed whatever they could towards its construction. They couldn't wait to inaugurate the sanctum sanctorum with the beating of the *dhol*. Ever since, the *namghar* had become the place to resolve all sorts of problems for the residents of Pamua village. When he was alive, Padmeshwar's father carried on the duty of reading the holy book and beating the ritualistic drums at the *namghar*. Attacked by a bear, he died about 10 years back. Padmeshwar thought if there was a heaven, his father would definitely be there in peace. The villagers could never forget the man who solved all their problems; Padmeshwar knew it.

Far away, an owl howled. Probably, the king of the jungle was on the prowl. Only a few days ago, a tiger had come inside a residential premises and killed a goat. Such things happened in Kaziranga. Not that there was a dearth of food in the jungle, but sometimes, when a tiger lost its track, it attacked villagers and domestic animals. Nobody could do anything about it. God only knew why a tiger would sometimes step outside its boundary to attack domestic animals. But it was somewhat accepted. If people could encroach upon the wild territory, why wouldn't a tiger do the same?

A melodious tune floated in the air. Blended with the rustling noise that the wind made, the tune created divine music. Padmeshwar remembered about the group which was staying with Rishi at the other end of the village. He had heard that the group had a blind flutist who could mesmerise anyone with his music. Lakhimi knew those people; they had come to visit his house.

There, the Petromax Lamp in the *namghar* yard was visible now. He couldn't fathom why the meeting was organised at the courtyard instead of the *namghar* floor. Probably, there were more people than it could accommodate.

Padmeshwar had an idea about the topic of discussion—getting legal documents for their land holdings. This had always been the problem area for the villagers inside Kaziranga. Even after spending 50 years there, most of them were not given a legal document to authorise them as the legal owner of their holdings. The village development committees were fighting their case, year after year. A few months back, Pamua village too decided to join the movement for legalising their ownership.

So, those isolated movements of several villages had now become a collective fight. Today's meeting expected the participation of a big leader from the central committee that fought for the cause of the entire people of Assam without legal documents. He was supposed to talk about a concrete plan for their future course of action.

A few months back, there was a huge procession from their area that blocked the Kaziranga highway in demand of land ownership documentation, erosion-related problems, rhino poaching and a few other demands. They raised slogans. The Highway No 37 had come to a standstill. The villagers of Pamua had not participated in that movement; they just stood far and enjoyed the scene. But that night itself, an urgent meeting was called at the *namghar* and there was a thorough discussion regarding the activities that took place during the day. The agitated youngsters of the village finally decided to be part of the ongoing movement. Their failure to solve the problem since last 30 years had left both the old and the young frustrated. Everyone reached a consensus—a fight in isolation would not fetch them the desired result. There had to be a collective movement. If the public was together, only then the government would give in to their demands. They had been pleading their case right in front of the clerks to officers to MLAs and ministers, but what happened?

Ever since, Pamua became an active participant in the revolution. In association with its neighbouring village, the village development committee of Pamua initiated a branch to fight for their right to legalisation of their land holdings. But Padmeshwar had heard that taking this issue as a base, even the sub-division of Bokakhat wanted to chalk out a bigger action plan by adding a few other demands. Probably, they were going to gherao Dispur.

People had already gathered at the *namghar* courtyard. Padmeshwar wrapped the *endi chaddar* neatly around him. The public was up and about today, thought Padmeshwar. Actually, busy the whole day delivering posts from one village to another, he remained ignorant of many things that took place in the village. His life moved in a definite circle. He got to know many things in the course of his daily grind, and many, he remained ignorant of.

Many *durris* were spread on the floor as sitting arrangement. A *tirpal* was also spread covering a wide area. In the empty patch of land in front of the *namghar*, Bipul, who ran a tea stall in the village, was distributing black tea and biscuits. It seemed he too wound up his stall to take part in the meeting. Yes, the issue affected everyone. Men were mortal alright, but to live, one needed land—life could not thrive without it.

Padmeshwar was just about to take a seat, when he saw a few young people on the link road running towards the *namghar*. They belonged to the village. Padmeshwar knew them well. All eyes automatically turned to those running figures. A curious expression writ large on everyone's face.

'Police, the police has come to the village,' one of them said in a hush-hush tone, just loud enough for the gathering to hear. Everything changed instantly. An unusual calmness engulfed the venue.

Atop an ant hill that grew on the southern tip of Pamua village, Dudul da was sitting in a meditative posture. Dudul da, alias Bimal Duara, in a saffron robe, sitting in a Vajrasana pose, was not an unfamiliar sight for Amal. The man he grew up with had long, unkempt hair and a fixed gaze now. A few years back, one fine day, this confirmed bachelor gave up a well-paying job and just disappeared. Later, his mother spotted him in a Nepalese television channel and persuaded Arunabh to go to Kathmandu and bring him back. Amal still shuddered when he recalled how he and Arunabh got bashed up by a gang of sanyasis when they travelled to the Himalayan country chasing Dudul da. They almost overpowered one of them who had an uncanny resemblance with Dudul da. But when the sanyasi screamed for help in chaste Hindi and his fellow sanyasis appeared on the scene, they had no other option but to admit that they made a mistake. It was a narrow escape. Both of them couldn't forget that incident for a long time. But now, time has dimmed those memories and lessened the pain. They have made terms with the thought that the elder son of the Duara family, who disappeared into thin air, was probably dead or maybe was one of those sanyasis who travelled around the world in search of moksha. Either way, he had denounced this material world. But why would a sanyasi, who looked like him, step into the periphery of Pamua village? Who was he? How did he trace out Pamua?

Amal felt the entire blood of his body rush to his head. A strange emotion overpowered him and it shook him to the core. Unconsciously, his fingers curled up into tight fists. A cry of helplessness, coupled with a feeling of suppressed anger, tried to escape from his throat. Who was he? Was he Dudul da or his ghost? No no, Amal didn't believe in ghosts. Okay, whoever he might be, even if he was an enlightened soul, this man was the number one enemy of the Duara family. Because of this man, the Duara family was living a life worse than death. While the entire family was mourning, this man was reaping the spiritual harvest. Fraud! Wait, he cannot escape this time…

His throat had dried up. Amal saw that the fraud yogi had his piercing gaze fixed on him now. Sometimes, like Dudul da used to do, he winked at him.

Amal was standing on the slope of the hillock. Only if he had carried a gun or something, he would have pumped a bullet into the forehead of that sanyasi, right in the middle where a long vermilion tikka ran. Wish Hridayananda was with him. Hriday would have definitely carried an arm.

Agitated, Amal looked around for help. Looking at his helplessness, the sanyasi sitting atop the ant hill smirked. Suddenly, with a thud, a heavy branch of a tree fell close to where he was standing. And at that moment, Amal lost his grip and started sliding down. He tried to hold onto the soil, but everything around was too slippery. With all his might, he clung onto the tree branch, but to no use. He was still sliding.

In his fit of anger, Amal saw the dry ant hill was engulfed in fire and smoke. The man who was sitting calmly on it started laughing, as if he was laughing at the fragility of life. As the fire became more intense, his laughter also became louder. The fire didn't have an impact on him. Fixing his gaze on the ant hill, Amal started climbing the slippery hillock. But it was a daunting task. The fire was spreading and along with it that scary laughter of the man in the saffron robe! Slowly, the ant hill and the sanyasi were totally engulfed by the fire. Only his laughter kept echoing all over. Amal too started screaming. His voice blended with the laughter of the sanyasi, creating a deadly tune…

Amal woke up with a jerk. He was sweating like hell. Everything was quiet in that pitch dark room. Amal was confused—was he dead or alive. What did he just experience? Was it a dream or reality? He had no clue. Where was he?

Probably, this is how the heart and the body function—always in tandem. Though the rhythm gets derailed at times, one never ditches the other till life is snuffed out. The heart always brings the body back to life. But it always leaves one with the important lesson of life. It rebukes the body for its momentary lapses.

Lying on the bed, Amal realised that he was indeed having a bad dream. Dudul was not a part of his reality any more. He died long ago. Even if he was alive, he was somewhere far away. Even the members of the Duara family had come to terms with it.

Amal took a deep breath. How come he dreamt of Dudul after so long? Was it that his subconscious mind was not ready to accept that Dudul was gone. He closed his eyes. He was feeling sad. What was the time? How chaotic a night!

Amal was sleeping in the guest room of the bungalow that belonged to the assistant manager of the Kapahtali Tea Estate, which shared its boundary with Kaziranga. Jiaur had been working with the tea estate for the past two years. He hailed from Mangaldoi. His wife, Riju, and their toddler daughter were living with him. Amal knew them for a long time. They both loved him. Once they learnt that he was coming there to start a resort, they insisted that he stayed with them in their bungalow. And Amal, though enjoyed certain luxuries, after considering all the pros and cons, decided to stay at Rishi's place. Both Rishi and Arunabh had convinced him that as the location of his resort was closer to Pamua village, they needed to win the trust of the locals. So, he didn't yield to the request of Jiaur and his family.

It was okay till then. But when he left the celebrations and joined Hridayananda in his hunt for the poachers, he fell victim to an accident. And, as a result he was forced to spend more than a week at Jiaur's guest room, where he was being treated by the company doctor.

On that fateful night, Amal had no other plans but to enjoy a few pegs of scotch and music with his friends. But when Hridayananda had to leave them in the middle of the party, Amal couldn't stop himself from accompanying his friend, even though nobody approved of him joining the search party, not even Hriday. Officially, outsiders were not allowed in such high-risk night operations. In fact, it was considered a punishable offence. There were often cross firings. People died on spot. Anything was possible when a chase was on. Conceding to the requests and arguments of Amal, Hridayananda had finally asked him to get in the car against his better judgement. And soon his adventure turned into a nightmare. The memories of that night still sent a shiver down his spine. Like a horror film, the sequences came flashing back to him…

After driving for about a kilometre from his quarter, as Hridayananda was about to hit the main road, he sped up the car. The vehicle skidded because of the rain. Then taking a right turn, he maneuvered it through a kutcha road, which was meant for the jeep safari. Because of the heavy rain, the road was getting muddy. Starting his walkie-talkie, Hridayananda tried to find out the location of his search party that was waiting for him at the designated spot. Hridayananda's source was supposed to inform them about the exact location of the poacher's gang in about half an hour. Before that, he was not supposed to divulge any information to any member of the team. That was the official rule.

The green Gypsy blended well with the surrounding. Hridayananda started his walkie-talkie again: 'Control…rhino calling. Over.'

'Dolphin, calling Dolphin. Over.'

'What's the news? Over.'

'Sir, Deputy Ranger Kalita is waiting. Will you contact him directly? Over.'

'Ask Kalita to come to the Ram Singh Camp. Pronto. Over.'

He switched off the walkie-talkie.

It was dangerous to use the walkie-talkie for a long duration in the forest. The poachers had learnt the techniques of intercepting the messages and used the information to their advantage. During the time of operation, they used mobile phones these days. Every technology had been hijacked by those bad elements.

The road was dotted with potholes. Hridayananda looked at Amal who was quietly sitting in the passenger seat. He felt a little irritated. His job would be in jeopardy if somebody reported to the authority about Amal. Why did he have to be so stubborn? As he jumped up and down, along with the vehicle in the potholed road, Hridayananda weighed the situation. This Amal was still the same old stubborn guy he used to be in college. So many years in the construction business didn't improve him at all.

Hridayananda brought the jeep to a sudden halt. It made a protesting sound before it stopped altogether. There was a huge wild boar standing right in the middle of that narrow road. Not one…in fact, three of them. It didn't seem to Hridayananda that they were in the mood to let them pass anytime soon. He quickly switched off the headlights. After a second, he switched it on again. The wild beasts, with humongous heads and short legs, were visibly shocked. Probably, they didn't like the disturbance. Hesitating for a while, they moved into the jungle.

Hridayananda started the Gypsy once again. Amal concentrated on the rearview mirror to see where the boars disappeared. In the rain, they didn't spot any other wild animal.

As they moved further, the road disappeared. Only two vague columns of tyre marks left by plying vehicles made for a motorable path here. After driving for about 10 more minutes, when they finally reached the Ram Singh Camp, it was almost midnight. It took them about an hour to travel that distance. The adrenaline rush Amal was experiencing in the beginning of the journey was ebbing out due to the jerking he had to endure. Parking the car, Hridayananda got down. Amal kept sitting.

The camp was a tree house made with bamboo. Beneath that rickety hut, the guards made a makeshift fireplace for cooking and the guards on duty took turns to sleep inside the hut.

Hearing the sound of the Gypsy, those armed forest guards came running towards Hridayananda. They were trying their best not to make any noise. One of them came up to Hridayananda and offered him the pouch that contained betel nut and paan.

'Have you all had your meal?' Hridayananda kept the decibel down as he asked them while accepting the paan. He plonked himself in the dirty old chair which was kept under the tree hut. Hridayananda himself dimmed the lantern which was the only source of light.

'We have had our food, sir,' someone replied. In the darkness, they couldn't make out who it was.

Hridayananda had to squint to look at his watch. He could make out that it was past 12. His source had informed him that the poachers were not making a move so far. They were waiting at the same position they were spotted at earlier. Probably, they would strike at around two. That meant they were in for a long wait. But making a move before they struck could mean giving them an opportunity to flee.

Hridayananda had asked Deputy Ranger Kalita and his team of four guards to join them at the Ram Singh Camp. But thinking of something, Hridayananda switched on the walkie-talkie and ordered Kalita and his team to move towards the Ghutlung Camp instead, which was about five kilometres away. Hridayananda had the information that the poachers had placed themselves somewhere in the middle from both the camps and were observing the movements of the rhinos. Maybe, they were planning to strike before dawn. From his many years of experience, he knew they either started their operation during the early hours of night or at dawn. But then there were no hard and fast rules. There were too many other factors, too. Many calculations were involved in such strikes.

There was nothing much to be done now.

Ordering the team of forest guards to go up the hut and rest for sometime, Hridayananda signalled the two guards on duty to sit on the bench next to him.

Hridayananda had been ignoring Amal all this while. Once the forest guards went up the hut, he signalled one of the two that remained on the ground and said, 'There is someone sitting in the car. Go and bring him here.'

Amal wanted to say something as he got down from the Gypsy, but stopped himself. Instead, he came close to Hridayananda and asked, 'The operation…I mean when are we going to strike?' Though he was whispering, the curiosity and excitement was getting the better of him.

'Sit quietly. You will get to know when the time comes. Now, total silence,' Hridayananda was a little rude. The sound of rain was drowning their voices anyway.

Saying nothing further, Amal started lighting up a cigarette. Hridayananda stopped him from doing that also. In a rude tone, he told how Amal's act of striking a matchstick or the lit cigarette tip could give away their position to the enemy.

This time, Amal reacted. 'Why? Don't they already know that you people have a camp here? They must be aware of the fact that a team of forest guards cook food, smoke cigarettes and vigil this area. Now if I smoke, everything will go wrong.' Though Amal's voice was controlled, his temper wasn't.

Conceding to his friend's argument, Hridayananda allowed him to have a smoke. But he warned him not to even think of a smoke once they left for the operation.

It seemed they would have to go without food for the night. Hridayananda started feeling hungry. They should have eaten something at his quarter before leaving. Forget about the sital fish and the chicken. Maybe, there was some leftover food in the camp kitchen.

'Hey, is there any food left in the wok?' Hridayananda asked Narah, the guard with a moustache.

Both the guards got up and looked at each other.

'There is enough rice for one person. Except for some cooked vegetables, there is nothing else. Sir, should we cook something?'

Hridayananda explained that one should not eat heavily before an operation. Besides, the night was almost over. So, whatever was there, they would share.

Taking the cue, both the guards immediately brought rice and a little sabzi in two discoloured aluminium plates.

Accepting a plate, Hridayananda felt sad. Yes, this is how a forest guard lived. They sacrificed their lives protecting the flora and fauna of the national park. Leaving their families in far-flung places, they lived in the jungle years after years. Before they realised it, their hair turned grey, and ultimately, they retired. Away from society and so-called civilisation, living in isolation, the forest guards were forced to be different from the normal people. Sometimes, they had to wait for two to three years to be with their family. They were at times not granted leave because there were not enough forest guards for the ranges. How many people were willing to work like that for a salary of ₹2,500–3,000?

Only recently, the forest guards had a hike and their salary had gone up to ₹10,000–12,000. Now, slowly, many casual staff were being made permanent.

Hridayananda was done eating, so was Amal.

Hridayananda went up to the drum that stored water, washed his dish and stacked it on the bamboo shelf. Amal followed suit. Hridayananda took out a paan from his pocket, smeared it with a generous helping of semi-liquid lime and put it in his mouth.

The continuous sound made by crickets and some unknown insects had made Kaziranga eerie at night. The sounds made by other animals and birds added to it. The mystery of the jungle was only deepening by the minute.

Chewing his paan, Hridayananda himself borrowed a cigarette from Amal; sometimes, he enjoyed one with his paan.

He just switched on the walkie-talkie. There was a message from the control room. 'Dolphin calling, sir. Deputy Ranger Kalita wants to talk to you. Over.'

'Rhino received. Okay. Ask Kalita to call on my mobile. Over.'

'Sir, your mobile is ringing. You have not picked up. Over.'

'All right. I am calling you. Over.'

The walkie-talkie was switched off. Everybody followed the strict order of keeping their mobiles in the silent mood before an operation. Kalita probably called while Hridayananda was having his dinner. Hridayananda knew the trick of carrying out a direct conversation with Kalita by switching on the one-on-one position. The first one among the 15 channels of the walkie-talkie belonged to the forest department. Within a short distance, he turned on the one-on-one mode to talk to the search parties. But it was now risky to talk to Kalita in that mode. The poachers might intercept the code language.

Amal was leaning on a bamboo pole and dozing off. The cigarette he was holding in his hand was still burning. He was getting angry with Hridayananda for waiting like this and becoming a feast for the mosquitoes and all kinds of insects around. He was angry with himself too. In a barely audible voice, he was mumbling to himself. Hridayananda, who was irritated with Amal earlier, felt pity for his friend. Poor guy, he didn't see what was coming. Amal's patience level was getting lower than what it used to be earlier.

Connecting with Deputy Ranger Kalita on his mobile, Hridayananda asked him to be on alert, as the operation could start any moment. Taking stalk of the arms and ammunition available with the forest guards at the headquarters, he disconnected the phone. But the mobile rang once again. This time, his source was on the line. Sitting straight in his chair, Hridayananda enquired, in a whisper, about the number of poachers and their exact location. Now, he was ready.

The poachers' gang had three members. They were camping under a huge jari tree near the pond that was situated on the north-east of Ram Singh and Ghutlung camps. They were waiting inside a plastic tent, probably drinking…

Hridayananda knew every nook and cranny of this range like the back of his hand. The location where they were spotted was about one and a half kilometre from the Ram Singh Camp and something between two and two and half from the Ghutlung Camp.

Hridayananda felt the adrenaline rush. In his mind, he chalked out the operation strategy.

He then called those two guards and asked them to call the rest of the team down. Dialling Kalita's number, Hridayananda asked him to march his team towards the location and take their positions, some 200 metres away from the spot. He strictly told Kalita to get ready for the ambush, but they were not to jump into action until further order. He explained to Kalita where exactly they planned to carry the ambush.

As Hridayananda stood like the general getting ready for a battle, his teammates stood in a row behind him. Save for the two security guards at the Ram Singh Camp, Hridayananda addressed the rest. Within two to three minutes, he explained the details about the location of their enemies and his own plan of action. After that, started the operation—tearing through the darkness of the jungle, their battle against the poachers. Hridayananda thought—it was the day of reckoning, a day to go for the kill. His department was constantly getting flak for rhino killings. These poachers were not stopping at anything. So, he would either catch them or kill them then and there.

Marching forward, Hridayananda glanced behind him. He spotted Amal, wearing a torn raincoat and carrying no arms or shield, following the group hesitantly. Hridayananda couldn't care less. Despite being told again and again, he came along. Now, let him face the music.

The rain had turned into a drizzle. The operation group had raincoats on. Some of them had a .315 rifle thrown over their shoulder and others, carried a 12-bore DBBL gun. Hridayananda usually carried a revolver.

The team marched on the water-filled, narrow footpath. They walked in silence. The jungle was full of adversities at night. There could be a surprise attack from animals—right from tigers and bears to snakes and poisonous insects. But what was the alternative? Unless it was totally necessary, they couldn't switch on the torchlight. But the team was trained for all these. Anybody who worked as a forest guard learnt the tricks of walking at night without any aid.

The forest guard, Lahan, who was following Hridayananda closely, knew the area well. So, Hridayananda was asking him for direction.

Some reptile type of animal slid over Hridayananda's right shoe. He stopped. The entire team stopped. Taking a deep breath, he proceeded again. Suddenly, a thin envelope of fog engulfed the jungle. The moist breeze carried the distinctive smell of tobacco. Probably, the enemy gang was smoking cigarettes.

Lahan raised his head and tried to sniff something. In the dark, he tried to find out where exactly they were. Then, he whispered something in Hridayananda's ear.

It was understood that they had already reached the spot. Probably, the enemy was stationed within 100–150 metres, for sure!

Obstructing the light emitted from his mobile with a thick hand towel, Hridayananda rang up Kalita. Kalita and his team had already stationed themselves in the position for the ambush.

Following Hridayananda's order, Lahan was about to crawl ahead to find out the exact location of the enemy. But a poke from Hridayananda stopped him in his tracks.

Poachers do commit mistakes. Like criminals leave some clue or the other at the scene of crime, so do the poachers. There...two small balls of fire shone at a distance. It looked like the tip of two burning cigarettes or bidis.

Hridayananda was still on the line with Kalita. From his kneeling position, he updated Kalita about the position of the enemy. Kalita confirmed that some people were indeed smoking and sometimes, switching on the mobile torch. Kalita's team was closer to the poachers and they were all set for the ambush.

Hridayananda asked Kalita to wait till his own team advanced. Closing in, he felt quite confident. He was not going to rest till this operation was a success. Just a few more minutes…

As he was crawling forward, suddenly the two burning points disappeared. What happened? Did they get a wind of the approaching forest guards? Hridayananda contemplated all possibilities. If they did, there was no time to think. The poachers' gang was within the shooting range for both his and Kalita's team. What to do? Should he go closer or should he fire? Hridayananda was thinking fast.

But he didn't get time to think further. There was this sound of a gunshot coming towards his team. Two more shots followed. The only thought that occupied Hridayananda's mind was that their own location was revealed and the poachers were firing at them.

Bringing the mobile close to his mouth and turning his head towards the team, he shouted, 'Fire, Fire! Action! Fire!'

In seconds, the solitude of Kaziranga was shattered with gunshots fired by his own team and also from the east, where Kalita's team was waiting. Rounds and rounds of bullets that were fired from .315 rifles and 12-bore DBBL guns targeted the enemy. Hridayananda too fired quite a few shots from his revolver. The firing and the counter-firing lasted for about five minutes. The five-battery powered torches illuminated the jungle. There was no place for darkness. Hridayananda's team bifurcated and moved forward as they fired. Kalita's team was also advancing towards the tent under the jari tree. The light from the torches were searching for the poachers, now trying to run for cover. There was gunpowder smoke everywhere.

Soon, the teams reached the tent. They searched the area, inch by inch.

There was no one. There were no signs of anyone being injured. The poachers dodged the bullets. They were like jackals. They knew how to escape. They would take risk to any extent. What a failure!

Hridayananda pulled his hair with his left hand.

No, it's not over till it's over.

He would chase them down. But before that, Hridayananda took a good look at the belongings of the poachers left behind in the tent. A water bottle, two packs of bidi, an *endi chaddar*, a matchbox, a half-empty bottle of whiskey, plastic glasses, a dirty *gamosa* and there...a sophisticated rifle.

Panting heavily, Kalita stood next to Hridayananda. Ceasing the rifle, Hridayananda thought about his strategy for the next phase of the operation.

The plastic tent was close to the bank of a small lake.

With the torch on, Hridayananda looked around. He suddenly remembered that two old boats that belonged to the forest department were moored there. One of them was missing. That meant they escaped through water. Right? There were fresh footprints on the mud near the lake. One party took the upward route around the lake.

'We are going by boat. Quick!' Hridayananda shouted.

Kalita's team was not allowed to follow the rest. Kalita joined Hridayananda in the boat. Where was Amal? Was he hurt? But there was no time to think. He ordered two guards to stay there.

Lahan was starting the boat. As it was about to sail, Amal, with a long jump, plonked himself in the boat. His weight rocked the boat. But Lahan was an expert rower. In the fog, which had grown much thicker, he maneuvered it through as if he knew which way the enemy had gone. Rowing with a long bamboo pole, he followed the water 'leak' to avoid the wall of water hyacinth. The oar made a chap chap sound as the heavyweight guard, Lahan, expertly took them ahead.

Amal remembered clearly…

As they moved ahead, their torches illuminated the lake. In that light, they saw the boat which was taking the poachers to safety.

Kalita and Hridayananda kept firing with their rifles at the retreating figures. Amal, who was sitting at the other end of the boat, was trembling with fear. Unable to bear the sound of the gunshots, he threw himself at the dirty floor of the boat and lay down on his stomach. He held both the sides of the boat tightly and prayed to all the gods he could remember in that situation.

To make the matter worse, the enemy started retaliating. Both the boats were moving amid all that firing and counter-firing. Amal had no clue for how long the firing continued. It slowed down from the enemy side. Probably, something had gone wrong. But it didn't stop altogether.

At that moment, Amal, to find his grip, raised his head slightly. Exactly at that point, a bullet came whizzing past just under his nose and hit the side of the boat. Amal could feel metal dust and splinters from the boat. He was sure that he had died. His brain stopped functioning. Was he to die in the middle of Kaziranga in a battle with poachers?

Trying hard to recall the faces of his parents, his children and wife, bewildered Amal shouted at Hridayananda, 'Hriday. I have died. Send my body back home.'

Almost sure that he was hit by a bullet in the head, eccentric Amal threw himself at the cold water of the lake. Slowly, his heavy body sank deeper and deeper.

After that, everything was a blank. He tried groping at the memory locked into the deep recess of his mind, but found nothing. He still drew a blank.

It was probably a day later…

After regaining consciousness, Amal found himself in a hospital-type room. Surrounding him were Rishi, Arunabh, Jiaur and a few unfamiliar faces, all looking anxious. A doctor and nurses were present as well. Opening his eyes for a second, he shut them again. They were moist.

When he got his strength back in the afternoon, Amal heard the rest of the story from Arunabh…

After Amal jumped into the lake, his body was filled with cold water. The team of forest guards fished out his unconscious body once the operation was over.

Hridayananda's operation was a success. Next morning, two bodies were found in the water. Those were riddled with bullets. A huge success. Yes, success at times shared a close connection with death. The battle between the law makers and law breakers. Amal had been a witness to the game of death which was played inside Kaziranga, known for its serene beauty. He tried to suppress the cry which chocked his throat.

For two days, Amal remained admitted in the hospital. After that, in a consensus from all, Jiaur brought him back to his bungalow. The dirty water which got trapped inside his body was playing havoc on his system. He was also suffering from pneumonia. Dr Mahanta, the doctor employed by the tea garden, would be able to treat him better there.

The next day in the bungalow, at the breakfast table, Amal heard the sad news from Jiaur. During that operation, the tall healthy guy, Lahan, who was rowing the boat, was hit by a bullet fired by one of the poachers.

By the time they could take him to the hospital in Bokakhat, he had already lost plenty of blood. The hospital referred him to the Gauhati Medical College in Guwahati. They tried everything they could. But Lahan responded to nothing. He breathed his last in the early morning. He was simply gone!

Tears refused to stop this time. Failing to control the welled-up emotion within, Amal broke down in loud sobs. The image of that tall, healthy but sober guy appeared in front of him. He had known him for only a couple of hours, but it was enough to develop a liking to that man.

'Goodbye, Friend. Probably, somehow, I too was responsible for your death. Forgive me.' A feeling of guilt overpowered Amal's senses.

You get to live only once...

They talk about this world and the other world. But is there life after death? If a person is born again and again, one should have at least faint memories of previous births. But there are none. No. There is just one life—not three. All those explanations about life after life were nonsense.

Lying on a hard single bed that had an equally hard slab of cotton for a mattress, Rishi was thinking about the philosophy of life. In the silent afternoon, when even the sound of a leaf falling could be heard, Rishi had all the time to do some soul-searching. Only a few mosquitoes buzzing around him were trying to disrupt his trend of thoughts.

It's been raining continuously for the past three days. The intensity of rain varied, but it did not stop, even for a moment. The neat and clean road was now all covered with slush. Though the season was setting in, looking at the rain, it seemed as if the monsoon had struck again. As if there would be a flood and it would wipe out the village once again. The climate was changing. It never happened like this before!

It was a Saturday. Usually, this was the day when Rishi would be busy at his music school. But the rain had turned Bokakhat into a mud bowl. Besides, the part-time watchman in the school called Rishi in the morning to inform that some local organisation had called for a 12-hour bandh. So, everything, right from shops to schools and colleges and even government offices, were shut down. If there was a call for a bandh, people usually complied out of fear. But the rain made sure that everyone stayed indoor. He said that Bokakhat looked like a graveyard.

God! For how long could Rishi stay at home? When he was not busy with his students, he would get irritated. The memories from the past troubled him. The regret of losing some precious moments of life, which he would never find later, tormented him whenever he was alone.

Actually, he didn't venture out of the village in the last couple of days, even when there was no rain. He kept playing the violin. Except for the time spent cooking, bathing and sleeping, his hands refused to let go of the violin. He was engrossed in playing a range of tunes and some out-of-tune compositions—as if he was into some kind of meditation. It happened to him sometimes. He would be completely consumed by his love for this instrument and ballad. He had travelled far and wide. He had met many musicians and bands in many countries. He had many friends all over the globe. Everywhere, he tried to explore music which transcends the language barrier. He attained success to some extent. But in life, he messed up big time. Even after taking tuitions on life, he thought he was a failure.

It was fast getting dark. It was also growing cold. By now, the place was filled with the chirping of birds that were returning home and the braying of cows trembling in the cold.

Rishi got down from the bed. His body was aching from lying there for such a long time. He made up his mind to venture out.

The raincoat he borrowed from Hridayananda that rainy night was still lying in his house. He grabbed it from the wall where it was hanging and wore it. His thin frame was drawn in the huge coat. He then reached out for the hat which was tossed aside in neglect. Closing the door, Rishi stepped out.

The rain had turned into a drizzle. It was windy though. Crossing the gate, the thought suddenly struck Rishi…where would he go at this hour? He dismissed that thought and started towards the main road. Where to go, he would decide later.

Kaziranga was crowded already. Rain didn't affect the flow of tourists. Many people booked tourist lodges in advance. Even those who came from outside Assam or foreign countries had spent money on their flight tickets, and paid those local car rentals and hotels much in advance to retract now because of the untimely rain. November, December, January and February were the peak months. Many people who came in these months with no prior booking were forced to go to nearby towns such as Bokakhat or Golaghat to find a place to stay. Cashing in on the inflow, many families in Kaziranga had started renting out one or two rooms to the tourists. The people in Pamua village were not rich enough to cater to the tourists. Rishi had initiated a co-operative venture in which women of the village contributed ₹50 each and ran a restaurant that offered traditional Assamese dishes. They operated from a hut which was constructed close to the main road. It had not yet completed one month.

Business was slow, but there was no lack of enthusiasm among the womenfolk of Pamua. The mud- and cow dung-coated walls housed a couple of long bamboo benches and tables as sitting arrangement. The main attraction was the Assamese thali. The women painted the words 'Assamese Meal' with bright red paint on an *endi chaddar* and put it up on the front wall. Rishi had organised it in such a way that most of the food items to be served there were coming from the members' kitchens. The small kitchen at the back was used to cook odd items. For ₹150, they served black lentils, small fish cooked in the tangy juice of elephant apple, chicken with spicy gravy, mashed potato, brinjal fry, *kahudi*, the edible part of a banana trunk cooked in *khar*, bamboo shoot, fried pakoras, homemade pickles and different types of chutneys. The meal was served on a banana leaf. After the meal, the guests were given the traditional Assamese mouth freshener, a mix of roasted *saunf* and sweet supari, and a small hanky as souvenir. Initially, it attracted only foreign tourists. But slowly, it was getting popular among domestic tourists too. Since they cooked everything in advance, most of the time, food went waste and the members had to take them back home. At night, though Rishi had asked them to keep it open till at least nine, no woman had the permission to stay out that late. So, as soon as the sun went down, they would be in a hurry to go back home. No one was willing to do business in the night hours. Everybody had problems at home.

Rishi tried talking to the head of their households, but no man was willing to let their women stay out till so late, except of course for Padmeshwar peon. Rishi was not giving it up.

Walking briskly, Rishi was about to reach the main road. Crossing the gate of Lakhimi's house, he stopped for a moment. There was no sound coming out of the house. There was a lantern burning in the verandah, but there was no light coming from inside. He resumed his pace. For no apparent reason, the feeling of loneliness suddenly weighed him down.

Reaching the main road, Rishi saw Assamese Meal was closed for the day. There was a lock hanging from an iron chain at the door. That meant the women entrepreneurs had already left. He felt amused. Though they had occupied more than 33 per cent seats in the panchayats, Assamese women were still the submissive type, and seldom went against their husband's wishes.

Rishi thought this restaurant would serve as a platform for the local women to take charge of the traditional food section for Amal da's resort which would be functional in another year. But looking at their professionalism, he knew it was a far-fetched idea. He was sure that they would have to hire cooks from outside.

It was almost a month since Amal da, after that fateful night with Hridayananda, had left for Guwahati. After spending quite a few days at Jiaur's bungalow in the Kapahtali Tea Estate, where he was being treated for pneumonia, Amal da spent about a week in a private nursing home in Guwahati. He had recovered completely and now was in Delhi. He was, of course, in constant touch with Rishi, discussing the resort and hinting at the fact that Rishi would have to play a major role in it.

Another issue that was plaguing the national park was the resorts there. Some people encroached government land and built resorts illegally. Some built without prior permission. The authority had demolished quite a few of them. Amal didn't want to be on the wrong side of the law. He wanted to do with proper documents and all—neat and clean business!

In the darkness, Rishi felt someone walk towards him. He stopped for a moment to see who it was.

'Who is it? Rishi da?' a rough voice came piercing through the darkness.

'That's me. Who is this? Cannot make out in this dark,' Rishi had to squint to take a good look at the man's face.

'Oh, it's me. Tarani. I live in the house next to the *namghar*,' the voice sounded relaxed.

'Oh, Tarani. Are you returning from the Jeep Safari Committee meeting?'

'Yes, Rishi da. The meeting got cancelled. There were hardly any members. It's been postponed till day after tomorrow.' Tarani seemed in a hurry to leave. 'I just had a call from my brother that my father has some kind of problem,' said Tarani, before parting.

Rishi knew Tarani sold packed tea leaves in the shop near the Kohora Chowk in evenings. In the daytime, he took tourists on jeep safaris in his second-hand jeep. He made a neat profit from selling tea leaves.

As Tarani passed by, Rishi could smell liquor all over the place. Tarani had this habit of drinking a few pegs of country-made liquor every evening before returning home. He was returning sooner than his usual time, but despite the fact that his father was unwell, he still had the time to drink. Rishi was aware of the fact that not just Tarani, but quite a few youngsters in Pamua were addicted to alcohol. In fact, not just Pamua, but in the nearby villages too.

It was time for the trucks and bigger vehicles to ply on the highway. They all were driving at breakneck speed. They never paid heed to the speed limit. They never cared for the fact that any moment, some wild animal could cross the road. Yes, no one was bothered about the law inside Kaziranga, neither the law-enforcing authority nor the public.

To protect the animals from such road accidents, there was a talk once about shifting this road to skirt around the area. Rishi recalled newspapers carrying the government proposal in big-font headlines. But then the debate started—the plus points and minus points, the pros and cons. That was the end of the matter. So many other such proposals were suppressed. Would they ever see the daylight?

Rishi had come to this place after a long time. Last time, he wandered aimlessly like this was when Amal da, Arunabh and Yashodhar were with him. Rishi analysed—yes he did like being alone, but if he had good company, it was also not bad either, even if it was a little crowded.

Inside the bamboo stall, Bipul was gathering his belongings and calling it a day. From where Rishi was standing, it seemed the fire in the hearth had already extinguished. So, he gave up his hope for a hot cup of tea. Even the lantern hanging on the wall was about to die out.

'Bipul, you closing down?' Rishi asked while standing in the dark.

Bipul could make out his voice. He also knew that Rishi was hoping for a cup of tea.

'Oh, Rishi da. Come, come. There was not a single customer today. Who would come out in this rain? A bad day for business. If you want a cup of tea, I can make it in a jiffy. Yesterday, I bought this pumping stove. Now even if the hearth is not lit, I can offer tea to my customers. But I have no milk today. I can make your tea with powdered milk.' There was a note of pride as the rolly-polly guy explained the situation.

'That's fine. Make me a cup of black tea. Strong. If you have, put some black peper too,' Rishi stood close to the half-closed shop as he instructed the young guy. Bipul already started pumping the stove. It made a hissing sound.

'Rishi da, what about the resort? Besides that boundary and filling of earth, I have not seen much activity in the construction site,' Bipul asked as he boiled the water.

'Things will move. We should get the clearance in a day or two. Once the documents are ready, we will start construction work in full swing,' Rishi replied in a calm voice.

He knew Bipul wanted to a job at the resort. His uncle's farm was not producing much. Even this shop earned him little money. He had no intention of going back to Majuli. A job at the resort would change his life. In fact, once he was settled here, his plan was to built a house on his uncle's land and bring his parents to Pamua. After their village was eroded by the river, his parents were living life like gypsies—on the river embankment during the rainy season and on the fields during the dry season. Life's been like that for them for a long time now. That they were homeless in their own land was killing them each day. Seeing them like that made Bipul sad too.

Bipul placed the cup of tea in front of Rishi as if he was his guest, not a customer. He poured himself some in a little plastic cup. They both started sipping.

'Rishi da, once the resort is built, please remember me. I am counting on you,' Bipul couldn't look at Rishi's face as he said this. His soft voice was laden with emotion.

'Sure! Let us get the permission first. Once the construction work starts, you will be involved from the beginning.' Rishi knew Bipul was a good boy. He didn't shy away from work. He was energetic and enthusiastic. Once he started something, he did not leave it midway.

Somewhere close by, a deer barked. Even in such places, they appeared suddenly at night. Sometimes, they lost their way and roamed around the village. Sometimes, a calf separated from its mother would bark like this. It was a very sad cry.

Rishi's mobile phone started ringing. Receiving the call, he put it to his ear.

'What are you doing, Rishi?' the deep voice belonged to Hriday da.

'Having tea at Bipul's shop,' Rishi's heart warmed up.

'If you are not busy, why don't you come over to my place?'

Rishi didn't even have to think. After all, he came out in the rain to go some place!

In a hurry, Rishi took out some cash and handed it over to Bipul, but he refused to accept it.

'Bipul, this is not your home. You offer a free cup of tea at home, not in your shop. It's your business. A business does not run for free. I am telling you, take it,' Rishi sounded authoritative as he forced the money on Bipul.

After that, Rishi started walking fast towards the Kohora Chowk. He was angry and sad too. Because of such misplaced generosity, Assamese people didn't do well in business. Right from Lakhminath Bezbarua, who ran a timber business in Orissa, to the present generation of tea planters, professionalism was lacking when it came to business.

It took about 15 minutes to walk to the Kohora Chowk. As he reached the chowk and was about to take a left turn, another light shower of rain started again. Covering himself with the raincoat, he walked faster.

The headlight of a vehicle came from behind. The car was approaching quite fast. This patch of the road was lonely and dark.

Making a screeching sound, the car came to a sudden halt. Rishi jumped aside. There was enough space for the car to pass. So, he resumed his walk. But then, why was the driver behaving so recklessly? Was he drunk? Rishi's antennae went up.

He could hear the sound of the passenger door opening. The headlights went off. The person who got down was coming towards him. Rishi stopped and turned around. Who was this person? What was his motive? Rishi tried to make sense of the madness. He didn't have any enemy. At least as far as he knew. He never hurt anyone knowingly…So?

He didn't have much time to think. Before he could draw any conclusion, the figure, which was closing onto him, jumped at him. Before he could react, the thought that had drawn on him was that he was not being attacked. In fact, he was in a tight embrace. His puny figure was tightly hugged by the body. And no, the body didn't belong to a man, but a woman. A pair of strong womanly arms were closing tightly around him…

'Who is this? What the hell are you doing?' Rishi was bewildered.

'You vagabond…you liar…you escapist…Can't you see me, you stupid Rishi?' Still holding onto him tight, the woman showered those adjectives in a loving tone. Her body was shivering at the impact of the emotion she was going through.

Rishi turned into stone. That voice, that touch, that emotional liberty…this was Lisa. Liz, that's how he used to address her. Ten years…no, more than 10 years…he had not heard that voice, felt that touch…Liz…the centre of attraction in the North Campus, and then JNU…This was, indeed, Lisa.

Overcome with emotions, his lean body started shivering. Was he dreaming or was it a reality? He couldn't decide.

The driver overtook the two figures locked in an embrace and parked the black Bolero aside. In the darkness, emerged another two figures. Rishi, who was still in the embrace of Lisa, saw a tall, good-looking man walking towards them. And holding his finger was a young, cherubic girl. As she hopped towards them, her two plaits started dancing in the wind. She looked like an angel. She was murmuring something in a sing-song voice.

After a long gap, Hridayananda was visiting his native village. His brother informed him that their father was quite unwell. He was admitted in the Lakhimpur Civil Hospital for a few days. He was discharged later and taken home, but soon relapsed. At 80 plus, Hridayananda's father, Dharmeswar Saikia, was a well-known figure in the region. He was a farmer and even though, he had stopped farming because of his age, he was still active in the sense that he gave his sons advice when required and supervised the farming activities. Every day, he got up before dawn. After taking a bath and singing the religious songs, he went straight to the fields. Like opium, the addiction to his paddy fields didn't let old Dharmeswar rest. So, when Hridayananda heard about his illness, he got scared. He had never seen his father unwell. In fact, Hridayananda couldn't remember the last time his father was sick. So, it was only natural that the news of his illness brought all kinds of thoughts to his mind.

Hridayananda rushed home. Usually, one is not sanctioned leave during the peak tourist season. But because of the seriousness of the situation, Hridayananda pleaded his senior to sanction five days of leave. As soon as he got it, he, in his small Maruti, hit the road that led to Lakhimpur.

Reaching home, when he saw the condition of his father, Hridayananda rushed to the most famous specialist in town. After conducting the tests, he did everything within his capacity to take care of his father. Before he appeared on the scene, his father was not getting proper treatment. His brothers were getting him the basic treatment, at times, desi medicine from traditional healers. So, once Hridayananda got him to the proper doctor, his father started responding to the medicine and was alright in no time.

When he was at home, except for the time spent on having meals and sleeping, Hridayananda didn't leave his parents even for a second. Actually, it was after quite a few years that he was staying at home for such a long duration. During his earlier visits, he stayed for half a day or at the most, one night. Staying at home for such a long time made everyone happy, including Hridayananda. His presence worked like a tonic for his ageing parents. Hridayananda too made the most of his stay. He brought staff for the house; shopped generously for his brothers, sisters-in-law, nieces and nephews. The night before returning, he organised a feast at his home for his friends who were still living in the village. He talked to them to his heart's content. In fact, he was surprised to see many of his friends ageing so fast. 'Why didn't you get married? Who will look after you in your old age?' they complained.

Hridayananda was shaken for a moment when he heard their complaint, but soon was in control. He thought, why think about old age. Who knows who will go first? Then who will look after whom? There were many lonely people in society. The whole talk about 'who will take care of you in your old age' was becoming ridiculous. How come so many orphanages and old-age homes were mushrooming? On top of it, who knows when a bullet would snuff out his life! In his case, the question of old age does not arise.

Devoting five days to his parents, his friends and the villagers, and giving his soul the food of love, Hridayananda returned to Kaziranga. As he touched his father's feet before departing, Hridayananda felt two teardrops trickle down his father's lifeless eyes. His father's silent tears and his mother's sobs were the blessings he needed to come back to his workplace with a renewed vigour. He felt free and fresh. Hridayananda managed to shake off the feeling of sadness that was lurking around as he moved ahead on that familiar path.

One morning, as he was having rice and dal sitting in his front yard, Hridayananda got distracted with the thought about his parents. Looking at the birds eating the grains, he recalled his own childhood days, his friends who had changed so much with time. Age spared none. Actually, there was more pain in life than happiness. What they said about life being priceless didn't sound all that true. The life of a bird was so much better, in fact—flying in the sky with no strings attached. In fact, the life of a migratory bird was even better. It's just about flying and flying, in search of a new horizon. North, south, east and west—nothing escaped them.

One day, Hridayananda was standing by a pond, close to a small guard post. This was the pond where a newborn elephant calf had fallen a few days back. The entire herd of elephants and also the forest guards tried to lift up the calf, but in vain. After two days of struggle, it breathed its last. The poor mother kept standing by the pond even after its baby died.

The sun was setting on the horizon. This particular post had only four guards. One of them made tea in the makeshift kitchen they had at the post. To go with the tea, they took out some puffed rice and spiced it up with radish, green chillies and mustard oil. Savouring the delicacy, Hridayananda leisurely chewed a paan.

From this post, one could see the landmass that was recently incorporated into the national park. The Brahmaputra river, the sandy banks and its catchment areas were more prominent in this portion in comparison to the green areas that existed in patches. The reserve forest of 1950 had become the national park in 1978. Because of its size and uniqueness, UNESCO had given it the status of a World Heritage Site. As the number of animals increased, the government was forced to incorporate more and more areas into Kaziranga. The forest, which initially was only 429.33 sq. km, soon grew to be an area of 1,002 sq. km. In the first phase, 43.79 sq. km of Burha Pahar was included in Kaziranga, then came 6.47 sq. km from Sildubi, .69 sq. km from Panbari, .89 sq. km from Kanchanjuri, and 1.15 sq. km from Haldhibari. The biggest inclusion happened in the sixth phase when a huge 376.50 sq. km was incorporated. This huge portion brought along the catchment areas of the Brahmaputra river.

Kaziranga as a forest land was huge. But over the years, many landless people had encroached it. Soon after Kaziranga became a national park, many suspicious elements, which had no local connections, also had appeared on the scene. After about 10 years, living in thatched huts, they assimilated with the locals and became a part of the local culture. No one had valid documents.

So, wherever there were talks of anti-encroachment drives in Kaziranga, there was a parallel drive among these newcomers to prove their identity. It spread a feeling of discontent among the local residents. Had the previous governments conducted some census without accepting bribes from these people, they wouldn't have to go through such fear of getting evicted.

Hridayananda had enough evidence to come to the conclusion that a gang of poachers was getting active in these areas of migrant population. None of the poachers nabbed in the recent past were Naga or any other tribal people, which used to be the case earlier. They belonged to these immigrants. This matter needed to be probed.

There was a trail of smoke that was rising from far. Probably, some land was being cleared to build another hut. Sometimes, the poachers used such smoke signals to deliver a message to their partners. Officials like Hridayananda were fully aware that those huts were the safe haven for many a poacher. But they could not do much because of the political pressure.

Last year, Hridayananda, in a surprise raid, had nabbed three poachers, along with their arms and ammunitions. But what came out of it? Following a strict order from higher authorities, he himself had to release those poachers even before he could register a case against them.

Opening the bundle of betel nut and paan, Hridayananda put another one in his mouth—the betel nut was not fully ripe and didn't taste good.

The afternoon sky was painted in red and grey. The sun was about to set in the heart of Kaziranga. Thousands of birds covered the skyline with their different colours; their twittering filled the air.

Hridayananda's mobile phone started ringing. The ringtone made a contrasting sound against the cacophony of the birds that announced their homecoming. Irritated, he pressed the mute button without bothering to look who was calling him. He didn't feel like talking. Let it ring. He was not obliged to take *every* call. He didn't want to deprive himself of the beautiful scene that was unfolding before him. Looking around, he saw all the forest guards enjoying the spectacular sight. A strange feeling of sadness overpowered his senses.

This post was not all that far away from the range office. As darkness was engulfing the land and the sky above, the noise of the birds were dying out. The fire in the faraway hamlet was still burning. It was still spewing smoke and ashes into the air.

The forest guards were making preparations for dinner and also getting ready for their night patrols. Hridayananda started walking towards the bamboo hut. One of the guards was shaking a lantern to assess how much oil was left for the night.

'Sir, how about another cup of tea?' asked Karuna Haloi, the oldest one of the guards.

'Not a bad idea!' Hridayananda replied, as he took a sip of water from the bottle he was carrying. Pulling up a chair, he sat down close to the hut.

The hearth was still warm. Putting a few dry twigs, Haloi started blowing hard into the bamboo cylinder to light it up. Then, he put the black, almost-distorted kettle on it.

Relaxing in his chair, Hridayananda brought the mobile close to his eyes and peered into it to see the missed call. It was Rishi's and he immediately dialled back.

It kept ringing several times before Rishi finally picked up.

'Yes, Rishi, why did you call?'

'Hriday da, where are you? Why don't you take my calls?'

'I am a jungle man, and I am in the jungle. I was busy when you called,' Hridayananda smiled, as he recalled what had kept him busy.

'Hriday da, do you remember my friend, Liz? I mean Lisa? She met you a couple of days ago.'

'Yes, yes. Of course! She is your friend. What happened to her?'

'Nothing has happened to her. It's about the documentary for which she had interviewed you. She wants some more information and wants to talk to you over the phone. She is back in Delhi,' Rishi's voice was full of enthusiasm.

'That's fine, Rishi. Give her my number.'

'Ok! I am giving her your number right away,' saying this in a hurry, Rishi disconnected the call.

Hridayananda remembered…Three or four weeks back, Rishi had brought this girl, Liz or Lisa, to his office. The tall, good-looking and smart girl was introduced to him as a representative from a famous Delhi-based television channel. She was a documentary filmmaker. She studied with Rishi in Jawaharlal Nehru University. Rishi dropped his studies midway and travelled around the world to play music. Since then, there was no communication between the two.

It was a chance encounter in Kaziranga that brought Rishi and Lisa back together. She said that even in the darkness, she could recognise Rishi's walk from behind. The following week, Rishi helped her with her documentary. As she interviewed the forest employees, she took a sound bite from Hridayananda too. Usually, Hridayananda avoided giving statements to TV channels or newspapers. It was an order from higher up. But he could not say no to Rishi. She could not get any official version for her documentary. Every official she met refused to comment. Hridayananda too avoided those controversial questions, playing it safe in front of the camera. But an expert journalist that she was, Lisa extracted maximum news and views regarding the politics of Kaziranga from him off the camera.

When Hridayananda realised his folly, he requested Lisa not to quote him as her source. She did actually promise not to put him in trouble. She realised that had it not been for Rishi, Hridayananda, serving in a sensitive area, would not have co-operated with a journalist at the first place.

Hridayananda liked Lisa. She was extremely practical, yet empathetic. He suspected Rishi and Lisa were involved romantically when they were students. Even if Rishi was not, Lisa surely had a soft corner for him. Hridayananda could make out from her body language and the way she talked to Rishi. He got curious about Rishi's personal life. What did love mean to Rishi, the wanderer?

Haloi placed a cup of hot tea and two rusks in front of Hridayananda. He used an old aluminium plate as a tray. Haloi, who was a casual staff, was contemplating on leaving Kaziranga to go back home, but Hridayananda was forcing him to stay on for a couple of months.

Originally from Nalbari, Karuna Haloi had been working at the Bagori Range as a casual staff for more than 20 years. He spent all his productive years in hope of becoming a permanent employee some day. His salary had become ₹3,000 per month only a couple of years back. Last year, with a generous increment, it became ₹4,000 per month. That's what stopped him from leaving Kaziranga. His wife and two sons kept nagging him to leave. Nobody cared about his ₹4,000 that kept him away from his family most of his life. The elder son started farming in the four bighas of family land and got married. The younger one got a job as a teacher last year. They wanted him around. But having spent all his life in the jungle, Haloi was now addicted to every little thing that the jungle had to offer. Even after getting two weeks of leave sanctioned, Haloi would get restless after spending just a couple of days in the village and longed to return to the jungle. Some people went through this kind of feeling. Hridayananda could relate to it. For, he too had been affected by this disease. Where did it end? Hridayananda reflected…He let out a deep sigh, without realising. No, there was no end to it… one should not even think about such things.

'What about food? What are you all cooking, boys?' Hridayananda asked, as he started for the Gypsy.

All four of them looked at each other's face.

'I have plucked some spinach leaves from our kitchen garden. Will make a gravy out of it.' The answer came from Haloi, because cooking was the department that he held dear.

'Only spinach gravy? No fish or anything?' Hridayananda asked, shoving another paan in his mouth.

'The market is too far away to buy fish. The boys had caught a few small fishes in the stream. Will make something out of them,' Haloi replied in a rude tone.

Hridayananda let it pass. Fishing in Kaziranga was prohibited and the law was strict about it. The lakes and swamps were full of fishes—a variety of them. But protected by the law, they died natural deaths in the water bodies, emitting a foul smell at times. It's not that those were not targeted by the poachers who came for the rhino horns. But catching fish under heavy patrolling was a difficult task indeed. Sometimes, the guards themselves caught a few.

'I am leaving. The walkie-talkie will be on. In case there is any news, don't hesitate to inform me immediately. We are expecting the minister any day. So, let's be on our toes. If another rhino is killed, we all will lose our jobs.' Giving them the parting shot, Hridayananda started the Gypsy and drove off.

After driving for about 15 minutes through the 'leak', Hridayananda reached the main highway. He headed straight to the Kohora Chowk. He had almost forgotten that he was supposed to meet his source in the local market. There was some big news. It was well past six in the evening, so there was only a slim chance of meeting him today. No villagers stayed out this late. And that man, his source, had this habit of enjoying his drinks in the evenings. That made their meeting at this hour almost impossible. The man owned a mobile phone. But he never picked up when Hridayananda called. When he felt the need, the source only called Hridayananda. And now, he had stopped revealing any secret while talking on the phone. There was this rumour doing the rounds that the talks and messages were being intercepted by some strangers inside Kaziranga. Everyone took it seriously. So, a panic was gripping everyone in Kaziranga—both those protectors and perpetrators.

Stopping his Gypsy a little away from the evening market, Hridayananda got down and started walking towards it. He had a shopping bag in his hand. The market was totally deserted, but he hoped against hope to find his source there. In case, he bumped into him, it should look like that he was there to buy groceries.

But no such luck. Looking around thoroughly, he failed to locate his source. Disappointed, Hridayananda bought a kilo of potatoes before returning to the Gypsy. Those who had spread their fare on a jute cloth, by the side of the road, had started winding up.

The owners of small shacks and permanent shops were sitting in boredom, which found an expression in a regular flow of yawns. Very few buyers were left. Only a few restaurants that served meals were getting ready to welcome tourists. A tantalising aroma of fish and meat curry filled the air.

As Hridayananda was about to speed up, a huge truck moving at breakneck speed tried to overtake him. Behind the truck were three motorbikes that were moving at an equal speed. Each bike had two riders. The truck was still speeding and chasing it were those bikers who were trying to stop it. People who were about to return home, stopped to watch the drama. Hridayananda stopped and thought of something before he too joined the chase.

Once the sun took charge of the day, people started pouring in on the national highway—hundreds of them! Talking excitedly in groups, many of them, tired, plonked themselves on the main road. They stopped the vehicles and soon, paralysed the communication system. In protest, they united together and created a situation that was soon getting out of control.

Kapahua village was situated close to the highway. It was considerably a large village that had about 150 households. But otherwise, it was a normal village, like any other villages in Kaziranga. The previous night, the police picked up two young boys from the village, Naveen and Dimbeswar, suspecting them to be poachers. The news spread overnight, thanks to the mobile networks. The people remained indoors at night, but at daybreak, everyone came out on the street to find out what had happened. Not just from Kapahua, but other nearby villages too.

Besides, a few local leaders, who were putting up a fight against the government's anti-encroachment drive in Kaziranga, were also present in the village. Those leaders and the village chiefs called a meeting early in the morning and arrived at a consensus to block the highway.

There was already unrest among those living inside and around Kaziranga who had no proper land documents, as the threat of getting evicted loomed large. The news of the arrest of two innocent men on the false charge of poaching stirred a hornet's nest. Blocking the highway it was!

A few young men from the village dragged some logs and placed them strategically on the road. One of them brought two old tyres from a nearby Punjabi dhaba and set them on fire. Before the police could go through all the paperwork and reach the spot, about 200 cars had come to a halt, creating a solid traffic jam. As the people from those cars got down and added to the chaos, a team of protesters went to the Kohora Police Station and gheraoed the place. Looking at the strength of the protesters in both places, the highway and the police station, the police didn't know what to do. Bewildered, the station in-charge called his higher officials. The slogans and the shouts of the protesters penetrated deep inside the jungle.

The animals too stopped for a second to sense the source of the noise. However, in all the hullabaloo, the huge rhinos remained blissfully unaware that they were the cause of the agitation—the agitation in which hundreds of people were coming out on the highway to protest against the politics that had roots in the killings of their ilk.

Only a few days ago, such an agitation had taken place at the same spot after two rhinos were killed in a single day. The only difference was that it was somewhat a peaceful one. They had burnt the effigy of the forest minister and in front of the photo of Mahatma Gandhi, they sat on a fast. No newspapers or TV channels failed to report anything that went in the name of rhino protection. They took it as their moral duty to report all the killings and the subsequent incidents.

The trend of the media assuming the role of a watchdog for any environmental issue started way back in 1873, when *Assam Mihir*, the newspaper, started criticising the government's role in protection of its forest resources. It was only when the newspapers started highlighting the issue of felling of trees for human consumptions, the government gave it a serious thought to formulate a forest policy to safeguard it from reckless cutting of trees.

Assam geared up for a forest department as early as 1886. Gustav Mann, the then assistant commissioner, who came on a deputation, put his attention on the forest areas of Assam. It functioned as an unorganised department till 1873, after which it was formalised by dividing it into two sub-divisions—one for Upper Assam and one for Lower Assam. The forest area of Guwahati and Goalpara came under the lower division, while Lakhimpur, Sibsagar and Naga Hills were grouped under the upper division. Before making it official, Gustav Mann had already conducted a detailed survey and submitted a report saying that about 4,565 sq. miles in Assam could be placed under the reserved forest category. At that point, the department functioned as a sister concern of the Bengal administration.

Two suited-booted elderly gentlemen were heard discussing on this serious topic as they stood by the highway after the traffic came to complete standstill. They were heading towards Guwahati from the Golaghat side. Both had retired as higher officials in the state government and shared the same wavelength in terms of knowledge and exposure, and that was exactly what led to the conversation.

A tug of war between Assam and Bengal followed after the forest department was put under the Bengal government. How could Bengal run such a huge forest area? In 1873, Gustav Mann was given the responsibility of the Assam section in the capacity of the assistant conservator of forest, ACF. That was the first step towards an independent forest department in Assam.

In the year 1878, as the post of chief commissioner was created separately for Assam, Gustav Mann was promoted to the rank of deputy conservator of forest, DCF. In the same year, the forest area in Assam was divided into five divisions—Goalpara, Guwahati, Tezpur, Golaghat and Kachar.

Recalling those historical facts, both gentlemen started walking towards the shaded area under the sal trees. Promptly, the uniformed driver produced an expensive flask and two cups. Pouring tea into the cups, he offered them to those gentlemen on a tray.

Poised, the two sipped their tea under the tree. After handing over the empty cups, one of them took out a sleek cigarette case from his pocket. The other one had already started lighting his pipe. Both started smoking in deep silence. The smell of expensive filtered tobacco spread all around.

The place where they were standing could be about a kilometre from the main area of protest. The protesters' slogans had not affected the serenity of this area. Their Toyota was the only private vehicle that got caught in the traffic snarl. The rest were trucks carrying goods, save for a tempo that was carrying three passengers.

Each vehicle caught in the traffic jam maintained the discipline by standing in a line towards the left side of the highway. Everyone was scared. If they broke the line and created a chaos, the police would get them or there were chances of angry protesters pelting a stone or two at their cars. So, everyone was behaving.

The sharp noise of siren pierced through the area as a police convoy passed by in full speed. It seemed some higher-up official was heading towards the spot. Looking at the police team, the gentlemen stopped talking. They looked at each other. God knows what was going to happen…What if the police had to apply force to control the situation? Anything was possible. Patience was a forgotten virtue these days. Both the administrators and the common men, they all were ready to erupt at the slightest provocations. Nobody was afraid to die. This restless psyche had spread all over the world.

The time ticked slowly. Everybody, including the drivers of the vehicles and the two gentlemen, was counting minutes in apprehension after seeing the police convoy. What would happen?

But they didn't have to wait for long to find out.

First, it was the sound of firing. Nobody could ascertain whether it was tear gas or blank fire or actual gunshots.

Soon, the sound of painful cries, angry shouts and screams came from that direction. Pure chaos ensued. As if a herd of wild elephants was let loose in the jungle. As if all the bells in a mental asylum were ringing without control. The protesters' scream mingled with the noise as they ran helter-skelter looking for a safe corner.

The police was wielding their lathis in full gusto. A few boys came running towards the place where the two gentlemen were standing. The police was hot on his heels. The whole situation was getting more and more chaotic.

The calm and serene forest area in a second turned into a battle ground. As if even the trees had stopped breathing and were training their ears to catch the heart-piercing screams of humans.

Throwing the remains of their smokes, the two gentlemen headed for the safety of their cars and waited in silence. Their lips were sealed, but their heartbeats were telling another story…

It took about two hours to bring the situation to its tragic end. Many protesting villagers fell prey to the cane. The police had arrested many men and women. The words doing the round were that the district magistrate himself would come and address the villagers. Even those who were arrested and sent to lock-up would be freed by afternoon. There was no telling if any of those statements were true or just rumours. Then there was this news that many protesters were seriously injured in the lathi-charge. This probably was true, because about half an hour later, an ambulance arrived and many men and women were seen being lifted up onto it. Many versions of the incident floated around in Kaziranga.

When the road was finally cleared and the long queue of vehicles that lay like a dead python for so long, started moving under the strict vigil of the security personnel, it was exactly 12 o'clock in the afternoon.

Rishi had left his hut early in the morning to go to Bokakhat. But the sudden turn of events had stopped him from going. He remained a silent witness to the entire sequence of events. He had heard about such road blockades and protests in Kaziranga before, but never had seen it happen. Today's events brought him into its fold. Though he was sitting on the bench of Bipul's shop, he was getting anxious. As he started towards the epicenter of the problem area, the police had started lathi-charging the protesting villagers. He didn't turn back, but was forced to stop.

Many issues about Kaziranga that had clouded his mind earlier had cleared up once he moved into Kaziranga. Still, he was searching for some answers. He was aware about the cold war between the forest administration and the armed forces or even with the general administration.

Most journalists of Golaghat and Bokakhat were close to Rishi. They respected him. They knew Rishi as Arunabh's friend. Many of them used to have get-togethers at his music school after work. Rishi's musical talent, his down-to-earth nature and his simple lifestyle got him many fans among this circle. He became the universal 'Rishi da'. Some of them were even interested in learning violin.

Many of the reporters had visited the area, taking quotes or bites from the local citizens. Rishi knew that the incident will be the breaking news in all TV channels and leading news in the morning newspapers.

The flow of traffic soon resumed like any other normal day. The news of the roadblock reached till Nagaon. The supervisor of the music school informed him on mobile that the incident had made even Bokakhat tense. Rishi felt dejected. He didn't feel like going to the music school. He thought of returning to his hut. But what would he do at home at this time of the day? Should he go and meet Hridayananda? But he immediately thought against it. In all likelihood, Hridayananda would be busy—with files, meetings, reports, inquiries and what not. Though the forest office was situated inside Kaziranga, it was no less than the Secretariat when it came to the workload. Whenever he went to meet Hridayananda, he always found him busy. There were altogether 152 forest camps in Kaziranga. These camps worked day and night at equal pace. There was always some emergency or the other.

'Rishi da, aren't you going to eat? Or, have you eaten already?' Bipul seemed concerned. His shop was packed with customers till sometime ago. Bipul did good business today. The majority of business came from the travellers who were stopped in the middle of nowhere because of the blockade. All the stale cookies, cakes and even two-day-old bread slices were sold out. No wonder Bipul was in a happy mood. His happiness radiated from his voice and his face.

'When did I have the time to eat? I just had tea and biscuit before coming out. I was planning to eat at Bokakhat. But you have seen what happened,' Rishi said in disgust.

'Alright then, Rishi da, eat with me today.'

'You have your lunch here at the shop?'

'Earlier, I used to go back home for lunch. But since my uncle has given up on farming, I am focusing more on my business. So, I don't like to shut shop in the middle of the day. I cook here these days,' Bipul's voice had a tinge of sadness.

'Have you started selling meals also now?'

'No, no. I just cook for myself in between attending the customers. How can I sell food? You need a lot many things to cook meals and even helpers. Besides, who would come to my shop to eat when there are so many restaurants at Kohora?'

Not waiting for Rishi's reply, Bipul put a wok on the stove. Pouring a little oil in the wok, he put the chopped cauliflower, pumpkin, brinjal and potato into it. In the expert hands of Bipul, the curry started simmering, emitting an enticing aroma. Lighting up his first cigarette of the day, Rishi started taking notes of the village way of cooking.

The traffic was getting sparse. A few cars stopped in front of Bipul's shop, but only to buy a paan or a cigarette. No one stopped for tea. It was time for lunch.

Bipul completed his cooking within half an hour. The menu consisted of a dal that was cooked without onion or turmeric, a vegetable curry, two boiled eggs and rice. Placing all the items on an aluminium plate, he called out for Rishi and offered him a jug of water to wash his hands. After that, he secured the bamboo panels of the door to have some privacy. Rishi sat on a stool. The plate was placed on the rickety table. Bipul sat in front of him.

Rishi suddenly realised that he was actually hungry. He didn't even realise when he wiped clean his plate as they ate indulging in small talks. Bipul was not a bad cook. And it was like a picnic to eat home-cooked food in the market place.

The clock struck two.

Bipul reopened his door.

Rishi took his leave. He didn't want to distract Bipul further from his work.

'You are leaving, Rishi da?'

'Yes. You carry on with our work.'

'Don't think too much about today's incident. Such things keep happening here. In all these years, the government has not got a clue as how to run things in Kaziranga. Kaziranga is saved by the love and involvement of the people who live here. The government cannot do a thing. Had it not been for the villagers, poachers would have wiped out the trees and the animals, turning it into a desert. But what's the point of talking about it? The government doesn't even realise the contribution of its people. They do not even trust us villagers.' Bipul gave his own explanation in the context of the day's event.

'They say, sometimes, villagers shelter poachers. Is it true, Bipul?' Rishi grabbed this opening to find out the truth. He went closer to Bipul as he asked this in a soft voice.

'Nonsense! Not in our villages. There, the poachers live at those Char areas,' Bipul also answered in a whisper. Clearing his throat, he added, 'So many times, we have caught poachers and handed them over to the forest authority. Everybody knows. The government levels such baseless allegations just to evict the villagers from this land.'

A high-end Sedan stopped in front of Bipul's shop. Three foreign tourists and a local boy got down from the car. They ordered tea. Though small, Bipul's shop was becoming popular in this area.

Making an eye contact to say bye, Rishi finally took his leave from Bipul.

Kaziranga was always shrouded in mystery. The more you tried to understand it, the more complicated it became.

Rishi started walking towards the Kohora Chowk.

Amal da was planning another trip to Kaziranga. This time, he planned to stay for long. He wanted to stay at Rishi's hut. The permission for the resort had been granted. But there were still many loose ends to be taken care of. Amal da, without wasting time, wanted to get down to construction. One of Amal da's friends was preparing the site plan. Very soon, Amal da's resort will be functioning on the line of a typical Assamese household. Amal da was particular that no one calls it a resort. He asked them to call it a guest house. The term 'resort', he felt, gave a very commercial feeling. Amal da wanted a small, intimate set-up, where one could spend a few peaceful days. There would be a flower garden, a badminton court, an arrangement for cooking outside in a bonfire, a small pond for fishing and a small kitchen garden. Amal da wanted to keep ducks and chickens, along with a cow for milk. He had conveyed his plans to his friend who was making the blueprint of the guest house. God knows how far Amal da could fulfill his dreams! This guest house, he intended to make, was different from the rest. Amal da didn't want to make staying there an expensive affair.

As Rishi was going through the project plans in his head, which was slowing him down a bit, a car suddenly pulled over near him. Its honks brought him back to reality with a sudden thud.

He looked at the driver. He saw the good-looking man, clad in sports gear and a stylish pair of shades, grinning at him from behind the wheel. That was Jiaur, the assistant manager of the Kapahtali Tea Estate.

'Get on. Where are you headed?' Jiaur asked, as he opened the door with his left hand.

'No idea. No fixed destination actually. Far away, wherever these feet take me…' Rishi gave a philosophical answer, as he made himself comfortable in the passenger seat.

Work on the resort was going on in full swing.

Amal had shifted his entire focus from building flats to building his resort. He had shut the construction work of a housing society in Guwahati midway and huddled his entire labour force into a truck and brought them to Kaziranga to start work on the war footing.

Obtaining the official permissions took a lot of time, thus delaying the execution of the project. A man of action, Amal was mighty irritated with the unnecessary delays. Now that the official part was over, he wanted to push work to meet the deadline. The permission for electricity was still pending though.

The tourist season was yet to commence; they did not come to Kaziranga in October. So, no rush. Bipul kept his shop closed during the day and helped with the construction work at the resort. He operated it only for a few hours in the evenings. Most construction workers were Bipul's customers who came for tea, paan or bidi.

Amal was living with Rishi. He got the Assam-type, thatched-roof hut improvised for his convenience. He built a small modern washroom; the original was a dirty kutcha type. He got a concrete slab made in the kitchen too.

An old woman from Pamua came to clean and cook on a daily basis for a monthly salary of ₹1,000. She took her meals with them. And when Rishi or Amal went for their work, she would go and recite the *naam* at the *namghar*.

Since the construction started, Amal became careful with his money. Rishi, for the first time, saw this calculative side of him.

Though, Amal's drinking habit after work remained the same as before, work on the resort continued till late night. Amal, who was constantly on the site, would come for a quick bath and a quick peg of whiskey. The workers were there till nine in the evening. Before they would wind up, Amal would go to the site and take note of every detail, including the things that they would need for the next day's work. After that, he returned to Rishi's hut to gulp down a couple of more pegs before having dinner and finally, calling it a day.

Sometimes, they both would visit other resorts in Kaziranga or nearby towns such as Nagaon, Bokakhat or Golaghat. Sometimes, they invited their friends and acquaintances and got together in the evenings.

Rishi's life had changed. He went to his music school on those fixed days in Amal's vehicle. He was, in fact, forced to use it. Amal da had told him with authority that other than his music school, he was to spend all his time on the resort, supervising the construction work. Just because he was Arunabh's friend, Amal da thought he had the same hold over him. Rishi didn't have much to do at the construction site, but once the resort was operational, he would have to do the managerial duty, right from taking care of the guests to looking after the kitchen staff. They had the plan to engage people from Pamua. Rishi was aware that the people in the village were already fighting among themselves for the coveted posts. So, he was trying to device a strategy so that none of the villagers were unhappy and at the same time, the poor people were engaged in some capacity or the other and can earn something from the resort. He was already facing problems in that respect. But these types of hiccups were only to be expected. By applying little shrewdness, he could make an all-pleasing plan. But he was only apprehensive about those families that were a little well to do and influential. They could pose major problems. But then, que sera sera…

Rishi, in this regard, had to visit Lakhimi frequently. She served as an important link for him. Interacting with her, Rishi had realised that for a girl of her age, Lakhimi was quite mature and practical. Only her shy disposition stopped others from getting to know her. Despite being practical, she was not a complex person. He was amazed that for someone who was so young and semi literate, she knew the pulse of the people, and could explain their psyche in the context of the village culture.

Lightening struck some place far away.

It's been constantly raining for the past two days. It hampered the construction work, but didn't stop it completely. Rishi and Amal were happy that before the monsoon arrived, the construction work would be more than halfway through. The skeleton of the resort was already built. Amal was now diverting his attention to other things than the main building. The digging of the pond would be completed in a couple of days. It had to be finished before the rains started. Amal had borrowed a Bihari mali from one of his judge-friends and assigned him the work of landscaping the flower and the kitchen gardens. Ten young boys and girls from Pamua were sent to Guwahati for a month-long training course in hotel management. Amal wanted only professionals for his set-up. Rishi also had this opinion that a business could never progress if started on an amateurish note.

Hridayananda wished he could do more for Amal's guest house, but was helpless because of his own responsibilities. He often expressed his regret over his inability to devote more time to it. But Amal was convinced that it was Hridayananda who paved the path for the foundation of the resort. Had he not helped in the initial stages, Amal wouldn't have dared to go ahead with it.

Hridayananda's workload had increased manifold. The issue of rhino killings had become a global one. The government was putting full pressure on the forest department. One wrong step and he would be transferred. Hridayananda didn't have the heart to leave Kaziranga. So, he was trying his best not to give them a reason.

In between his office duty and field visits, Hridayananda managed to visit the construction site on and off. During his free time in the evenings, he sometimes joined Amal and Rishi at the latter's place. Still, he tried to keep his friendship with Amal under wraps. He had many enemies—right from the forest office to the administration, from poachers to the ministry level—everywhere. There was some kind of conspiracy going on in his department. Though they lived in the lap of Mother Nature, the complexities of life had turned them somewhat cynical.

Despite his hectic schedule, Amal was missing Arunabh. He didn't like it without him. Though Arunabh, his first cousin, was quite younger than him, Amal had full faith in Arunabh's decisions. So many times, his timely advice had bailed him out of sticky situations.

Amal was close to Arunabh since the latter was an infant. They played together on the banks of Brahmaputra. Only Arunabh had the guts to criticise Amal whenever he made some mistake. Nobody else in the family dared to do that. Without Arunabh, Amal felt lost.

Actually, Arunabh had gone to South India. The newspaper that he worked for was celebrating its anniversary in a big way. All out-stationed journalists were invited. Alongside the celebrations, there would be a meeting to chalk out their future strategy. Arunabh wanted to tour the entire South India before returning home. Amal spoke to him just the other day. From his excited tone, Amal could make out the he was having a good time.

The rain was beginning to irritate Amal. This year, it rained even during the winter months. Now, before the monsoon hit the state, it started again. Such rains created havoc on daily life. Despite all the rains, they said Assam received rainfall that was 20 per cent below normal.

The proprietor of Duara Construction, Amal, made some mental calculations, according to which, the guest house would be ready by October, that is just before the tourist season starts. The building part was his department, but for other things that required to make the guest house functional, he entirely depended on Rishi. He just wished Arunabh would return soon so that he could breathe easy.

Rishi had gone to Bokakhat. He had taken Amal's car. Amal was getting worried when he did not return even at this hour. The night was getting deeper by the second. He tried calling him, but Rishi didn't pick up his call. That worried him all the more. The driver was also new to this area. God knows if they were in some trouble!

Amal was bored sitting at the construction site. It was Saturday; Amal loved Saturdays. He had no intention of working on a Saturday evening. Not that days and dates meant much to people like him, but the idea of a relaxed Saturday evening and a holiday on Sunday stayed with him like a tradition.

Now that the work was progressing as per the schedule, Amal was feeling quite confident—confident enough to allow his fun-loving side resurface.

Amal's huge, black vehicle at last alighted on the main road and stopped by the construction site. Amal saw a smiling Rishi coming out, holding a packet in his hand.

'What took you so long, Rishi? It's Saturday,' Amal asked, as he took a long puff of his freshly lit cigarette.

'Don't ask, Amal da. I got badly tied up. There was a meeting in Bokakhat to discuss the agitation for land holdings. They forced me to speak on the issue. Do you think I am equipped to talk in a meeting? I don't even have an understanding of the subject. So, mumbling a few lines in support of the agitation, I sneaked out.' Rishi was both excited and agitated, as he said that.

Amal was surprised. Did the residents of Kaziranga see this artistic person as their leader? Hopefully not! He was depending on Rishi to look after the guest house. He couldn't afford to let him go.

A little worried, Amal threw the stub of his cigarette.

'Let's go out, Rishi. Let's not cook today. We will eat out,' Amal said with a calmness that he didn't really feel.

Both sat in the car. The driver started it immediately, towards Nagaon.

It was quite dark by then. The traffic on the road was thin. People preferred to be home by this time. And the night-service buses that started from both Upper and Lower Assam would take some time to reach Kaziranga.

After driving for a while, the driver pulled the car into a resort called Green Peace. Amal had been to this place several times. It was a nice and expensive place with a well-stocked bar. Not everybody could afford to walk into this one.

Amal told Rishi that they would drink and have dinner there and then go back to Pamua. Rishi didn't complain. He knew the futility of doing so, once Amal da's mind was made up.

There was no one at the bar. Amal, occupying a corner table, ordered for two large pegs of whiskey with soda. Rishi, in Amal da's company, was getting into the habit of drinking almost regularly. But as he got high very fast, Amal kept an eye on the quantity he took. Amal was strict about it.

They were just sipping on their drinks as a white man in a white tee and khaki shorts, donning a red cap, walked in. As the bar was empty, he came towards them and asked, 'Hey, can I join you guys? I need a drink.' Without waiting for a reply, he pulled one of the empty chairs and sat down with them.

Seeing a foreigner in his bar, the manager came running and greeted him.

Ordering a particular brand of wine, the foreigner pulled his chair closer to Amal's and shook hands with both Rishi and Amal. Introducing himself as Thomas, he said that he was from London, working on wildlife conservation. Reading about issues such as rhino killings, flood and encroachment in Kaziranga on the Internet, he decided to visit Assam. This was his fifth day in Assam. He would stay for three months to study wildlife in Kaziranga.

Amal talked about his new venture as a part of the introduction and how in a way he is also interested in the goings-ons of Kaziranga.

Thomas was curious about Amal's resort, as he himself was staying at one of the resorts in Kaziranga. Rishi explained everything in details.

Thomas was an attentive listener, a curious one. He posed meaningful and technical questions—as if he himself was interested in opening a resort in Kaziranga. The evening was getting interesting. Having drinks with a foreigner and talking about one's business was not a bad idea after all.

With slight hesitation, Thomas asked how true it was that many resorts were opened illegally on the farming land. Why were a few resorts demolished? Was it true that the government was using this particular issue for not giving valid land documents to the local residents? If the cultivable land was converted into commercial land use, what would remain of Kaziranga? A load of resorts? He even asked Amal if he had obtained the necessary permissions to open his.

Amal was shocked with Thomas' volley of questions. How did he know so much? In just five days, he had gathered so many facts! He got suspicious about this innocent-looking white man. He started asking pointed questions to Thomas about his business.

In a very calm and normal tone, Thomas replied to all his questions, saying that he came from Manchester, and worked in a zoo called Chester for three months, where he had to take care of two baby rhinos. That's why his interest in Kaziranga. He gathered that to know more about rhinos, he had to visit Kaziranga. Keeping that as his aim, Thomas worked in a restaurant for a few months and saved money. Thomas was quite young, he had not even completed his graduation. After spending three months here, he would resume his studies as a science student. He would, in fact, love to dedicate his life towards the conservation of rhinos and other wild animals. He wanted to know why people were so greedy about its horn that they would go the extent of killing such an innocent animal.

Amal looked at his watch. It was nine in the evening. After a hard day's work, he was feeling tired, both mentally and physically. Thomas too looked at his watch. The resort, Danshiri Echo, where he was staying, was located at Agaratali that was quite far from that place. Amal was aware of this small resort, by the bank of Dhansiri river, that was famous for its true Assamese flavour. He felt a surge of emotion for this fair-skinned boy. They knew the meaning of the word 'commitment' and whatever they did, they did it with complete dedication. They won't do anything just for the heck of doing it, but would go to the roots of things. Little wonder the British could rule over so many countries once. This young guy was a fine example of his race.

Amal, in the adjoining restaurant, ordered food for all three. Thomas meekly protested, but Amal insisted on having food together. But sensing his discomfort when Amal asked him what was troubling him, Thomas said he was looking for a place to spend the night, as the tempo that brought him here from Kaliabar refused to take him back to Danshiri Echo. As the driver belonged to this area, he just dropped him here, leaving him to fend for himself. With no public transport available at this hour, he saw this place and walked in for a drink. But basically, he was looking for a place to spend the night.

As spending a night at this particular resort would cost him a bomb, Amal assured him that after dinner, he would drop him at Dhansiri Echo. There was no need to worry. Rishi offered to host him for the night at Pamua village, if he wished. Thomas, however, opted for Amal's offer to get dropped off at Dhansiri Echo, as he had some morning assignment to carry out.

They ordered food according to Thomas' choice of dishes. By the time they sipped the last peg of whiskey and had food, it was 10 o'clock.

The road was deserted, so the driver drove the car at full speed. The few cars that crossed on the highway were also at full speed. There were signboards indicating the speed limit within the Kaziranga, but nobody paid any heed. Rules were meant to be broken. In fact, they laughed at the administration, comparing it to Blind Dhritarashtra.

Lighting a cigarette, Amal tried calling his mother at Guwahati. The network was poor. Rishi and Thomas kept chatting, non-stop.

With no traffic to slow them down, it took them about half an hour to reach Dhansiri Echo. Dropping Thomas there, Amal got back to the car with a promise to meet up soon. Amal assured him that once his guest house was ready, any time Thomas came to Kaziranga, he was welcome to stay there for free. Thomas loved it. He shook hands twice with them.

As they reached the side road that led to Pamua village, the driver was forced to stop the car. There was a huge gathering of people on the road. This was something unusual considering the time of the night. The entire village otherwise goes to bed by nine. So, what caused the commotion?

Once the car was pulled over, Amal and Rishi got down. They started walking towards the group. Rishi noticed that most people were standing in front of Lakhimi's house.

Something was wrong. Leaving behind Amal, he rushed towards Lakhimi's place.

The people were talking in a hushed tone. Most of them were, in fact, silent. The whole atmosphere seemed spooky.

Among the shadowy figures, Rishi saw Tarani, the member of the Jeep Safari Association. He was standing silently, wearing just a *gamosa* to cover the lower half of his body.

'Hey, Tarani. What happened? Why have so many people gathered here?' Rishi couldn't conceal his anxiety.

Seeing Rishi, Tarani came close to him and whispered, 'Don't ask, Rishi da. A horrible accident. After having his dinner, Padmeshwar daity came out to close the bamboo gate. God knows from where a hungry tiger came and attacked him, biting off a chunk of meat from his shoulder. Daity didn't have a chance. He fell then and there. A scream came out as he fell. Hearing that, Lakhimi came out with a lamp and saw him lying there. Following that, there was a huge ruckus. The villagers, who were about to sleep, came out with *dhol*, *taka* and *taal* to scare off the tiger.'

Narrating the incident left Tarani tired. But he added that he himself took Padmeshwar peon to the government hospital in Bokakhat immediately. But Padmeshwar had already lost plenty of blood. God knows if he would survive or not!

It was not one of those usual, rushed mornings. Hridayananda got up late from bed. On a gazetted holiday, sometimes, he could avoid going to the office. Though today was not an official holiday, he could afford to take it easy. There were a few days in the year when he could break the monotony of his hectic routine.

He was expecting a few members of a well-known NGO from Guwahati. Every year, this organisation called Friends of Forest visited Kaziranga and set up health camps for animals. Not the wild ones, but the domestic animals living in the interior villages of Kaziranga. They carried out preventive measures to stop all kinds of epidemic. Since most diseases spread through such domestic animals, once they were vaccinated, it made the wild ones less susceptible to these diseases.

The NGO got in touch with the chief conservator of forest, CCF, for permission and co-operation. He permitted them to hold the camp at the Bagori Range after apprising them of the guidelines. Because of the Bagori Range's geographical location—it is often submerged in stagnant water—it had proved to be a vulnerable spot when it came to diseases.

This was the reason why Hridayananda was relieved from his routine duty for a day. The NGO would be carrying out its camp during the day. Hridayananda just had to supervise, that's all.

Actually, the forest department had a complete network for such work. It employed departmental vets and officials. But if someone from outside volunteered to hold such camps, the department usually obliged. Many people alleged that the forest department didn't conduct these activities in the interior areas. Though Hridayananda never admitted it but, in the heart of heart, he knew that those allegations were indeed true.

The NGO people were supposed to reach by 10 in the morning. They were planning to work throughout the day at Bagori and probably move to some other location the next day.

Today, Hridayananda carried out his morning rituals at a slow pace. Actually, he was not feeling himself for the past few days. He had a persistent cough. He was feeling weak and was finding it difficult to concentrate. The cough was creating problem during his night vigils. The sound got carried far and wide at night and was a total giveaway for the poachers.

He did consult a doctor who gave him some antibiotics. It was some throat infection. He was advised to stop having betel nut. But how could he leave this dear, old habit just like that? He was just afraid of contacting malaria. So many people in Kaziranga die of this disease every year. Nobody outside Kaziranga is aware of this fact. Most patients die due to the lack of proper treatment. Malaria is, indeed, the most dreaded disease in the national park.

Dijen was done with his cooking.

Hridayananda was planning to have lunch with the NGO people. But he never left his quarter without having food. This has also been an old habit with him.

After the food was cooked, Dijen cleaned up the kitchen in a hurry. Then, without even serving Hridayananda the meal, he picked up his bicycle and left. He said there was some trouble at the tea garden. The big boss was getting strict. His duty started from eight in the morning, but he had to mark his attendance even before that.

There are four tea gardens and more than 200 villages inside the official boundaries of Kaziranga. It is a roughly estimated figure. Most of the villagers are poor people. Only the garden owners and managerial-level employees are well off.

During the dry season, when fodder for the animals was scarce, many villagers left them in the grasslands in Kaziranga. They had no other alternative. It was a difficult task for them to source out a square meal. So, what could they do about their herd?

These domestic animals fed on the wild grasses and trees, and also spread the germs that then gets passed on to the wild animals. This also has an adverse impact on the progenies of the wild animals.

The main problem, however, comes from the fertilisers and pesticides that are liberally used by the tea gardens. Such chemicals are the silent killers. There was a cold war going on between the owners of those gardens and the forest people. But at present, there is not a solution in sight.

The Numaligarh Refinery, which was set up by the Dhansiri in 2001, brought along with it a host of problems for the flora and fauna of Kaziranga. True, the refinery is an asset for Assam, but why couldn't the policy-makers think of a way so as not to patronise one asset at the cost of another?

Hridayananda heaved a heavy sigh. Who would hear about these endless problems and who would act upon them?

His phone started ringing.

Who could be calling him before eight in the morning? The number belonged to Amal.

'Are you up? I have something important to discuss,' Amal sounded slightly agitated.

'What kind of a hell has broken loose so early?'

'I cannot talk over the phone. We have to meet. Can I come over to your quarter right now?' Amal sounded anxious.

'No. Not now. I am about to leave. I have a busy schedule today. Come in the evening. But give me a call before you come,' Hridayananda said in a calm voice.

Amal, probably, was a little disappointed. But Hriday's serious tone conceded him to say yes to the evening programme.

Keeping the phone down, Hridayananda reflected. He had not met Amal for a long time.

The construction of the guest house was in full swing. Amal was hell-bent on inaugurating it this season itself. It seemed possible. Most of the construction work was nearing completion. Amal was proceeding with proper planning and calculations.

Hridayananda was getting late.

Hurrying up with his bathing ritual, he got dressed before plating up his morning meal—dal, rice and a vegetable fry. Exactly after 15 minutes, Hridayananda started his Gypsy.

He drove for about eight to 10 kilometres down on the highway before maneuvering his jeep onto a kuccha road, adjacent to a resort towards his left. The animal health camp was being organised at the *namghar* of a village situated at the foothills. As he got closer to the *namghar*, he could see three Tata Sumos being parked outside. Those, he was sure, belonged to team of the NGO.

Hridayananda was aware that such camps carried out the vaccinations for diseases such as anthrax, foot and mouth disease and black quarter. The bovines often suffered from these three diseases and when they went to the jungle for grazing, they passed on their germs to the wild animals.

Hridayananda walked fast. He felt happy. Probably for the diversion it provided from his monotonous routine.

Before the inauguration of the camp, there would be a talk by the organisers on their aims and objectives. They would be making an appeal to the villagers to remain vigilant against any syndrome of such diseases. They would, at the end, distribute small gift items.

A worn-out tent was pitched on the courtyard of the *namghar* to block out the sun. A man was already delivering a lecture in front of the gathering of village people and their animals.

Seeing Hridayananda, a few youngsters came forward to welcome him.

Hridayananda felt a tremor inside. Probably, he was also expected to deliver a talk. He suffered from stage fear. But if the situation demanded, he would recite the good old government mantra.

He was taken to the dais and made to sit on a chair.

But it seemed luck was on his side. Looking at the huge gathering, the organisers decided to cut short on the lecture part. So, just introducing Hridayananda to the people and also offering him a *gamosa* as a token of respect, they brought the whole procedure to an end. They soon started examining the animals.

Hridayananda was acquainted with quite a few people in the NGO. They had been visiting Kaziranga for the past two consecutive years. Unlike many others, they worked with sincerity.

The whole place buzzed with activities. The four vets, who belonged to the NGO, started examining the animals and injecting them. Except for sitting and watching them, Hridayananda had nothing else to do. He decided to take a round later.

If they could vaccinate all the domestic animals, the wild animals would be safe at least for another year.

Breaking his trend of thoughts, a pretty girl offered him a steaming cup of tea. Taking a good look at her, he realised that she was not an Indian, but rather a foreigner. Probably, she was working with the NGO.

He thanked her as he accepted the tea. The girl gave him an endearing smile.

The chief executive of Friends of Forest, Madhurya Barua, came to meet Hridayananda. 'Here you are, Saikia da. We got a little delayed today. Look at all these animals! We will be able to wind up only by late evening.' Madhurya's smile reflected excitement and a sense of achievement.

'Your dedicated service here has really made an impact. Though we have our own hospitals and a full-fledged team of vets, we have not been able to work like you guys. These remote villages have not been benefiting from our health schemes at all,' Hridayananda said, hesitantly.

Madhurya did not make any comment. He was aware about the ground realities. He knew about the bureaucratic red tapism. But he was a polite young man.

Hridayananda got up and took a round of the camp with Madhurya.

Not so far away from where they were standing, there was a commotion of some sort. Walking towards it, they saw a huge buffalo being forced to lie down on the ground. Its legs were tied up. The buffalo was protesting with all its might. They were trying to vaccinate it, but it was not an easy task. The buffalo refused to lie still, even for a moment, and it seemed to have the force of a thunder inside it.

The vet, at his wit's end, pushed the injection with force. The buffalo tried hard to protect itself from the jab, but failing to do so, let out a piercing cry. It was a painful scene to watch.

The entry to Kaziranga for tourists is closed in April. It reopens only in October. This is the period when the herd of tamed elephants used for various government projects get time to relax. But these are also the months in which the herd gets affected by diseases. Another NGO worked towards the vaccination of the entire elephant population working in Kaziranga.

Not too many people are aware of how dedicatedly some NGOs are working for the ecosystem in Kaziranga. The prominent among those are Early Birds, Walt, Evergreen, Aaranyak, Assam Anglers' Association, Gharua, Nature's Society, Manas Bandhu, Nature's Beacon, Nature's Banyaprem, Kaziranga Wildlife Society, Hornbill Prokriti Sangha, Lachit Rover Cruise, Environmental Training Centre…Hridayananda couldn't recall all the names. The NGOs offered their service with sincerity and without making much noise.

The day that started on a busy note, soon became afternoon and the afternoon gave way to dusk.

The lunch at the event was organised by the village head at his place. Cooked in wood fire, it was a simple meal of rice, dal, sabzi and fish *tenga*. Hridayananda enjoyed the home-cooked meal, especially the fish *tenga*. The ponds, lakes and swamps in Kaziranga were filled with fish, but as the law prohibited fishing of any kind, there was no way one could savour those fishes. One could admire the big fishes, but that's about it.

Like rhino poaching, there were instances of illegal fishing in these water bodies. They fished at night and smuggled their catch out to sell in the nearby towns. In fact, a couple of forest guards were also found hand in glove with the fishermen. A few also got suspended from their jobs, as there was enough evidence against them.

When Sarat Chandra Sinha was the chief minister of Assam, he allowed fishing at the Kalmua Lake a day before Bhogali Bihu. But that tradition soon became a commercial activity and the forest department was forced to stop that practice. Such experiments go wrong at times and the boomerang effects come to the fore.

After completing the health check-up and vaccination of the all the domestic animals that were brought to the camp, the mood of the NGO workers was that of jubilation. They were planning to spend the night at the forest guest house, Aranya Lodge. They had to conduct another camp at Bokakhat the very next day.

By the time Hridayananda finished signing a few documents as the forest department's representative at the camp and returned home, it was already eight in the evening. Amal had called him thrice towards the end of the day. Amal was the serious kind; if he got stuck on an idea, he would not stop before solving it.

Parking his Gypsy, Hridayananda was about to open the lock of his door when Amal's car pulled up at his gate. He could not see Amal in the dark, but could make out that he had got down from his car. Hridayananda switched on the light of the portico. Seeing Hridayananda home, the white cat came forward to welcome him. As he entered the house, the cough started. There was no sign of stopping…

Springing a surprise on Hridayananda, Amal pushed the curtains aside to show his presence. Beside him, stood a young woman. Almost paralysed after the coughing attack, Hridayananda could not make out if she was a young girl or a married woman. Then, taking a good look at the beautiful, serene face, he could make out she was not wearing the vermilion mark, the symbol of a married woman, on her forehead.

Hridayananda didn't know how to react. Who could this woman be, coming to his place at this hour? From her dress and mannerism, he could make out that she was from some village.

'Do you recognise her, Hriday? Do you remember meeting her ever?' Amal threw the question at a bewildered Hridayananda. Amal sat down in a chair and asked the woman to occupy the other one.

'I think…I am sorry, but I cannot place her…Who is she?' cornered, Hridayananda asked with hesitation.

'Huh! All government officers suffer from selective amnesia. You are also one of them. Ungrateful…no humanity at all!' Barking those words, Amal started pacing up and down.'Why, she is Lahan's wife—Lahan, for whom your midnight mission was accomplished…It was Lahan's presence of mind that saved you and me from getting shot. It's been a year now, but your department has done nothing for his family.' Amal was angry and disappointed, both.

Suddenly, everything became clear to Hridayananda. Could he ever forget the sacrifice that young, dedicated forest guard made that night to save them? After his death, his family was facing hardships. But he made a resolution to do something about it. He must save the family from getting destroyed. It was already late.

Actually, there was no provision in the rule book to help out the family of a deceased. There was a proposal to appoint Lahan's younger brother as a casual staff. There was some communication to the CCF to that effect. The CCF was okay with the idea. But even though, there were a lot of vacant posts in Kaziranga, it took time to get sanctioned by the government. One had to wait…

Hridayananda had never met Lahan's wife. She had never come to him. Only the brother was in touch. He only handed over the body to his family. The woman, who had gone berserk with grief that day, had no resemblance to this woman sitting in front of him. This one was a calm, quiet and distant entity.

Hridayananda's cough had subsided on its own. An uneasy calm had descended on the room. Hridayananda was feeling angry with himself. Lahan had literally given his life and soul to his job. But after his tragic death, the family got nothing in compensation. If the minister felt it deemed, he could have done something. Otherwise, the government was not bound by any rule. He felt disgusted.

The atmosphere in the room was charged.

Then, there was a sound of sobbing. Lahan's wife broke down. The tears from her eyes joined the stream of water running down her nose. That beautiful face was now distorted with uncontrollable sobs and it made the whole situation all the more unbearable. It was almost as if the airflow in the room had suddenly stopped.

Amal walked out. The light went off. Load shedding…

Darkness outside and darkness inside…Amid the sound of soft cries, Hridayananda stood stupefied.

The hospital at Bokakhat was not equipped to treat Padmeshwar Bora. The part of his body where the hungry tiger had sunk its teeth was badly infected. The wound would require some time and medication to heal. Luckily, the tiger didn't snatch away the arm. If the tiger had one moment longer with Padmeshwar, his life would have ended then and there. He was admitted in the hospital for a week. He had lost plenty of blood and was unconscious for one whole day. After seven days, the doctor told Lakhimi that whatever they could do, they did. But he was not healing, so they would have to refer him to the Gauhati Medical College. They preferred Guwahati over Jorhat or Dibrugarh medical colleges, though those were closer, for medical reasons.

Lakhimi's worries multiplied at the doctor's decision. She was not familiar with even Jorhat, the town closest to Kaziranga. There was no reason for her ever to leave the village. Girls, who were born in the village, grew up in the village. And once they attained the marriageable age, they were married off to someone from a nearby village. They grew old in that same village.

Because her father was in the government job, they had an opportunity to travel to a few nearby towns. At least, she had seen the Rang Ghar and Kareng Ghar at Sibsagar and visited a few relatives at Golaghat. She had been to as far as Nagaon. None of her friends were lucky enough to visit even Golaghat or Jorhat. Unbelievable, as the world has shrunk to a global village for many, but that's the way life has been for the villagers in Pamua, a village, where many tourists flock to sample the ways of village life and have a proper Assamese dish at the restaurant, Assamese Meal.

In her hour of need, Amal, Rishi or Hridayananda didn't leave Lakhimi's side. Every day, they took stock of the situation and helped her accordingly. Amal had provided his car to her brothers to commute to the Bokakhat Hospital. When the doctor advised Lakhimi to take her father to Guwahati, Amal and Rishi were also present. They understood what was to be done and Amal assumed the role of her guardian.

Employees from the post office where Padmeshwar worked visited him frequently. The department was ready to pay for the medical expenses. Padmeshwar was entitled to earned leave, medical leave, etc. If his treatment overshot the number of leaves left, then he would be sanctioned leave without pay. That would not affect his job. Lakhimi didn't understand the official mumbo jumbo. But Amal and Rishi found out everything that they needed to know.

Lakhimi was standing in a dark corner of the hospital verandah and crying softly, holding the *chaddar* over her eyes. The younger brother was holding her, wearing a blank expression.

'Hey, Lakhimi. Why are you crying? Don't worry. Everything will be okay. I know most of the doctors in Gauhati Medical

College. We will take your father there. In no time, he will be alright,' Amal tried to console her, as Rishi stood there by her side.

All the arrangements were made to take Padmeshwar to Guwahati. But the biggest problem was to leave the house without anyone around to take care of the boys, the farm and the livestock. Besides, the boys had their school to attend.

The village head and the young boys of the village came to their rescue. Rakheswar took charge of the cattle and goats. Rakheswar's daughter, Tora, would make sure that Lakhimi's brothers were fed and they attended school. Tora was Lakhimi's best friend. All her friends—Tora, Rupeswari, Nirala and Rupahi—were with her all the time. They cried when she cried. They were with her in every sense of the word.

Without delaying any further, they decided to take Padmeshwar to Gauhati Medical College the very next day. Amal rang up his doctor-friends to start the admission procedure. They decided to take Padmeshwar in an ambulance; Lakhimi would accompany him. Rishi would go in the morning by bus and do the necessary paperwork. He too had a couple of friends in the medical college.

Rishi's house in Roopnagar remained closed most of the time. One room was rented out to a young couple. Rishi's elder brother was based out of Mumbai for his job. His sister was settled in America. Whenever Rishi visited Guwahati, he barely went to his house. Rather than going to an empty house, he preferred to stay with his friends. Once or twice in a year, he got the house aired and cleaned. The couple looked after the campus well. It was a relief for Rishi.

Rishi had a friend who ran a small lodge close to the medical college. He arranged one room for Lakhimi to stay till her father was admitted. Rishi reached the hospital at nine in the morning. He spoke to his friends. The ambulance carrying Padmeshwar arrived at one in the afternoon. The initial work was already done. They managed to get a bed in the medicine ward. Since Padmeshwar required treatment from both medicine and surgery, it suited them fine. The doctors from the surgery department would visit him there.

Once done with the hospital formalities, Rishi took Lakhimi to the lodge in a cycle-rickshaw. Lakhimi seemed to be in a daze as she tried to take in the hustle and bustle of the city life. She felt intimidated by the traffic, huge buildings and busy market areas. Without Rishi by her side, she would have felt utterly lost.

In the village, she used to treat Rishi like her guest. But now, this lean, bearded man looked so much in charge of everything. It seemed as if he owned this huge city and she was *his* guest.

It was a small lodge—just three rooms. Each room had one stove and a few basic utensils. This Assam-type house, which was situated at the foothills, was neat and clean. The main hall had a television set. The owner of the lodge, Kamal Kalita, and Rishi went to the same school, Cotton Collegiate. Now, he ran a small chemist shop on the premises of the medical college. He started this lodge about two years ago. There were a couple of such small lodges in that area that catered to the patients and their relatives.

When they arrived, Kamal was still at the shop. His wife, Savitri, gave Rishi the key to his room. The small room had two single beds, a clothes rack, and a table and a chair. An old ceiling fan buzzed over their heads.

Lakhimi was quiet. Never in her life had she imagined that one day she would have to take so much of responsibilities.

In the last few days, the life that she had known had changed altogether.

Keeping their luggage in its proper place, Rishi explained to Lakhimi what she needed to do. The hospital would provide food for Padmeshwar. She would have to cook only for herself. Looking at her pale face, Rishi assured her that everything would be alright; only she needed to be patient. And since there was no need for an attendant by the patient's side, her trouble had been reduced considerably.

As Rishi explained everything to her, Lakhimi just kept staring at him with a blank look.

Savitri came in carrying a tray with two cups of tea and a plate full of biscuits. She had already heard about the incident from her husband. Now, putting her hands around this innocent village girl, she assured that she would not face any problem there. She would personally take care of her needs and with Rishi around, there was absolutely no reason to worry. Everyone loved Rishi.

Listening to Savitri's high praise for Rishi, Lakhimi looked at him. Sipping from his cup, he was busy making the list of things that needed to be purchased from the market. He was too busy to notice what was going on around him.

Collecting the plate and the cups, Savitri went out of the room. Rishi was still busy completing the list. Running his fingers through his hair, he was thinking hard if any more additions were to be made to the list.

Lakhimi, without even realising, kept staring at him all this while. Once done, Rishi lifted his head and looked at her. His eyes met hers. Lakhimi felt embarrassed. She tried saying something, but words did not come out quite. The words chocked her. Rishi too tried to say something, but he just turned red. As if the air in the room had grown heavy all of a sudden. And their incoherent sentences collided with the heavy blanket that the air had spread in the room. Just then, Rishi's mobile started ringing. It was Amal da.

Rishi hurriedly updated him on the day's events. He wished the phone had not rung at that precise moment. His mind was playing all sorts of games on him…After listening to him, once satisfied, Amal disconnected the phone.

'Lakhimi, you rest for a while. I will go to the market and buy the stuff. Before that, I will visit Uncle. If the doctors have prescribed some new medicines, I will get them. You visit him in the afternoon.' Rishi got up to leave. But before leaving, he taught her how to operate the stove and told her to lock the door after him.

Lakhimi bolted the door once Rishi left. She then spread a clean bedsheet over the mattress. The ceiling fan was making an irritating buzzing sound. She switched it off. But soon the room became hot. She opened the back door to let the fresh air in. There was an iron grill at the verandah. It was safe. Fear. The word raised all kinds of emotions in her mind. What was fear? Who should she fear? The jungle of Kaziranga or this concrete jungle of Guwahati? After her father had been attacked by a tiger, the feeling of fear had lost all meaning for her. After the sudden death of her mother, and now, a near-death experience of her father, what was there to fear? Maybe, there was. But she didn't want to think about those right now.

As she stretched on the bed, immersed in her thoughts and still staring at the fan, sleep took over her senses. Her tired body, the uneasiness that arouse from an unaccustomed surrounding and sadness of the mind were all too much for her to bear.

Sleep took her back to her familiar jungle and the whistling sounds. Someone stood by her bed. Who could that be? Was it her mother?

'Aaijani, don't be nervous...I am there with you!' the voice of her loving mother came from somewhere far. As if it was an echo.

Lakhimi had no idea for how long she lay there inert. A loud knock assaulted her senses. For a moment, she couldn't figure out where she was. She trained her mind to focus. Darkness had already descended on the earth by then.

Pulling her *chaddar* around her, Lakhimi peeped through the window. Seeing it was Rishi at the door, she opened it. He was carrying two heavy bags. His shoulders were drooping with the weight of those bags. Running towards him, she took one of them. Rishi was sweating like hell.

Lakhmi felt bad seeing him in such a condition. He was just a casual acquaintance, and here he was, being forced to do so much for them! She had no clue if Rishi had ever done such work. But what he was doing for her and her family, who else would have done? They say it's a selfish world. But she could not find any selfish motive in Rishi. Or, in whatever he was doing for her.

Carrying the bag inside, she tried to take hold of her emotions. But it surged with all its force. Pressing the corner of her *chaddar* over her eyes, she started crying.

It was now Rishi's turn to be surprised. He had no clue about how a woman's mind worked. He didn't have much experience with women. Yes, he was in love before...But even after doing so much, what made Lakhimi cry was beyond him. He had some vague idea, but he could not put it into perspective and that made him angry with himself.

But then, he was in no mood to analyse human psychology. Rather, he would focus on Padmeshwar's treatment. Once things were moving, he could go back to Kaziranga. Amal da would face problems with the resort if he was not around.

Lakhimi went to the washroom.

Taking out the stuff from the bags, he started stacking them neatly at the kitchenette. He had no problem carrying out such chores. Perhaps, Lakhimi thought he was not cut out for such a job. Perhaps!

As Lakhimi came out of the washroom, Rishi looked at her face. Though her eyes were still puffy, he could make out that she was in control. She better be...Lakhimi rushed to cook rice and dal for him, but Rishi said no. He should rather visit her father in the hospital. He would drop her back at the lodge and leave a little early. He would have to clean up his house in Jyotinagar to make it liveable.

But Lakhimi was adamant that unless he ate with her, she would not cook for herself.

Rishi didn't know what to do. Lakhimi had no idea how far Jyotinagar was from Roopnagar. Though he felt agitated inside, he didn't let it show. He left the room asking her to get ready.

Closing the door behind him, he started to smoke. Lakhimi, after five minutes, joined him. They were ready to leave for the hospital. As they walked towards the hospital, Lakhimi stayed close to Rishi. The crowd and the traffic were frightening the hell out of her. Every step proved to be a new experience to Lakhimi, who had never seen such a bustling city in her entire life.

Padmeshwar had managed to eat on his own. He was a strong man. He had faced the adversities of life in that remote jungle-village head on.

Looking at her father lying quietly on the hospital bed, Lakhimi felt relieved. Yes…he was going to pull through. And soon. Her father was a good man. That's why so may people were there to help them out. God will also be kind to him.

His medical investigations had already started. The professional atmosphere of Gauhati Medical College and the strength of the doctors and nurses gave Padmeshwar a fresh surge of hope. This hospital was a lot different from the Bokakhat Hospital.

The visiting hours for attendants were already over. They were asked to leave. Rishi explained to Padmeshwar and Lakhimi that there were fixed visiting hours. The patients needed to rest.

As she climbed down two flights of stairs, Lakhimi was much more at peace—a lot more positive now too. She was almost sure that her father would walk back home, completely healed.

On their way back, Rishi showed Lakhimi the important points on the hospital premises. The chemist's shops towards the east, the auto-stand, the market and the short cut to the lodge.

Rishi wanted to scuttle from having dinner, but Lakhimi without changing her clothes, headed towards the kitchen. Rishi had no chance to protest. An expert cook, Lakhimi didn't take long, even though she had just one stove to do all the cooking. Even before the clock struck nine in the evening, she produced a thali in front of Rishi. There was no dining table in the room. So, Rishi pulled the small corner table and put the thali on it. It was a new experience.

None of them had eaten the whole day. He asked Lakhimi to join him, but she wouldn't. She wanted to clean up the kitchen before she took a bath, only then she would eat. She had plenty of time to pass. Rishi didn't force her. Only then, he realised how hungry he was. As he ate the hot rice, he started sweating all over. The fan was not helping at all. Seeing that, Lakhimi took out a newspaper and started using it as a hand-fan.

Rishi was overwhelmed. He had never been fed with so much affection and care. Travelling around the world for concerts, he had eaten in many five-star restaurants, but this simple meal of rice, dal, mashed potato and *patal* fry was something priceless.

A strange emotion overcame this bearded, lanky, about-to-be-middle-aged guy called Rishiraj Duara.

Wiping clean the plate and enjoying every morsel, Rishi went to the washroom. He splashed water over his face with force as if he wanted to wash away the surreal feeling that was enveloping his senses. When he came out, his hair was totally wet. The campus was quiet. The other two rooms were vacant. Kamal's wife seemed to be busy in the kitchen, though the sound of the television set was coming from her living room. Kamal would be home only after 10 at night. Most chemists kept their shops open day and night, but Kamal preferred to close it after 10.

Rishi took the *gamosa* that Lakhimi had handed to him. He gingerly wiped his face and his hands. It was time for him to leave. But something was holding him back. He remembered Lisa. Had she been there, she would giggle and push him out. But Lakhimi was a village girl. She didn't know those playful acts. Fiddling with the corner of her *chaddar*, she just kept looking at the floor.

'Lakhimi, I need to go. Will you get scared? You are safe here. Kamal and Savitri live just a stone's throw away. If you have any problem, just call them,' Rishi said in a soft voice, as if not sure of what to say.

Lakhimi didn't say a thing. She kept staring at the floor—as if she was mesmerised by it. Her eyes were glued to it.

Rishi got up, walked slowly towards the corner where he had kept his bag and picked it up. Against his better judgement, he looked at Lakhimi's face. Internalising the entire pain of this world, she stood mute, only her tears flowing, like two streams in full spate. She didn't try to obstruct that flow. She looked like a figurine carved out of stone. She was the source of a river.

Rishi didn't know what to do. He had no idea how to save this delicate situation. He tried to delve deep into the recess of his memory, but found nothing there to equip him to handle it.

Even as his mind was telling him to bolt, he stood beside her, like a statue. Forgetting his past, and the future, he also stood there like a stony figure. No, anything but stony. He started shaking like someone suffering from fever. What was he going to do? But then, he had lost the ability to know what was right or what was wrong. Without realising what he was doing, Rishi placed his right hand on Lakhimi's left cheek, which was wet with tears. Letting out a deep sigh, he closed his eyes...The stream that flew from the peak of a mountain, came down with full force. Endless flow...Rishi felt he was drowning, deeper and deeper.

How much time had lapsed or when was the exact moment that he tenderly embraced Lakhimi's sobbing figure, he had no clue. The only thing he was aware of was his own feverish body holding onto Lakhimi's soft one. The rational part of his mind stopped functioning long back. He was only aware of this young woman in his arms, of his desire...the contours of two bodies burning with desire...of an erect peak and a welcoming valley.

Time was ticking by...and then, the two feverish bodies united to become one entity. None of them could tear apart from the other. The shameless, lusty world remained a mute spectator to this union. The volcanoes of the heart kept erupting...the fire, the smoke and the ashes...

Time just flew by, and Amal thought it moved at this rate only in the big cities, where one was immersed in the grind of daily life. But he was proved wrong. How the days turned into weeks and weeks into months, he could never tell. Life was actually busy in Kaziranga. Something or the other started early in the morning, and before one realised, it was evening.

The resort was at its last leg. The interiors were getting the finishing touches. The garden, which was started at the onset of the rainy season, was at its prime. A few varieties of flowers were already in bloom, others were just about there. Going by the frontal view of the guest house, one would believe that it was already functional.

But no. There were still some minor details that needed to be taken care of. And by a rough estimate, it would be operational sometime in the tourist season itself. Near the entrance of the guest house, was a small room made of glass, which would serve as an outlet for Assamese *riha mekhela*, *gamosa* and other ethnic items to cater to the tourists. Amal also made an agreement with Jiaur to sell tea leaves from his estate. The shop was already doing business. Amal had devised this strategy. Once the shop starts functioning, it would garner publicity for the resort. And there was nothing like the word of mouth. Rishi named the shop Hajon-Kachon, meaning 'deck-up'.

In fact, the shop was becoming quite popular, specially among the friends of Hridayananda. Whoever travelled from Upper Assam to Lower Assam or vice versa, made it a point to stop over at Hajon-Kachon and buy tea leaves or other knick-knacks. Hridayananda boasted, once the resort was ready, it would be packed with his friends alone during the tourist season.

Everything was finally falling into place. Amal was already feeling a sense of achievement. He decided once the resort started bringing in business, he would give up his real-estate work, which was nothing but a headache. He had had enough of it. Now, he wanted some peace.

After his extensive tour of South India, Arunabh had come back to Guwahati. He made a flying visit to Kaziranga. But he had a purpose. His magazine editor had asked him to do a feature on rhino killings in Kaziranga, a subject which had already become a hot topic for debate. He visited in the capacity of a journalist.

When Arunabh's article was published, Amal felt a little resentful. It talked about the international nexus that was killing rhinos and predicted doom for Kaziranga. It also touched upon the resort-centric government policies, among other businesses, which were earning revenue. He concluded his article by saying that if rhino poaching was allowed to continue at this rate, the one-horn rhino, as a species, would become extinct and Kaziranga would soon lose its attraction for foreign and domestic tourists. That would sound the death knell for the thousands of hotels and resorts operating in this area. And if those were to close down, the locals would lose the only viable source of income.

Amal read it with full attention. Arunabh was a good journalist; he had his facts and arguments right. He was popular too. But did he have to be so blunt about the closing down of hotels and resorts? As he read it, Amal felt sad about the bleak future. It was depressing. Goddamn it!

Amal could never hide his feelings. When he talked to Arunabh over the phone, Arunabh could sense that something was wrong. So, he assured him, Kaziranga, despite being plagued by all sorts of problems, would manage to sustain itself for years to come. Till then, Amal would have recovered his investment on the resort with full interest. Arunabh assured him towards the end of their conversation that in a couple of days, once he was done with his political story and sent it to his magazine, he would join Amal da in Kaziranga. Amal tried to take it positively. Good that Arunabh was sending out the warning signals when the going was still good. It was not his age to get overexcited about things in life. So, he decided to be careful with his business.

One Sunday morning, Amal, along with Rishi, left Pamua village. Both were casually attired, in tracksuits and white caps. Their destination was the village that bordered the Karbi Anglong district. It was a unique village.

Two kilometres ahead of Kohora, one needed to go towards the south to reach Rangsina village. It was known for its rich handloom and handicraft items. It was a poor village by and large. It didn't have cultivable land. Neither had it plain areas nor hills to provide scope for jhoom cultivation.

The situation of the villagers was neither here nor there. The district administration of Diphu ignored it and the Kaziranga administration or Assam government paid no attention to the development of this village.

Hridayananda advised Amal to market the handloom items woven by the women of this village. Marketing means selling those items in the outlet of his resort. That would be a win-win situation for both him and the villagers. In future, he could send those to markets outside too.

That was the reason why Amal wanted to visit the village and asked Rishi to accompany him. Anyway, Amal was putting on weight sitting there idle and eating. Walking to this village would help him reduce a bit.

The wide metal road gave way to a narrow kutcha lane. The road had hills on both sides—a beautifully undulating landscape! They could not help but notice the lack of greenery in this area. It seemed people were cutting trees mindlessly. How could they?

Rishi was hopping ahead.

He had visited Rangsina village several times. Rishi had this wonderful quality of making friends wherever he went. He just divulged how only a few days back, he had chicken cooked inside a bamboo pole and *harlung*, a home-brewed liquor, in one of the villager's house. Amal was surprised. When did he have the time to do that?

'Huh! You are a smart one,' Amal sounded slightly envious. The more he got to know Rishi, the more surprised he was. He was like an alien visiting this planet. Only Arunabh knew Rishi well. After all, they were thick friends.

Amal was drenched in sweat. He must have burnt quite a few calories already.

The climb became a lot steeper. Amal's lower thigh started hurting with each step. God knows how far he would have to walk!

Rishi was oblivious to Amal's discomfort. He was all energy, with a spring in his step. Sometimes, he would stop to catch some beautiful birds, butterflies, even clouds and fauna in his camera. Taking out the water bottle from his rucksack, he would gulp down water. He was getting far ahead of Amal.

Amal shouted, 'Rishi…wait…wait.'

In seconds, his voice was echoed back—wait…wait… wait…

Amal was shocked. It sounded eerie.

Rishi stopped. Looking at Amal's pitiable condition, he came running back.

'What, Amal da! You are already tired,' he said in a condescending tone. He himself was running out of breath.

'Go slow. We are not here for a business deal. We are just exploring. We can take it easy!' Amal was also getting irritated.

Rishi took another swing from his water bottle. Amal lit up a cigarette and pressing his mobile button, checked for network coverage. No, there was no signal. The phone was useless here.

Rishi did not allow him to rest for long. 'Get going now. The villagers have already left for work. We must meet at least a few people,' Rishi physically pulled him up. Their journey resumed.

After walking for a distance, they could see a few houses on the leeward side of the hill—few and far between! Rickety huts with thatched roof. A couple of huts had tin roofs though. Mostly *chang ghar* and a few huts like those in the plains.

The village was quiet. They could hear only a few children chatting here and there. A few dogs barked randomly. The huts were far away from one another. Looking at the condition of those, they could make out that the people here lived well below the poverty line.

'Hey, boss, how far do you plan to go? Who are the people you want to meet?' Amal whimpered.

'Come, come. Just beyond that turn is Mansingh Rongpi's house. We are visiting him,' Rishi sounded detached.

Rongpi's house from far struck him to be quite a lively one. Eight or 10 people had gathered in the front yard. Looking at the approaching figures, they all hushed up.

A young, well-built guy, who was naked from his waist up and wore just a loin cloth to hide his modesty, came up to the bamboo gate to welcome them. Amal and Rishi sat on two *mudas* placed under a jackfruit tree. Immediately, a pretty, young woman wearing a bright-coloured ethnic dress offered them lemon water in two aluminium mugs.

'Rishi sir, rest for a while. The villagers who had gone into the forest would come back soon. I have already told them about your visit,' the young guy rubbed both his hands, as he said this in a humble tone.

The lemon water was the most refreshing thing Amal had tasted in a long time. The water must have come from a natural spring—pure and cold!

Amal surveyed the scene. To the north of the courtyard was an Assam-type house made of bamboo and wood. There were big trees all around the courtyard. Mostly papaya, guava and jackfruit trees. There was a bamboo bench under one of those trees. Six or seven people tried to adjust themselves on that bench. They looked simple and innocent, faces contoured with extreme poverty. Adjoining the house, there was a raised platform where six or seven young girls and married women were standing. On the eastern end, there was a pigsty. Roaming around were a few hens with their chicks. A few healthy-looking dogs sat leisurely amidst them.

Within half an hour of their arrival, the courtyard was packed to its maximum capacity. The villagers who had gone out to collect edible roots, herbs and wild animals had come back for the meeting.

The sun was almost overhead now. Mansingh Rongpi looked like the leader of this village. Bringing a low, half-broken *muda*, Rongpi sat under a guava tree. He started his talk. The humble, young man turned serious.

'Honourable guests! We welcome you with our open heart. We are living in a pitiable condition. We vote for the district council. But they don't care about our plight. Even the Assam government does not bother about us. Then what are we supposed to do? No government official has ever paid us a visit. So, as you suggested, we will work on our handloom with complete dedication. Only, you will have to take care of the marketing side. This is what our public wants me convey to you.'

Though Rongpi delivered the speech in a formal way, each of his words was heartfelt.

The courtyard was packed, but not a word was uttered. Everyone was looking at Rongpi's face as he talked. Now that he completed his speech, they all turned their gaze towards Amal and Rishi.

It was obvious that Rongpi spoke for the entire community. He was the undisputed leader and the speaker.

Rishi looked at Amal. It was their turn to talk. Amal signalled him to go ahead and explain everything to the villagers.

It was Rishi's turn to become serious.

The discussion he earlier had with Amal, Rishi tried to simplify things point by point. He explained how they could start a co-operative society and they would be made partner in the business. The profit would be shared on the basis of work. But the products had to be of superior quality. There won't be profit sharing for the initial six months. Rishi, Amal and his company would provide the principal amount. And the money would be disbursed through the co-operative committee.

Rishi explained with such simplicity as if he was addressing the some primary school students. Even a few doubts that Amal had about co-operative societies were cleared now.

A few villagers raised questions that Mansingh translated for Rishi. Rishi could satisfy them with his answers. After about 40 minutes of interaction, the villagers looked happy and convinced.

Mansingh didn't want to linger on with unnecessary details. The people got up to leave. Offering an awkward bow, they left one by one in the most disciplined manner.

Soon the courtyard was empty. Only a few women remained inside the house. As soon as the people left, two young girls brought out a small cane table and placed it in front of Amal and Rishi. One of them spread a beautiful cloth on it.

Mansingh disappeared into the house, only to reappear with a pitcher. The mouth of the pitcher was stuffed with banana leaves.

The hearth on the western side of the courtyard was lit. Two girls placed a big wok on the fire.

Mansingh came closer to the table.

'The day we got to know that you all are visiting us, our women started brewing this for you. It has matured today. Quite tasty to drink,' Mansingh explained, as he poured the white liquid in tall aluminium mugs.

One girl brought a plate covered with a banana leaf. It contained piping hot meat and green chillies.

'Start, sir. By the time you finish your *harlung*, the rice will be ready. You must be hungry,' Mansingh offered.

Amal was happy. What could be better than relishing country-made liquor in this pristine, picturesque surroundings with natural breeze caressing you? And to top it all, it was home brewed. Talk about luck! This feast was written in bold letters in his destiny.

The feast had just begun…The liquor was divine. They cooked the pork in *til* and herbs. Putting a succulent piece of meat in his mouth, Amal felt blissful. Rishi had already drawn half a mug of *harlung*. Demolishing quite a few pieces of pork, he was licking his fingers, wiping off the gravy.

Talk resumed again during the drinking session. Amal was looking for answers to a few questions that were in his mind. He wanted to know if Rangsina village fell within the boundary of Kaziranga or not.

The question seemed to offend Mansingh Rongpi.

'How do we know? According to the district council, we fall inside Karbi Anglong district. Sometimes, people from Kaziranga threaten us with guns, forbidding us from extracting wood from the jungle or practicing jhoom cultivation at the foothills. But then, how do our people survive? It is the government's duty to settle the matter, to decide whether we belong to Kaziranga or

Karbi Anglong.' Rongpi sounded agitated, as he mentioned that they had received a notice of eviction sometime back.

On 20 January 2013, a meeting was organised in Kohora to protest against the government's move of eviction. Rangsina village had sent their representation to that meeting. Thousands of people followed it up with a rally that shook Kaziranga. Mansingh was also present. After listening to the very articulate farmer-leader, Akhil Gogoi, the participants of the meeting were inspired to protect their land with their lives and had raised slogans to that effect.

Rishi, throwing a look at Mansingh, started pouring some more *harlung* into his mug. Seeing their empty plates, a girl went running into the house and brought out more meat.

Having two city-bred, rich gentlemen for an audience, Mansingh got encouraged to pour his heart out.

He felt the administration of Kaziranga had failed in protecting the forest that fell into its jurisdiction. Bangladeshi migrants were continuing to make new colonies. They killed animals mercilessly. Last year itself, 40 rhinos were killed and most poachers caught in connection of rhino killing, turned out to be illegal migrants.

The government cannot do anything about that. Then, what right do they have to evict the local people who established their villages some 40 or 50 years ago? Officially, Kaziranga was declared a reserved forest in 1974. Kaziranga had only on papers 1,000-sq. km area. The patch of land that ran parallel to the Brahmaputra was a mini Bangladesh that followed their self-styled governing system. Everyone, right from the forest department to the ministers, was aware about it. But nobody took any action. They just targeted the peace-loving, hard-working local people.

By the time they finished their talk and lunch, the clock struck three in the afternoon. Amal burped twice. With the non-stop supply of sumptuous pork, he indulged in overeating.

Amal took a good look at the girl who had come out to clear their table. She was nature's primitive woman—very beautiful. Her beautiful eyes, taut breasts and well-toned body wore a shy veneer and that added to her beauty. Amal felt overwhelmed with the beauty all around him.

Finally, it was time to say goodbye.

Before leaving, Rishi went to the thicket behind the house and relieved himself.

Amal was feeling heady. He folded his hands to say namaskar to each of the family members. His steps became heavy. Rishi's eyes were dilated.

To see them off, Mansingh threw a *gamosa* over his shoulder and started leading the way.

Lighting up a cigarette, Amal offered the pack to Mansingh. Hesitating for a moment, he took out a stick.

Amal saw a packet of banana leaves in Mansingh's hand.

'What is that, Mansingh?' he asked.

'Pork. Uncooked. For you all. Rishi sir said he would like to cook. You don't get this often.'

'Often meaning? From where do you all shop for your daily needs? Or, do you buy and sell meat in the village itself?' Amal was curious.

'No, sir. This one is a wild boar. I killed it myself this morning.'

'My God! What are you saying? You killed a boar that belonged to Kaziranga? That's a crime,' Amal almost screamed.

'Sir, why would we kill what is Kaziranga's property? In fact, we save a lot of animals that come floating in the flood water. We guard them. This one belonged to the jungle in our hills. Sometimes, we do kill one or two,' Mansingh sounded a little sad.

Rishi intervened and stopped Mansingh from getting into the self-praise mode. He steered the conversation towards work, asking him to start the co-operative society in the first week of the following month. Rongpi was entrusted with the responsibility.

After walking with them a little further down the road, Rongpi turned back. Rishi asked him to go back. They would manage on their own.

The sun was hiding behind a hill on the west. Its light was devoid of heat now.

As soon as they reached the turning point on the road outside the village, there were three boys standing. They were carrying big and sophisticated arms.

Amal felt a shiver run down his spine. 'Who are these boys?' he asked, in a low voice.

'Don't look at them. They are rebels. Karbi. They belong to KPLT, Karbi People's Liberation Tiger. They are aware of our visit. They won't harm us,' Rishi also whispered back.

At midnight, the flames that engulfed the boundary of Kaziranga, could be seen from far. The fire started from a small hut in the Bagori Range, which was a part of the settlements that lined the Brahmaputra.

The breeze that came from the Brahmaputra faned the fire, making it spread faster. The dry grasses and dried-up leaves caught fire easily.

Within a short span of 20 minutes, the fire had spread to anything and everything around.

Luckily, there were not too many people sleeping inside those huts. A few of them were just lying empty. It's been only a month since those huts were built. Those huts meant another illegal colony was in the offing.

That is the standard practice in Kaziranga. They first occupy a space and wait for the authority's reaction. If no one, the government or otherwise, objects to it, then they slowly start moving in. About eight to 10 men and women start living in those small huts. The next step is to build a courtyard. Then, another hut across the courtyard. In no time, the open field would turn into a hamlet or a thickly populated village. In six-months' time, the village would fall into the category of an old village. The next phase is to seek voter's identity card.

Officials like Hridayananda made it a point to inform the higher authorities when such colonies started. But nobody, higher or lower, gave a damn. And if the Hridayanandas of Kaziranga took some initiative to remove those fresh encroachments, there would inevitably be some warning from above—from the local political leaders to associations to even ministers! After that, there was no stopping for the encroachers.

Hridayananda was on a nocturnal mission when the fire broke out. He was actually at the other end of the Bagori Range, where he was looking at the details of a night raid they had planned to spring on a gang of poachers. It was then that he saw the bright orange flames of destruction.

The raid had to be abandoned midway. Why did this have to happen in *his* range? On one side, the poachers were creating chaos and now, on the other, a fire was unleashing havoc. At this rate, he would soon have to wash his hands off his job. Bagori was getting notorious for rhino killings.

Stuffing a betel nut into his mouth, Hridayananda switched on his walkie-talkie to talk to Deputy Ranger Kalita. He briefed him about the fire. Kalita, at that moment, was stationed on the Northeastern boundary, which was completely opposite to the place where the fire was spreading.

Hridayananda was somewhere in the middle of the range—about eight- to 10-kilometre away. There was no time to lose. Whatever may be the reason for it, or whether it was a legal or illegal colony, even it fell outside the boundary of Kaziranga, he would only be answerable. The whole thing may even take a political hue.

There were only a handful of forest guards with him. He formed a team big enough to fit into his Gypsy.

Asking Hareswar, his driver, to get down from his jeep, Hridayananda took the steering. Hareswar understood his boss's need to drive at times. Meekly, he got down and sat in the passenger seat.

Those six guards and Hareswar sat in complete silence. Looking at the bright flames shooting skyward, they all realised the gravity of the situation. Such disasters happened very rarely.

The Gypsy roared in the expert hands of Hridayananda.

Hridayananda felt helpless. No matter how hard he tried to save the park, reality had something else in store. He felt he was not going to last here for long. Even if the government didn't take such a step, probably he himself would be forced to seek transfer from Bagori.

There was fire inside his head too. Whose conspiracy was this? Who were those people, minting money by killing innocent rhinos? People he knew?

Sometimes, he had this urge to hold a press conference and reveal everything he knew and suspected.

They were getting closer to the fire. He was still driving at full speed on the river bank. The flames were getting aggressive and the smell of smoke and ashes assaulted their nostrils. They finally came to a halt, as there was no proper road to lead them closer to the site. They would have to walk about 2 kms to reach there. They all were tired, as they had been running around the whole day. Nobody had the time to eat even. Two of the guards were just about to cook a simple meal when they had to leave.

They were looking forward to a hurried meal before the raid, but then it proved to be just a wishful thinking.

If now, those poachers taking advantage of the fire killed a rhino, then he was doomed. Facing this huge dilemma, Hridayananda asked his deputy to take charge of the night operation.

Hridayananda and company got down from the jeep. This place was not all that safe. It would not be wise to leave the jeep unattended. He had only six forest guards. In fact, even driver Hareswar was a forest guard. Deciding to leave Hareswar behind, he handed him a gun.

Explaining everything to Hareswar, Hridayananda started walking towards the area now engulfed in flames. Two of his guards walked ahead of him, chopping the shrubs and vines that obstructed their path. The path was also filled with puddles.

By the time Hridayananda and his guards arrived at the spot, the flames were dying out. The fire had broken out almost two hours ago. Adding to that the half an hour that took them to get there, the fire was already on the downslide. From far, they could make out eight or 10 human figures hovering around, but by the time they reached there, they all disappeared.

This particular forest area was devoid of dense vegetation. It was more of a sandy piece of land covered with kahua and other varieties of grasses. It had a huge swamp. The old Luhit flowed around it just a few metres away. On the southern side, there was a big lake.

The team took positions. God knows what was plotting! Hridayananda had this nagging feeling—what if the poachers started this fire just to distract the forest rangers?

Hridayananda focused on his surroundings, absorbing every single detail. Indeed, this was an encroached colony—and quite a recent one too. Many years of experience helped Hridayananda arrive at these conclusions like a professional detective. But where were the encroachers? Seeing the forest team approaching, they must have ran away. . .

Cordoning off the area, the forest team started their inspections from the east to the west. By the time they were through, there was no doubt that these huts belonged to encroachers, not local people.

All those huts were of makeshift kind. On four bamboo poles were thinly woven thatched roof. The conglomeration had about 11 such constructions.

Everything had been burnt to ashes. The fire had totally subsided. But for a fire of this magnitude, there was no ember. A few cracking sounds could be heard every now and then as the bamboo poles were slowly reduced to ashes. That too died down soon and the whole area plunged into silence.

The ones sleeping in those huts must have escaped by the Brahmaputra by then. Or, maybe, they were hiding somewhere in the jungle itself. They were too smart.

'Huh, if you people have the guts, why don't you come out? We have come for your protection only. Why have you now run away like jackals?' Unable to resist his anger, Hridayananda spat out the words at those invisible figures.

Hridayananda lingered on for a while, trying to find out more about the fire.

How did it start? Was it an accident or some trick? Did the people themselves start the fire for some financial gain?

Suddenly, an arrow-like object, piercing the earth close to

a felled tree trunk, attracted his attention. What was it? He couldn't make out in the dark.

He would have to report this fire to the CCF first thing in the morning—a detailed report. So, he could not ignore any clue. Duty is duty.

Taking the torch in his hand, Hridayananda started walking towards the tree trunk. He put the light on it. Yes, indeed, it was an arrow—a long arrow that was slightly bent. It was barely lodged to the ground. He put on his thinking cap.

Someone had shot the arrow from far…Who could the archer be? Dislodging it from the ground, Hridayananda brought it up to his eye level to examine it.

Well, there was a dried-up seed of amara fruit lying nearby. The six torches of the forest guards were now illuminating this particular area.

'Sir, sir! Here is another arrow,' the excited, but muffled voice came from one of the guards.

'There, there…here are some more…two…five…so many actually,' another one reported.

A couple of them had amara seeds, half burnt or intact, at the sharp edge. Those arrows missed their target.

Slowly, the mystery of the fire started unravelling itself. It was not accidental. Neither was the fire started by the encroachers themselves. Sharp arrows with kerosene-soaked amara seeds were fired from far to attack those huts.

In Assam, such attacks with arrows having inflammatory substance at the tip was common in the older times.

Probably, some one who didn't have much faith in the government machinery when it came to controlling unlawful settlements in Kaziranga was trying to remove this illegal colony by deploying these old-war techniques. But who were those people?

A smile touched Hridayananda's lips. He gave out a sigh of relief. Yes, there was someone watching, who could not accept what was going on. Locals had a way of protecting themselves.

Tomorrow, he would have to submit an official report about the fire. But still, he felt happy and content at that moment.

'Sir, someone gutted this encroached settlement with bow and amara-seeded arrow for a purpose,' one of his team members finally understood the whole thing.

'Huh, Idiot. Now, you got it,' Hridayananda said, under his breath.

'Good job! There was no other way to evict these encroachers,' another guard chipped in.

Hridayananda ignored the comment. 'Here, give me a betel nut,' he said, aloud. Putting the betel nut in his mouth, he took out the revolver from the belt around his waist. Without giving any indication, he pointed it towards the sky and fired two rounds continuously. A flock of birds nosily flew away.

The guards stopped in their tracks, but none of them was surprised. They knew why Hridayananda did that. Having accompanied him on many such missions, they were well acquainted with his shrewdness and leadership abilities. One could sustain in this jungle only by playing such games. The report Saikia sir would be submitting tomorrow to the CCF would have a strong case now.

By the time they walked back to the Gypsy, it was dawn. They were hungry and exhausted, but there was no relief from duty. Once the sun was out, they would have to be on their toes, again—with their mission to protect wildlife.

Hareswar started the jeep. Now, for a return journey…

After taking a bath, Hridayananda sat in the chair on the verandah of his house. His eyes were burning. He did not have proper sleep for the past few consecutive nights. Having spent many years in Kaziranga, Hridayananda realised life was not the same any more. Gone were the days when one could relax in his job. The problems of Kaziranga had taken new colour. Now, it required them to be alert 24×7. It was more like keeping vigil on the front.

In the kitchen, Dijen had started his morning duty. In between, he placed a cup of tea in front of Hridayananda.

Dijen was looking subdued. The tea garden he was working in had some management problems. His job was also at stake.

Before Hridayananda could finish his cup of tea, his mobile started ringing. He was about to stretch out, but thought against it. It was from his office.

There must be something terribly wrong if they had to call Hridayananda this early.

It was Deputy Ranger Kalita.

'What's up, Kalita? Did you find anything? Was a rhino killed again?' Even before Kalita could say a thing, Hridayananda fired the questions at him.

'No, sir. We couldn't find any trace of poachers. It was an uneventful day. But the rumour is that an observer team of the Centre is visiting Kaziranga. In fact, it has already reached Guwahati. They are expected here any moment now. I just wanted you to know.'

Hridayananda felt disgusted. Kalita went on talking, but nothing registered in his head.

Finally, Kalita kept the phone down. Or, probably it got disconnected. Team after team—of bureaucrats, politicians, experts—kept visiting Kaziranga. But to what effect? The non-functional drone, the CCTV cameras, and now, the recent proposal for rhino protection—were those enough to save the rhinos from the cruel onslaught of the poachers? They said as the horn was nothing but a cluster of hair, if severed, it would grow back. But if the horn gets severed, how would a rhino protect itself from the attacks of other animals?

Hridayananda was aware that once in Tanzania in Africa, the government had imposed the law of severing the rhino horns in order to protect them. But still poaching did not stop.

He was feeling drowsy, but there was no time to go to bed. If he even lay down on the bed, he would be fast asleep. So, he leaned on the chair and closed his eyes. A light sleep immediately took over his senses.

Hridayananda dreamt of his village. He saw that he was riding a huge rhino as he reached the gate of his house. His mother and father both were waiting for him, holding a *gamosa* in hand. Behind them, were his brothers, sisters-in-law, and the bunch of nephews and nieces. They were enjoying the sight of him riding a rhino. Carrying a bucket of water, his father came forward on his wobbly feet. He then washed the legs of the rhino. He washed away the mud. His mother put a bunch of hay in front of the rhino. Receiving such a warm welcome, the rhino made a pleasant sound before starting to eat out of his mother's hands…

Bengmara village, adjacent to Pamua, had a surprise visit from the police department. They raided the village in the middle of the night. The villagers, after a hectic day of sowing and tending to the ripening sali rice, had been fast asleep. And suddenly, a few officials from the Bokakhat Police descended on the village with a police team from Kohora.

The huge police force gheraoed five or six houses. Kicking open the doors, they hauled up the owners, so much like soldiers in a war movie.

Every household had young boys. After interrogating them and matching their names and surnames with papers that they had carried, they detained five boys. In one of the households, not finding the boy they were looking for, they hit the old father instead. The old man went down like a felled tree. His son was not on the run. In fact, he had gone to Jorhat to call on his sick sister who was married off there. The old man tried hard to explain, but all in vain. The police demanded that the leader of the revolutionary gang, who was in hiding, be produced immediately. But how could this old, innocent man produce his son out of thin air? So, accusing him of lying, they thrashed him a little more. The old man started moaning. His breathing becoming erratic.

Looking at the condition of her sick father, his daughter came running to him, her body trying to shield the old man. Seizing this opportunity, one of those over-zealous constables pulled her blouse. The cheap cloth could not withstand the assault. It gave away at the seam, the free end flying like a flag hoisted on Independence Day.

After rounding up five young boys, the police team left Bengmara village, looking smug.

As soon as the police left, the village, which till then was in the state of shock, broke down in sobs. It was a small village. Everyone was related to the other somehow or the other. Even if a duck was slaughtered in someone's house or someone cut a grapefruit, others got to know. The arrest of five youths created a huge commotion in this small village. Nobody knew what to do. Most people were semi literate and economically backward. Not knowing what the provocation was or what steps to be taken, all—right from children to elderly—started crying in unison.

This Bengmara village was a little isolated. All those five boys, who the police took away, were carefree youngsters. Sometimes, of course, they participated in the protests that took place frequently in Kaziranga against encroachments or rhino killings. But they were mere participants, none of them was the leader type. Only one of them had gone to Dispur to gherao the Secretariat last year. He was bashed by the police there. So, what was the reason? To find out the answer, the most elderly people gathered in front of the village head's house. The sun was still asleep.

A team, comprising the younger lot of the village, started for Pamua. Waking up the village head, they gave out a call for the public to gather at the *namghar*. Within an hour, the entire village was up. By the time the sun made an appearance, the news reached all the surrounding villages.

Only a few months ago, the police had picked Nabeen and Dimbeswar from Kapahua village, which was not far from Bengmara, on false charges of rhino poaching. The entire Kaziranga had protested that time. The fight in demand of documents for their land holdings was at its peak. They had challenged the administration by blocking the road, and thereby, paralysing the entire traffic. Though the police tortured the protesters, they were forced to free Nabeen and Dimbeswar. Sensing the ire of the public which was tired of living under constant threat of eviction, the administration had been keeping mum all this while.

Earlier, more than 200 villagers had staged a dharna against the government's inaction in stopping of rhino killings. Though the outside world was not aware of the magnitude of the protest, the government machinery had understood the underlying unrest. So, why suddenly unleash terror on the villagers again? There was no answer. The mute Kaziranga too was seeking answers to a whole lot of questions.

The wind that lashed Kaziranga from the east to the west, sounded like a deep sigh heaved by nature!

Rishi woke up at the sound of knocking at his door. It was barely dawn. Amal da had left for Delhi. Arunabh, who had come from Guwahati, was also sleeping in his hut.

Rubbing his eye, Rishi opened the door. He was surprised to find a huge gathering outside his hut. Rishi sensed something grave must have happened overnight. The presence of few members of the Pamua Development Committee among them confirmed his suspicion.

Rishi just needed to ask 'What's wrong?', and quite a few voices started explaining the incident of police atrocity passionately, in unison. They were mighty agitated. Things couldn't go on like this. They could not go on living in insecurity. They needed a closure to this state-sponsored terror.

Rishi was shocked.

He had only recently moved to Kaziranga. His life revolved around music and gardening. Agreed, that he was a sympathiser when it came to the cause of the local people and the environment. But was he equipped to find out a solution to their problems? No. He was not the leader type. What did they take him for? He was not even remotely connected to politics. Who had advised them to come to him? Scratching his head, Rishi did some quick thinking.

'Rishi da, you are well connected. You know many powerful people. You need to help us out. We cannot live in such indignity,' Homeshwar, who said this, looked angry.

The crowd sat down on whatever was available—chairs, *mudas* and benches. Bipul, from the tea stall, was also there among them. Rishi gestured him to take his bicycle and fetch biscuits and plastic cups. Rishi wanted to serve them tea.

Arunabh, who was sleeping inside, with his journalistic instinct could make a fair guess as to what must have happened. Trying to catch the words, still lying in bed, he finally got up and joined the group. He was in his pyjamas and a vest. Rishi, who was soberly nodding to the people still narrating the incident, felt relieved seeing Arunabh. He was intelligent and aware—a senior journalist! If anyone could find a solution, then it was him.

The tall trees and bamboo groves in the adjacent area were trying to stop the sunrays from reaching Rishi's courtyard.

In a record time, Bipul brought cookies and plastic cups. Starting the stove, Bipul took the responsibility of serving tea to everyone. Gulping down tea and cookies, Rishi ordered Arunabh to participate in the discussion.

Arunabh was aware of such problems in bits and pieces. He never gave much thought to them to put the whole issue in the right perspective. But since Rishi was now a resident of Pamua, the villagers' problem was his problem too. Something needed to be done. At least for humanity's sake.

After discussing in details for about an hour, Arunabh convinced them that there was no other way but to approach the court with a petition to stop the police brutality. But there was another problem. Pamua village would not be able to approach the court on its own. They should go either under the banner of the Kaziranga Sangram Samiti or the victims from all the villages together to have a strong case against the police. But then a petition was already filed in the court seeking legalisation of their land holdings. So, they needed to discuss with the Samiti as to how to approach the matter. That will be a long process. On the other hand, the government, which was unable to stop rhino killings, was already angry with the protesting public. The higher officials and ministers thought that the issue had become international only because of the public outcry.

Hearing Arunabh's statement, the people started arguing and counter arguing. Instead of finding a solution, the situation was becoming more complex.

Arunabh stepped in again. He offered that taking this latest incident as the moot point, the people of Pamua, Bengmara and Kapahtali should engage in a discussion. Many residents of these villages possessed legal documents for their lands. They were also part of the ongoing fight. With the Samiti's co-operation, they should make a fresh appeal in the court. At no cost, should they give up on their unity.

Arunabh also assured them that he would request all his journalist-friends, who were working for national and international newspapers, to visit these villages and take stock of the situation. Once the issues were highlighted in the national and international media, the central government would be forced to act upon it. If necessary, they would take the matter to the international human rights organisations as well.

Arunabh's assurance worked at last. Hearing the logical argument, the young boys who had given up, felt hopeful again. Without wasting any more time, they left. It was the harvesting season. If they didn't pay attention to farming on whatever small holdings they had, they would have to go hungry for the rest of the year.

Soon, the courtyard was empty. Only Bipul stayed back. Taking a spade, he started digging at the flower and kitchen gardens. Then, he got busy weeding out the unwanted growth.

'Bipul, only another cup of tea would wake us up. Will you, please?' Arunabh said, stretching himself.

Giving him a smile, Bipul immediately went into the kitchen.

In the bamboo thicket nearby, a huge flock of egrets started chirping. Though the size of their habitat was shrinking, they were still not homeless completely. God only knew what they were trying to convey in that cacophony! On the banks of Muna and Daphlong lakes, one could see pelicans, chickens and a variety of ducks. They crowded during the dry season, but were present during the monsoon too. Kaziranga consisted of 5.88 per cent water body, 66.44 per cent grassland and 18 per cent evergreen forests. Every day something or the other happened at the lap of this wonderful nature. The monsoon had just lashed the region. As a result, each tree, shrub and creeper looked rejuvenated.

The flora, in turn, passes on its positivity to the animals and birds. But rhino? Why was the rhino proving to be Kaziranga's undoing? The Kaziranga Sangram Samiti was not the only organisation taking up the poaching issue. Many other organisations, from Kohora to Dispur, had been protesting, thus making everyone concerned sit up and take notice.

Sometime back, Arunabh had done an investigative story. Taking a complaint by an NGO as the peg, he made an observation that a few higher-ups in the forest department were hand in glove with the poachers. And he hinted that those officials were protected by ministers. He also raised the question about the misuse of crores of rupees which flew to Kaziranga from the government and non-government sources, and why the ministry was not monitoring it. He criticised the government's plan to cut the horn from a rhino in order to protect them from falling into greedy hands. He also criticised a few international NGOs that had planted the idea. His write-up also included the warning a few students' unions had given to the forest department saying that they would teach all guilty parties a lesson in their own turf, if the situation did not improve. Actually, Arunabh did not comment directly. He put his words into the mouth of the NGO members, student leaders and a few local people by quoting them extensively.

Though, the fortnightly magazine was based in the South, the news from the North-east found a prominent place in their display. Especially, ever since Arunabh joined the magazine.

But a few days ago, Arunabh was intimated from the headquarters that a ₹10-crore defamation case was slapped against the magazine by the forest department for the allegations.

But then, neither his editor nor his publisher was worried about the lawsuit. Such things kept happening all the time. His editor himself called Arunabh to convey that he should be writing about the government irregularities and corruptions that plagued Kaziranga, especially the rhino killings. Only, he should focus on facts and have ample evidence.

Getting the go-ahead from none other than the editor himself, Arunabh became a lot more enthusiastic. It was inevitable that they would drag the magazine to the court to save their own skin. But Arunabh vowed to keep highlighting such atrocities and corruptions in order to save the park.

'Hey you, musician…lover boy, would you reveal your day's itinerary, please?' Sipping the strong tea, Arunabh asked Rishi in a sarcastic tone.

'What possible itinerary can I have? Till Amal da comes back, I have to supervise the construction work at the site for the entire day,' Rishi sounded a little sad.

'Alright! You remain there. I need to roam around the whole day. Don't cook for me. I will eat whenever I find time. In fact, if you can give me mashed potatoes and a boiled egg with joha rice for breakfast, that would be great. Ask Bipul to make it,' Arunabh advised Rishi. Rishi agreed.

One of his friends from Bokakhat had lent an old scooter to Rishi. Arunabh borrowed it from Rishi for the day. Amal da's car was not there.

Taking a bath, all three had piping hot rice, mashed potatoes and boiled eggs even before the clock struck nine in the morning. Arunabh asked Bipul to take the scooter to the construction site and wait for them there.

Letting out a burp or two, Rishi and Arunabh lay down in bed luxuriously and lit up a cigarette each. Before going out for the day, they wanted to enjoy this little time they had to themselves.

Outside, the sun was shining bright. The summer had still a few weeks left. However, the Weather God was playing a crazy game by shining bright at one moment and coming down in torrential rain in the other. One moment it was hot, and the other, chilly. The road of Kaziranga was constantly muddy. It won't dry till the monsoon is over.

'Hey, Rishi, how is Lakhimi's father doing now? Will he be alright soon?' Arunabh remembered Lakhimi's father all of a sudden.

Rishi inhaled the smoke from his cigarette deeply. He started coughing. 'No, man! Forget about getting better soon, probably he won't pull it through. His condition is deteriorating by the day. His wound is not healing at all,' he sounded worried.

Arunabh kept quiet. Padmeshwar's innocent face came to his mind. His entire life was a struggle. As a postman, he had served the people in Kaziranga all his life, and finally, had fallen prey to a deadly tiger. Life seemed so unfair. In this mysterious world, who kept records of one's deeds? What was written in destiny was beyond human comprehension. One could only hope that whoever was in charge of people's destiny got his calculations right…

Hurrying up, both slipped into their working gears. Rishi locked the door. The lock was just symbolic—one pull and it would easily give away. Rishi himself had to break his lock twice after losing the keys.

The grasses were growing taller. Carefully, both friends tried to walk on the dry surface of the road.

The village was quiet. Most of them had gone to the fields, and those who were not into farming, went about their respective jobs. The children were in school. Except for the womenfolk and the elderly people, no one was around.

After walking for a distance, Arunabh stopped in front of Lakhimi's house. He looked back at Rishi. Their eyes met. Giving out a signal, Arunabh opened the gate.

The house, too, had plunged into silence. Only a stray dog was moving about. Seeing Arunabh and Rishi intruding its territory, it started barking. They stopped.

Hearing the barks, Lakhimi came out of the house. Her dress was all out of place. Both her hands were covered with ashes, the tell-tale signs that she was washing utensils. She wore a gloomy expression. She was the poor shadow of the Lakhimi Arunabh had seen earlier.

She was not expecting Rishi and Arunabh at this hour. Seeing them at her doorstep, she was taken aback. Conscious and helpless, she did not know how to react.

'Oh, it's you! Please come in. Have a seat,' she said, pointing at the verandah.

Arunabh and Rishi looked at each other. Rishi looked sad.

Without saying a word, they both sat in the chairs. Lakhimi went inside.

A dove started crooning somewhere. In that pindrop silence, the noise was sounding a lot louder.

After quite a while, Lakhimi reappeared, this time wearing a clean *chaddar*. She was still looking sad and dejected. Her gaze was locked on some object far away.

The atmosphere was getting nerve wrecking.

Arunabh finally opened his mouth. 'Lakhimi, how is your father…I mean Uncle. How is he feeling now?' Arunabh spoke in a soft voice, as if he was reluctant to break the silence.

Lakhimi didn't reply. She was stoic. Surprised, Arunabh looked at her. She was now looking at the floor. Her eyes welled up. Arunabh turned away his eyes.

He usually kept himself away from such delicate situations. But then one cannot do that all the time!

He thought what to say next. He could think of nothing intelligent to ease the situation. 'Lakhimi, take us to Uncle,' he said, instead.

Lakhimi looked at Arunabh, puzzled. 'You can see him. But do you want to see him?'

'Let's go. We just want to say a quick hello!'

They followed Lakhimi as she dragged herself to her father's bed.

The inside of the house was in utter chaos. It looked as if Lakhimi was unable to handle the responsibilities that so suddenly had befallen upon her. At least, she was managing to send the boys to school. So, everything—from bathing her sick father to giving him the bed pan to medicine to cooking and cleaning and taking care of the livestock—fell on her shoulders and it was taking a huge toll on her.

Crossing the main room of the house, they found Padmeshwar Bora sleeping on an unkempt bed. It was not exactly a bed, but a huge wooden trunk that was made into a makeshift bed. In the cloudy weather, the room was dark even in the daytime.

Walking closer, Arunabh stood next to the bed. A sharp stench of urine and medicine assaulted his nostrils. He felt like puking. But what met his eyes was not something he was prepared for.

Padmeshwar Bora had turned into a living skeleton. His body had turned black, like burnt coal. He made a strange sound as he breathed. There were flies hovering around him. He was wearing a dhoti and vest. The wound on his shoulder was covered with a checked *gamosa*. Arunabh did not have the heart to look at him for long.

Padmeshwar was having trouble with his speech too. He could barely whisper. Only Lakhimi understood what he was trying to say.

After looking at Padmeshwar Bora, Arunabh did not feel like sitting there any longer. His chest grew heavy. Why is human life so fragile? Life can take a drastic turn at the blink of an eye.

Hesitantly, Lakhimi asked them if they would care for a cup of tea. But without looking at her face, Arunabh replied, 'We don't want tea, Lakhimi. Take care of yourself.' Saying that, he headed straight to the gate. Rishi was just a few steps behind.

From there to the guest house, Arunabh did not utter a single word. His mobile rang once, but he did not pick up. No matter how hard he tried to block the image of the ever-smiling

Pademeshwar Bora pedaling his bicycle with a huge stack of letters and parcels, the images kept flashing in his mind.

Reaching the guest house, he splashed water on his face, as if he was trying to wash away the image he had just witnessed. He wished it was just a nightmare. Lighting up a cigarette, he drank a glass of water.

After half an hour, Arunabh started his scooter. Seeing him leave, Rishi came out. Without turning off the ignition, he kept looking at Rishi's face. 'What will you do now, Rishi?'

'What will I do? What do you mean?'

'I mean, how long will Lakhimi suffer like this?'

'But what can we do?' Rishi closed his fists, unsure of what was coming next.

'Listen carefully. We can do just one thing…' Arunabh stopped midway. He swallowed hard. 'If you have not vowed to remain a bachelor for the rest of your life, marry her and rescue the family from getting destroyed.'

Emphasising each word carefully, Arunabh zoomed off.

Rishi, as if struck by lightening, kept standing there. Soon, Arunabh was well out of sight…

'Have you seen a white tiger?'

'Yes.'

'Where?'

'In the zoo. Where else?'

'No, yaar! I am asking whether you have seen one in Kaziranga,' Rishi sounded irritated with Arunabh.

Arunabh kept quiet. As if Rishi had seen a white tiger in the open in Kaziranga! After shifting to Kaziranga, Rishi sometimes made absurd comments. Arunabh knew for a fact that Kaziranga had no white tigers. The park had rhinos, elephants, water buffaloes, deers, spotted deers, wild boars and about 60 leopards. There were about 38 to 40 varieties of animals in Kaziranga. The population of the spotted deer was the highest, counting up to a few thousands. In the number two position was the wild boar. Only the 1966 census showed two white tigers. It was strange! Then God only knows where they disappeared! God knows what greedy poacher got to them finally!

'Listen, as per records, white tigers existed in India from 1556 to 1605. Kaziranga figured nowhere when it came to white tiger population. Nobody believes that Kaziranga has white tiger. But I have seen one myself. One day, I had gone inside the jungle with Hriday da. It was there, basking in the morning sun, cleaning its paw. I pointed it out to Hriday da. But the moment he turned his face, the tiger jumped and disappeared into a dense thicket.' As Rishi narrated his thrilling adventure, he got visibly excited.

In fact, he was so excited that he tried to stand up on the moving boat. It upset the balance and the boat started rocking. In alarm, Arunabh and the boatman started shouting, 'Hey…hey!'

Realising what he was doing, Rishi sat down again. The boat became stable.

They were undertaking this boat journey in a lake inside the Agaratali forest. Taking an official boat, Arunabh was inspecting the plight of the wild animals of Kaziranga caused by non-seasonal floods. The irony was that the forest department had filed a lawsuit against the magazine for which Arunabh was working, and here he was, enjoying the hospitality of the same department to investigate the wildlife problems. Actually, the top brass of the department did not know Arunabh or rather was not bothered about his presence. It was only to save their skin, or their self-respect, they slapped the lawsuit. It was a routine matter. Most people knew about that.

This Agaratali forest fell under the Bokakhat sub-division. It was at a short distance from the headquarters of Kaziranga and about 20 kms from the Kohora Range. As it had several lakes, this forest land attracted plenty of birds. It was also home to swamp deers, boars, rhinos and buffaloes. But it was famous for its colony of pelicans.

A huge portion of this forest had been eroded by the Brahmaputra. Not just Agaratali, but as trees and jungles were slowly disappearing, the mighty river started eating up the banks, slowly but steadily.

On one side, the human beings were on the rampage, destroying the greenery. And on the other hand, taking advantage of people's foolishness, the mad Luhit was spreading itself at the cost of the national park and the villages that fell along its route.

The forest department washed its hands off saying the erosion of the banks did not fall under their purview. Actually, there were only a handful of people in the headquarters who actually bothered about such problems. Strangely, there were a few outsiders who were keen about resolving these issues.

But a few greedy employees and officials, who were empowered with an Assamese name and surname, had endangered the future of Kaziranga. And the sad thing was that there wasn't be a single Assamese official in the key positions in forest department in the coming years. Arunabh, who was minutely studying the administrative set-up of Kaziranga, was sure of it.

The water had inundated 80 per cent landmass of the national park. Animals came out in hoards searching for a dry place. Rhinos, buffaloes and swamp deers took shelter on any spot that remained above the water level.

The boat was heading towards a forest guard post. Such posts were built with bamboo, wood and hay. All these posts looked as if they had gone past their retirement age—jaded and faded. How could anyone expect these foot soldiers with no arms and not even bare minimum facilities to fight with those poachers, who had the state-of-the-art firearms and technology?

Back in 1964, the first guard to fall prey to a poacher's bullet was Boloram Dutta, who was patrolling in Sildubi, in the north of the Diphlu river. It created history of sorts. Later, many helpless guards lost their lives in such fights inside Kaziranga. Last year itself, when Arunabh and Rishi were busy finding out such stories of sacrifice, they lost Lahan in the most tragic manner. Hridayananda and Amal were the eye witnesses…

A portion of the post was submerged in water. There was a rickety ladder that connected the ground to the floor of the *chang ghar*. Since the ground was uneven, assessing the depth of the water was also dicey—at some places, it was knee deep, and at some, it came up to the waist.

A forest guard tied up the boat to the bamboo pole of the hut with a strong rope. Then, he held the boat firmly as Rishi and Arunabh climbed up the ladder.

Inside the hut, Amal and Hridayananda were sitting on a *durri*. They looked tired. The whole day, Hridayananda had been running around looking after the animals which were displaced from their habitats by the sudden flood. He was constantly on boats or walking in water to make sure no harm came to the animals. He had recently recovered from a fever—still weak. A responsible officer that he was, after hearing about the devastating flood that struck at midnight, he could not remain in bed. He was up and about, and within minutes, he was surveying his range from end to end. There was no time to even pause and eat.

In fact, nobody, other than Rishi and Arunabh, had time for a meal. All the forest guards had to make do with puffed rice, flattened rice and jaggery that they had stored for a rainy day. That and a few cups of black tea in the name of nourishment!

Amal was a foodie. He had to have rice. Not having a proper meal, he was irritated and throwing tantrums. When Hridayananda gave him a piece of his mind, then only he remained silent. Hridayananda explained, 'We eat proper meals every day. But look at these guards. The have no ration, no money.' So, if Amal wanted to see the ground reality in Kaziranga during the flood, he would have to forget about food—at least for a day.

Hridayananda's lecture worked. Yes, Amal himself had volunteered to come along, despite Hriday asking him not to.

The sun was about to set on the horizon.

Taking Hridayananda's prior permission, Arunabh and Rishi had taken the boat to assess the flood situation. They were worried after seeing the real flood fury, which was far more dangerous than what they had read in newspapers. There were so many things that neither words nor the camera could capture. Hridayananda was the only one who was accustomed with the devastating effects of flood. Having grown up in Lakhimpur, seeing the horror that Ranganadi unleashed every year, he knew what all he could expect with a flood of this magnitude. Someone or the other would inevitably lose his life to flood in Lakhimpur.

Agaratali, where Rishi and Arunabh were roaming in, today saw a fatal incident. Gutimala's elder brother dropped her off on the other side of the river in a boat for grazing the cow. When her brother did not come back to pick her up in the evening, she held onto the tail of the cow and tried crossing the river. She had done that several times earlier. The river was a small one, but the current of the water proved too strong for Gutimala. She tried to hold on, but got entrapped in a whirlpool. The circular current tossed her tiny body hard before washing her away. Nobody could find her. It happened just an hour back. Somebody narrated the sad incident in the walkie-talkie. Rishi and Arunabh did not know about it.

Hridayananda got up from the floor. 'You guys wait here. I saw a few rhinos out in the open in bad condition. If they are still there, we would have to shoo them off to a safer place. Otherwise, they will fall prey to poachers at night.' As he explained this, he climbed down that shaky ladder and got into the boat. The boat started immediately and vanished amidst big trees and shrubs.

Darkness was conquering this part of the world once again. The sound of birds was reverberating everywhere. Swamp deers, boars and rhinos were making some nasal sounds. Hearing a monkey's shrieks, a bird made a strange sound, as if it was anticipating something sinistrous to happen. The whole thing evoked fear.

The flood had devastated Kaziranga. The animals were not normal today. Everyone was worried, fearing something terrible would happen. Many claimed that during such times, many forest guards had seen paranormal activities in Kaziranga. They had even seen many strange reptiles; some had seen huge birds. Hridayananda didn't entertain such talks.

The forest guard who stayed back, lit up a kerosene lamp and tied it onto a pole of the *chang ghar*. The flickering light in the vast expanse of darkness created an image of isolation and loneliness.

On the floor of the *chang ghar*, a guard boiled water to make tea for them. His officer had ordered him to offer tea to all three. In an aluminium thali, he poured puffed rice and mixed it up with chopped onions, green chillies and salt.

Nobody had the courage to break the silence of the night. No sound at all, except for the slurping of the tea and the crunching of the puffed rice.

Suddenly, breaking the silence, the guard broke out in a fit of coughing. There was no sign of stopping. His entire body was convulsed in pain. Keeping his glass on the floor, Amal rushed to the guard. So did Arunabh and Rishi.

The guard was by now rolling on the floor, coughing non-stop. He was sounding like a sick animal.

'Hey, Brother, what happened?' Amal asked, concerned. The guard could not answer. He was only coughing. Amal shook him.

Somehow, he managed to say in a feeble voice, 'Have been suffering from fever and cough for the past few days. I told sir that I needed to go home. But no leave. Staff shortage. If I go away, one person would be less. Those bastard poachers keep track of such news so that can lay their trap, sir.'

He was moaning and groaning as he said that.

The guard was quite young. But poverty was making him older even before age could do.

'Have you taken medicine?'

'I have. Sir had given me some. But nothing seems to be working. I must have been possessed by some spirit.'

Rishi and Arunabh made him sit up comfortably.

His name was Tilen Das. He belonged to Biswanath Ghat. He had been working in this range for the past six years. No transfer. Everybody was aware of the fact that there were very few forest guards in proportion to the area of the park. But, not allowed leave even for medical treatment was something inhuman. Once a forest guard called Rabilal Hazarika applied for leave. But he was not sanctioned, and ultimately, he died.

There was no end to their woes. There was no proper arrangement for food or rest.

They were modernising some posts by replacing the bamboo poles with concrete posts and thatched roof with tinned ones. But that's about it. That was the reason, whenever the opportunity arose, any employee or forest guard, would seek transfer and never even look back.

Amal was feeling low. Arunabh had told him that just by visiting the water-locked Kaziranga for one day, he would not be able to assess the ground reality. Now, he knew what Arunabh had meant.

Tilen had stopped coughing. He was leaning on the wall for support. He had this fear that either he had contacted TB or malaria.

Amal made a mental note to confront Hridayananda. How could he not grant leave to such a sick man?

They could see the blinking light from what they imagined to be a boat; got to be Hridayananda. Soon, they could hear him talking loudly on his mobile. He was probably having an argument. He sounded positively angry. 'Amal, come down. Let's drop you home,' he shouted from below. He said something else, but they could not make out what.

One by one, all three started climbing down and reached the boat. Amal was the last one to leave. Before leaving the post, he took out a 300-rupee note and thrust it in Tilen's hand, and asked him to go the very next day and see a doctor.

Tilen was taken by surprise. But he returned the notes. 'I don't need money, sir. What will I do with money? If you can please get my leaves sanctioned and send me home…home.' His voice trailed off towards the end of the sentence.

The notes fell onto the floor. Amal had started climbing down. He felt useless and helpless as he saw Tilen rejecting his offer.

Focusing the torch on Amal, who was slowly climbing down, Hridayananda screamed, 'What's wrong? Why are you not coming down, you pig?'

Amal became alert. He increased his pace. Hridayananda was in an odd mood today. He was really angry with someone. Amal knew his friend inside out. But today, he felt he did not know this Hridayananda. Something must have gone wrong somewhere.

The boat was moving steadily, cutting the dense darkness with a dimmed light coming out of a torch, whose battery had seen better days. The chop-chop sound of the oars and that made by insects were making the atmosphere mysterious. They would have to row for about a kilometre to reach to the highland where Hridayananda's Gypsy was parked.

Amal had no idea how Hridayananda was going to provide shelter to all the animals of his range. There were areas that weren't submerged along the national highway. But will the animals come to these highlands? Will the rhinos, tigers, elephants, boars and deers not be afraid? Why did they not think of constructing some raised platforms inside the park itself? There were some international donors working for the welfare of the animals. Had the forest department put forward such a suggestion, they would have definitely listened to it.

Amal was tempted to ask this question. But looking at Hriday, he did not have the courage. Still, he could not stop himself from pleading for Tilen Das' case. 'Ehh…Hriday. Tilen

Das in the camp was pretty sick. He said his leave was not sanctioned. Can't anything be done?'

He trailed off in anticipation of a volley of shouts. He kept his mouth shut and ears open.

But lo and behold, no such thing happened. Hridayananda did not see red, nor did he criticise his friend.

After keeping quiet for a while, Hridayananda opened his mouth. His voice was barely audible amid the continuous chop-chop sound the oars were making as they broke the watery barrier.

'Huh! Do you feel I am not bothered about his health? I am aware of everything. But who do I grant leave to? There is no staff. I am working with a limited number of forest guards. When such flood occurs, poachers too try to kill rhinos, adding woes to our misery. The deers and other animals are easy targets. In such a case, if I grant leave, the top officers would hold me responsible. I am going to leave this job…Soon, I am going to resign. How much can I take? I stayed back just for my love for Kaziranga. But it's useless. Nobody understands me…nobody understands the pain of the Tilens.' As Hriday poured his heart out, his voice was filled with anger and a sense of helplessness.

'Hriday da, many reserved forests or national parks outside Assam have opted for health insurance for their employees. Why are we not following that here?' Arunabh opened his mouth after a long time.

'Arunabh, you are a journalist. You will know it better than me why and at what level such policies get stalled from being implemented here.'

Arunabh remained quiet. He was well aware of the fact that Hridayananda was going through a rough time. It was better to keep shut. State governments in Orissa and Andhra Pradesh had chalked out many beneficial plans for their forest guards. Arunabh had read when the news was carried by media regarding a pact made by those governments with the Oriental Insurance Company. If someone got injured while on duty, he was given ₹75,000 and if someone died, up to ₹15 lakhs was given to his family as compensation. That was done almost 10 years ago. They must have added a lot more facilities by now. Only in Assam…

The boat got stuck. It refused to budge. The water level was shallow. But it had to be untangled in order to move forward. The guard who was rowing the boat tried his best to free it.

Handing over the torchlight to Rishi, Hridayananda wore his gumboots and got down from the boat. They both applied full force to free the boat. The nose of the boat was stuck in a gap of a felled tree trunk. After some serious effort of pushing and shoving, they managed to untangle it.

'You people walk from here. I don't want to take it any further. It might get stuck again,' Hridayananda said, almost like an order.

Amal and Arunabh were a little hesitant. But it was Hriday's order…So, they started rolling up their trousers. Rishi was already in the water.

Leaving behind the two forest guards on the boat, Hridayananda led the team with his torchlight. His quick steps in the water made the chap-chap sound.

Amal was frightened. So was Arunabh. Rishi didn't care much. Danger lurked in every step of this knee-deep water in this jungle—especially, from poisonous snakes. But what was the alternative?

So, dividing the muddy water with their forceful steps, all four proceeded towards the highland.

Suddenly, something round and thick tightened around Arunabh's leg. He got scared. He felt he was attacked by some reptile. He tried to think fast what to do next. 'Hriday da…I think a snake has wrapped around my right leg. I cannot move it…' screamed this city-bred guy.

Hridayananda stopped. He walked back to where Arunabh was standing. In a swift action, he thrust the torch into Arunabh's hand and started examining Arunabh's leg with both hands. Where was the snake? Was it a snake?

Trying to feel the object around Arunabh's feet with his hands, Hriday pulled out a three-inch-thick creeper from his heel. Not a creeper; actually, it was the root of an old jari tree. It resembled a deadly snake.

Hridayananda was aware that the forest had many old and strange snakes. He had many such strange and scary encounters. He was now immune to such incidents. The tourists, who flocked the park in the winter, had no idea what lay beneath this serene-looking national park. How could he forget the incident when a bullet from an AK 47 zoomed past just three inches below his ear and injured a guard who was standing close to him? Or, the incident when he had to run for his life after coming face to face with a hungry tiger?

They could now see the jeep that was parked some distance away. They would have to walk 50 or 60 metres to reach there. Hridayananda would feel relieved after he left all three home. Then, he would decide what to do for the night. He was sure that his source would not give him wrong information. Only some last-minute changes may occur in the operation. In all likelihood, tonight, one such operation would take place. Hridayananda felt the rush of adrenalin.

Hridayananda was showing the torchlight to all three following him. His mind was occupied with the thoughts of the night raid. Even as he looked on, Arunabh, Amal and Rishi ran towards the jeep as if they were taking part in a race. They didn't wait for Hriday to show them the way with the torchlight. Yes, all three were scared out of their wits. They will remember this experience of walking in water at night in Kaziranga for the rest of their lives. Hridayananda started laughing in the dark, without making a sound.

Amal and Rishi were the only two living beings walking on that otherwise deserted road. The sky was clear, bright with the moonlight. Two days ago, there was a full moon. So, the moon was still round and bright. The green fields on both sides of the narrow road were covered with grey as far as the eyes could see. It was difficult to say whether it was fog or smog.

This time of the year, when the winter is about to set in, the countryside of Assam becomes alluringly beautiful. Both city-born and bred, Amal and Rishi, could not get enough of this beauty. Living inside Kaziranga was a unique experience for them.

Only a few days back, Kaziranga was made open for tourists. It was an elaborate affair, with the minister and all the big shots in the forest department taking part in the inauguration. It was a day-long function. Amal, too, was invited. But his enthusiasm for the function soon ebbed out. He noticed that except for the minister and a few big bosses, no employee was enthusiastic about the function. They were just mechanically playing their parts. Even the participation from the local people was less.

Only the members of the Jeep Safari Association were present at the event.

Actually, this year, the flood had devastated Kaziranga to a great extent. Some areas were completely washed out. No one could say for sure what all were lost. Every element associated with life—emotions, a sense of security, fights for territory—made Kaziranga what it is—a habitat for such a wide variety of life. But one flood could wash away all those emotions, that sense of security for both animals and humans. Since 1950, Assam has lost as many as 2,534 villages to flood. A stretch of 8,000 hectares of land has been claimed by rivers in their full spate. That makes a huge impact on Kaziranga and its nearby villages.

Amal and Rishi were still walking. The whole atmosphere had a calming effect on them. They had just witnessed the destructive side of nature. Looking at this Kaziranga, one could not gauge its destructive streaks.

Mother Earth was generous when she created Kaziranga.

Both of them sat down on a concrete slab that was built over a culvert. After a long time, Amal had the craving for a cigarette; he lit one up. The smoke spiralled up and disappeared into the pristine surrounding. Rishi, sitting quietly, enjoyed the aroma of filtered tobacco.

'Rishi, when do you think our guest house will be ready?' Amal's business acumen resurfaced, even amidst the bounty of nature. He sounded a little unsure of himself.

Rishi's mind was somewhere else. Amal's question brought him back to reality with a thud. 'Amal da, the main work is already complete. They are working day and night. I feel from the first of January we will be able to open it up for tourists. You can ask your clerk in Guwahati to get the bedsheets, curtains and towels. It will take time to get those things in proper place.' Rishi talked like an experienced manager.

Yes, there was so much to be done! Starting a resort was not a kid's play—that too in such a short span of time. One had to think about every little detail, right from the kitchen to cooks to beds to dressing tables to sofa sets and what not! But then, the checklist for each department was satisfactory. So far so good.

The co-operative venture called Assamese Meal was given the responsibility of providing lunch and dinner to the guests. It was done on a contract basis. It saved Amal a lot of headache and benefited the women entrepreneurs of Pamua. The breakfast and fast-food section were handed over to the team trained in Guwahati. They would work as waiters, security and helpers. Bipul would have to close down his shop, as he was made the leader of the team. After doing a thorough survey of the salary structure in the nearby resorts, Amal made a pay structure for his own employees. He made the pay scale with benefits, like a Provident Fund. Pay day was fixed on the seventh of each month. The first pay day was just around the corner. Thankfully, he was not required to pay all of them this month.

Though everything was falling into place, Amal still had anxiety attacks. A few incidents reported in Kaziranga were the reason for that. Disappointment and confrontation were becoming the order of the day inside Kaziranga.

Recently, Forest and Environment Minister Prakash Javadekar had visited Kaziranga. He made it clear that the Centre was worried about rhino killings. He had announced that a task force would be constituted to stop poaching. He also mentioned about involving the local youth in a rhino protection committee. Later, addressing a press conference along with the state forest minister, he said that it was the responsibility of the State to protect its wildlife. Touching the subject of encroachment, he said the state government had to take strict measures against encroachers. He added that the task force would also look into this issue.

Once the minister had left, came the CBI team. The CBI was handling two rhino poaching cases. The team was likely to take up more such cases. The team based out of Bokakhat met many people to probe the matter. The alert team wanted the details of the two guns used in the killings from the district court in Bokakhat.

It seemed the entire nation, hell-bent on stopping rhino killings, was coming down heavily on the poachers. All these happened in the first week of September. But then, the enthusiasm evaporated and things got back to being normal once again. The Centre, too, cooled down—a strange situation!

Such developments disturbed Amal. Would the resort business in Kaziranga fetch him any profit? Or, was the government planning to stop such business centres from Kaziranga altogether by imposing some new law? If something like that happened, he would go bankrupt. Crores of rupees had been invested in it already.

Taking puffs of his cigarette, Amal started pacing up and down. Against the moonlight, the shadow of his tall body looked like that of a dwarf. The fog was enveloping the area. But his mind was far from being cool. Fishing out for the packet in the pocket, he took out another stick and lit it up. As he inhaled it deeply, he broke out in a terrible cough.

Rishi was observing the whole scene. He knew what was bothering Amal da. Amal da's fear was not totally unfounded.

But to start something, he had to believe in himself. He could not abandon it midway. That too in anticipation of something bad! Had that been the case, no venture would have been fulfilled in this world. Such insecurities and uncertainities were part and parcel of life in the 21st century.

He tried to divert Amal da's trend of thoughts. To be honest, it was because of him and Arunabh, Amal da invested so much money in this project. So, it was his responsibility to keep Amal da's spirit buoyed.

'Amal da, let's go and have a drink. The weather is right for a peg or two,' Rishi insisted.

Amal agreed with Rishi. 'Where do you want to go, Rishi?'

'Suit yourself. We can go to a bar or visit Hriday da or simply sit at home. The bottle of scotch you brought from Guwahati is still there—at least half of it.'

'Forget home. Let's just drive some place,' Amal shoved his worries to the corner of his mind.

The car was parked at the guest house. And the guest house was about two kilometres from where they were. Both started walking towards the resort. There was a sense of urgency in their steps this time. It was not even eight in the evening.

The driver had been suffering from fever; he was sleeping in the outhouse of the resort. Taking the key from him, Amal sat in the driving seat. The cold engine revved up to Amal's expert touch. Soon, the vehicle was on the highway.

There was not much traffic on the highway. There were cars, but definitely the number of pedestrians, cycles and bikes were few and far between. In the last few days, the highway was often raided by tigers and wild elephants.

Since the devastation caused by the last flood, there was shortage of food for the animals. And this time, more than elephants in search of paddy and grass, it was the Royal Bengal Tigers that were out in the villages looking for goats and cows. Last week, tigers killed an elephant too. That elephant was tied to an iron chain and left inside the jungle to graze. Suddenly, it disappeared from the spot. The mahout who took care of the elephant searched for it everywhere. He was puzzled as to how the huge elephant could escape the tight iron shackle. After three days, following a foul smell, he saw the elephant's decomposed body behind a thicket. Major portions of the huge body were devoured by tigers.

There were reports from nearby villages about tigers killing cows and goats. After the news of the attack on Padmeshwar broke out, villagers of the surrounding areas avoided coming out of their homes at night. They had been terrorised.

Amal and Rishi, too, while returning to their place at Pamua had come face to face with tigers, not once but twice.

But it seemed even tigers were afraid of city people. They were not attacked on both the instances, but sufficiently warned. This peculiar attitude of tigers could generate enough curiosity among wildlife scientists to start research on this subject.

'East or west? Which direction, Rishi?' Amal asked, without stopping the car.

Rishi thought for a moment. Bokakhat? Nope. Kaliabar would be a better choice. There were quite a few dhabas on both sides of the road. They could treat themselves in one of those.

Following Rishi's advice, Amal turned the car towards the west.

After driving at a moderate speed for a while, Amal pulled over onto the side of the highway. He looked puzzled as he shut the engine.

'Rishi, there used to be a resort, I mean, a restaurant with a bar somewhere here. I don't remember the name, but do you remember once we met a British boy, who we later dropped at the Dhansiri Echo camp? Do you?'

'I do, Amal da. But the government bulldozed the resort last week. You could still see its remnants here had it not been so dark. The owner had built it without permission. So, it was destroyed,' Rishi answered, calmly.

Amal was taken aback.

Was the Assam government, which had been marred with corruption charges, become efficient all of a sudden? It was, indeed, unbelievable. Or, was there more than what met the eye?

'Are you sure? Was it actually the forest department that demolished that resort?' Amal was still finding it difficult to believe it.

'Hundred per cent! This is the result of the people's constant protest against the ineffectiveness of the government machinery. The government or the government departments are also run by people like you and me. There are some good people there. When the public makes a noise against corruption, they feel empowered to take up such steps. They are also worried that Kaziranga would one day disappear if such practices were allowed to continue.' Rishi was upbeat, as he explained the whole thing.

Amal felt a little reassured. Yes, everything was not lost. There were good people. There were people who genuinely felt for Kaziranga. There were people like Lahan and Hridayananda who were ready to sacrifice their lives to protect the wild animals. So, there were possibilities for good business…

Arunabh had questioned Hridayananda as to why the forest department had not implemented the medical insurance policy for its employees. But then, the Central Minister Javadekar had assured to implement the insurance scheme for the employees. Not only that, he also promised to keep a tab on the crores of rupees sanctioned for Kaziranga, whether the money was being used properly or not.

Amal started the car. His chaotic mind was now somewhat calm and he was in control.

The speed of the car automatically slowed down. This usually happens when the driver is having such melancholic thoughts. Suddenly, both saw a row of flames coming towards them—an unending line of dancing fire. It looked surreal. Amal parked the car aside. Rishi too was shocked.

Both came out of the car.

Only then they could make sense of the dancing flames. Actually, it was a long procession of people carrying torches, which was coming from the opposite direction. Even though the moon was shining bright in the sky, the 200 odd people were carrying red flames, illuminating the road and inundating the area with slogans in support of the protection of wildlife and condemning rhino killings.

Amal and Rishi stared as the procession passed by. It was moving towards the Kohora Chowk. They would, in all likelihood, attract the attention of the foreign tourists. The tourist, thus, would be aware of the problems that plagued Kaziranga. The awareness would grow.

Both sat in the car.

After driving for a while, Amal entered the premises of a guest house and parked the car in the parking area. It was a mid-level guest house, which was filled with people—mostly families.

Entering the bar, they saw three of the tables were occupied by some middle-aged men. Choosing a corner table, Amal ordered for whiskey and fried chicken. Relaxing in his chair, Amal lit up a cigarette. After working continuously at the resort, both were dead tired. Amal had lost a few kilos.

Sitting comfortably, they started sipping their whiskey. Someone from the other corner came towards them.

'Hey, Amal? Remember me?' offering his hand, the stranger smiled at him.

Amal took a good look at the man. Cropped hair. Bald. The eyes were bright and shiny, even in the dim light. Amal tried hard to recall. This man looked so familiar…

'Well, my face has changed a lot. Earlier, I sported an unruly crop. Now, I am bald. I am Anirudh. The history department… do you remember now?' the man said, pulling a chair with the free hand, his other still clasping Amal's.

It was now Amal's turn to be surprised. Yes, the history department in Cotton College. The topper in the class and the best graduate Anirudh…Anirudh Kakoti. But was this bald guy the same Anirudh of his college gang?

'What have you done to yourself, yaar? How on earth would anyone recognise you? My God! It's been 20 or 25 years…'

'But I did recognise you, Amal.' Anirudh included Rishi also in the conversation as if he too was an old friend.

Suddenly, it became a happy place.

Amal updated his college friend about his life. He didn't forget to mention that he was in Kaziranga to build a resort, that he was not just a casual visitor. Anirudh was posted at the Dergaon Police Training College. After topping his batch in Cotton College, he went to Delhi for further studies. There, he cleared the IPS, and now, he was a top-ranking police officer. Anirudh had come from a very poor family. It was necessary for him to get a job immediately after completing his studies. His wife was a professor at the Gauhati University. Both kept updating about their lives and talked at length about their old classmates.

'You know, now the domestic responsibilities and career problems are settling down. When the children were in school, there was no time for anything else. Now, I have started reuniting with old friends. Probably at this age, one tends to relive those old times. What say?' Anirudh said, as he ordered for his last peg.

'Yes! Good we met. Dergaon is not far from Kaziranga. We can meet once in a while. Sometimes, you drop in, and sometimes, I will come visit,' Amal had the plan all chalked out.

The man who was sitting with Anirudh had gone long back. As he was still missing from the scene, Anirudh went out to look for him.

Anirudh reappeared about five minutes later. This time, his face was gloomy. Amal threw a questioning look at him.

'Amal, there is a firing incident in Burapahar. I don't know whether it is between the forest guards and poachers or with the KPLT terrorist outfit. My people are investigating. Will come to know about it soon,' Anirudh's body language was that of a police officer, as he said this.

Amal signalled the waiter to order for food. All three had selected a few dishes. Anirudh ordered for his security men too.

'You know trouble brews only in Kaziranga. There are so many reserved forests in Assam, but nothing untoward happens in those jungles. I feel the army should be given the responsibility of protecting Kaziranga. Then only things will be under control.' There was a ring of regret in Anirudh's tone. He, in a way, admitted that the forest department and the Assam Police had failed in giving protection to the national park.

A few days back, a few armed men abducted a young man called Biren Pegu right in front of his house in a Mishing village in Bokakhat.

Later, his body was found in the jungle. The villagers, suspecting that it was the handiwork of the forest department that carried out the secret killing thinking Pegu to be a poacher, gheraoed the Bokakhat Police Station.

On the other hand, the forest department gave a statement that Biren, aka Bakasur, had been involved in rhino killings. After getting a tip off, they laid an ambush on the poacher's gang. Biren died in the shoot-out, while the three other poachers managed to escape.

This incident made the area tense. Such attacks and counter-attacks kept happening in Kaziranga. People often questioned the claims made by the forest department.

Completing their meal, Amal and Anirudh walked out. The outside was completely deserted now. The moonlight seemed to be fading away.

Anirudh's security men were sitting in a Gypsy right at the gate. His assistant was talking on his mobile in a low voice.

Amal suddenly realised that Rishi was not with them. Where did he disappear? Amal got worried. Rishi was not good at handling his drinks. It would be a big problem if he passed out.

'Rishi...Rishi,' Amal shouted. There was no response. Amal was getting restless.

Amal shouted a few more times, and as if taking the cue, Rishi reappeared on the scene with the same deftness as he had disappeared earlier.

'Where the hell did you go? You were giving me a heart attack. You should not drink more than two pegs,' Amal was irritated.

Rishi kept quiet. Looking down, he kept standing close to Amal. Amal was surprised.

'Amal da...' Rishi sounded different, as if his voice was coming from far away.

Amal threw a questioning look.

'Amal da. Bipul called. Lakhimi's father, I mean Padmeshwar uncle passed away,' Rishi said in an unusual voice without looking at Amal.

Amal clasped Rishi's hand.

It was getting terribly cold. With the increase in felling of trees, the vast area of Kaziranga and the villages around it were feeling the pronounced cold wave. And as the cold increased, the activities in the villages decreased. As more and more tourists, draped in colourful woollens, thronged Kaziranga, the presence of the village people was getting sparse.

There was a mobile theatre group that had come to the Kohora Chowk. They were camping there for three days. Such theatre groups did visit Kaziranga around this time of the year. The many cultural organisations in Kohora held such shows. People loved to watch plays and movies.

After the harvesting, there was plenty of time at the villagers' disposal. So, people from all the villages came out in hordes to watch plays. In fact, even the tourists, both domestic and foreign, grabbed such opportunities for some additional entertainment. Sometimes, the demand was so huge that the visiting teams were forced to stage two shows in a single night.

This time, the rush was all the more. The ticket counters opened at nine in the morning and were sold out by mid-day.

The villagers preferred the first show. For the second show, the audience comprised government officials and tourists.

Quite a few shops selling parathas, chole, pakoras, paan, and even, meals mushroomed around the makeshift stage. They were doing brisk business, thanks to the plays which were such a crowd puller.

Today was a lean day to start with. It was cloudy since morning. The clouds only became dense by the mid-day. It was expected to rain any moment. But no. Throwing a cover of mist, Varun, the God of rain, made a vanishing act. Towards the afternoon, the sun came out with a shy look. People had no clue what to expect from this erratic Weather God.

A few people of different age groups gathered around the pandal. They had come to watch the play. But there was still half an hour left for the play to start. So, most of them were busy either chewing paan or puffing a cigarette and catching up with one another.

There was a big meeting scheduled for the coming Wednesday at Kohora. Around 20 odd organisations joined hands to discuss issues such as rhino killings to land holdings to erosion of the river banks. Everyone living in and around Kaziranga was expected to attend. Preparations for this meeting were on since one month. This was going to be a significant one. Do or die was their motto. All organisations, keeping their petty issues aside, joined hands for a larger goal. They had enough of the government apathy. They were not scared any more about the future. Who cared what would happen tomorrow when their today was at stake? Many years had gone by as they protested in a democratic manner. Now, the time had come to fight and they were ready to fight hard.

Representatives from different districts of Assam and even outside were expected to participate. Many of them had already confirmed their participation.

A long siren signalled that the play was about to start. The people who were still loitering outside went in. The dance-drama had already started. One of the late entrants, in a hurry to take his seat, banged into a pole and sat on the floor holding his head. Nobody noticed him. They were mesmerised with the lovers on stage, who were dancing blissfully as they finally reunited in heaven.

Hridayananda, who was sitting in the second row of the first class, felt the vibration of his mobile. Should he check or let it ring? He was in a dilemma. After so long, he had come out for some entertainment. But it seemed the Jungle God could not tolerate his momentary happiness. Why would his deputy keep calling non-stop otherwise? Five missed calls. It has got to be important!

Cursing his rotten luck and ignoring the embracing lovers on stage, Hridayananda got up and started towards the entrance. He didn't bother to reply to the questioning looks of his fellow rangers who were sitting with him. It took him two minutes to maneuver through the packed hall and come out in the open.

Once out, he tried to connect with Kalita.

'Sir, bad news. We found a dead rhino near the Ghutlung Camp. Our search party found it lying near the pond…' Kalita sounded breathless.

'The horn? Did they get it?' Hridayananda was equally anxious now. The sound of music coming out of the pandal was making it difficult for him to hear clearly. So, he thrust the mobile to his right ear and covered the left ear with his other hand.

'No…I mean…gone. We didn't get to know—didn't even hear a gunshot,' said Kalita.

Hridayananda felt a chill run through his spine. Why did the poachers attack only in his range? Why such heinous activities took place here only?

Kalita was still on the line.

'What will we do now?' pulling his hair with his left hand, Hridayananda almost screamed. Even before he realised it, he was in the Gypsy.

Hridayananda remembered the minister was scheduled for a visit the very next day. He was coming with his family and friends. They all were supposed to have lunch in Kaziranga. What the hell was he going to do now? His brain stopped functioning.

Reaching out to the dashboard of his vehicle, Hridayananda took out the pouch of betel nut and paan. Putting one in his mouth, he rang up Kalita again. 'Kalita, I am coming. There is no use trying to hide this incident. Let the minister come. You start the formalities,' saying this, he disconnected the phone and immediately started the engine.

These days, if a rhino is killed, they have to first report it to the police. Then only comes the post-mortem or other fomalities. After doing all these formalities, the dead rhino is left in the jungle for the carnivorous animals. The forest department keeps an eye on the dead rhino from far. Sometimes, the animals devour the huge beast within the night itself. There was no need to bury it.

It was foggy.

Hridayananda used to like such cold and foggy days. But now, his mind did not register such miracles of nature. There was no time or inclination to indulge in such sensitivities.

His mobile started ringing again. Slowing down the car, Hridayananda glanced at the screen. It was Amal calling. His guest house was going to be launched in a few days. It was almost ready. Hridayananda was amazed at the speed Amal had executed the entire project, right from buying the plot of land to constructing it. Hridayananda had seen many resorts coming up in this area. He was also aware that many of them were either sold off or closed down, as they did not do good business. Still, Amal did the unthinkable.

'Tell me...I could not watch the play. Had to leave as soon as it began...there was no other way...' Hridayananda said in a sad voice, as he picked up his friend's call.

Amal wanted to invite the forest minister for the inauguration. He was organising a cultural programme in the evening. He had already invited a popular singer from Guwahati. He was calling Hridayananda for his support.

Hridayananda didn't support the whole idea. What was the need to attract people's attention by doing such shows? Instead, they could have got Yashodhar and made him play the flute and sing. In the daytime, Amal would have to do the puja. He was a businessman, he should think like a one too. And about the minister? Would he come just because Amal invited him?

Hridayananda also knew that the fun-loving Amal would not like his advice. But then, as a friend, it was his duty to tell Amal what was good for him. Let him feel bad.

Hridayananda pressed the accelerator harder.

His thick sweater was not enough to protect him from the icy wind. This was one problem with the open Gypsy.

The fog was floating around making myriad patterns on the road. The trees on both sides were becoming hazy. It would take him 20 minutes to reach the spot where the rhino was killed.

Driving a little further, he switched on the walkie-talkie. On its network, he could hear the careful words that were being exchanged among the forest guards within his range. Everybody was measured in their talks. They knew Hridayananda was on the line.

'Charlie calling…Charlie calling…everyone on duty? Over,' Hridayananda whispered.

'Everybody has taken their positions, sir. Over.'

Hridayananda lowered his vehicle onto the kutcha road. The jeep started dancing as it moved on the uneven surface. Its headlights flooded the jungle.

On his way, he would have to pick up a team before reaching the Ghutlung Camp. If the horn of the rhino was already gone, the poachers must have reached a safe place by now. They had a strong network. After killing a rhino, they immediately cut off the horn and disappeared without leaving any trace. It did not take much time to dislodge the horn from the body. In fact, they knew the trick of chopping it even before the rhino died.

After travelling for quarter of a mile, Hridayananda could see the searchlights. A team of four guards was waiting for him. The moment he stopped his jeep, the guards jumped on board with the swiftness of guerrilla warriors. Without any delay, Hridayananda sped up.

The Ghutlung Camp wore a deserted look. Everyone had left for the spot where the carcass of the rhino was lying. It was a black day for Hridayananda's range. Poachers killing a rhino even before dark, when the range was abuzz with tourists and tourism-related activities, didn't speak well for the forest department at all. It would create a sensation in the media. The tourists would also get to know about it. Everything amounted to a blow below the belt for the Kaziranga administration. Hridayananda was doubly worried. So many people had seen him entering the theatre. The bosses would find out about it. Eventually, the minister too. So, the entire blame would fall on him. Because of his carelessness, the poachers got the opportunity to strike.

Hridayananda got angry with himself. Of all days, he had to find this day to watch a play.

He had reached the end of the motorable road. They got down. Nobody uttered a word. Everybody was aware of the gravity of the situation. His stoic expression also added to their fear.

Someone switched on the torch to lead the way. Stepping on the fallen leaves, Hridayananda and his team proceeded. There was a narrow path that led to the lake.

This path was actually made by the footsteps of animals that often came by this way to drink water. After covering some distance on foot, they saw the carcass lying under a huge tree, by the lake. It was a huge one. From the broken twigs and disturbed surroundings, it was evident that the rhino gave a big fight before it took the final fall. The guards, too, cleared the area to facilitate investigation.

'Where is Kalita?' Hridayananda's voice boomed.

Immediately, Kalita materialised. 'Here I am, sir.'

'Where were those guards in the Ghutlung Camp? Did they not hear any sound? We should have been able to kill at least one of them,' the lava inside Hridayananda was coming out through his voice.

But he realized his own folly. The poachers had made away with the horn. Now, which battle was he expecting to win by being nasty to his guards? The poachers must be sailing somewhere across the Brahmaputra, or must have taken shelter in one of those numerous villages. It would not be surprising even if they took the road.

'Have you informed the police? When are they coming?'

'Sir, there is a shortage of staff at the police station. It will take some time for them to come here.'

'Huh! So, now we have to guard the carcass? What if they strike elsewhere?' Hridayananda shouted.

'No, sir. I have sounded a special alert in every post. Except for two persons, everyone will go back to their respective camps. We were waiting for you.'

Once the police was there, they would be able to lodge an FIR, and then, send the body for post-mortem. Still, they sounded the departmental vets.

Deputy Ranger Kalita ordered all the guards to go back to their posts. Soon, one by one, the people left. Only five remained, including Kalita and Hridayananda.

Holding the torchlight, Hridayananda moved around the rhino. He knew quite a few rhinos that lived in his range. He wanted to find out whether this rhino was a familiar one or not. He could not be sure. Wild animal! That too in death, it had become pale. It bled like hell. The bullet went straight to its heart. That's what he deduced from the wound.

There was a trail of blood. That meant the rhino was shot somewhere else. Focusing the light on the trail, Hridayananda walked on. But midway, he aborted the journey. No point. It would be wise to carry out the investigations once the post-mortem was over, and that too in the day light.

Hridayananda put a betel nut and paan in his mouth.

His brain refused to function logically. The news must have reached the minister by now. After this news, he probably would abort his visit. Not 'probably', he would definitely not come. If the newspapers and television channels found him here, they would not leave him.

His mobile started ringing. It took him by surprise. God kows who! The CCF? Minister? Or, someone else?

Bringing it close, he peered into the screen. Yes, it was a journalist from a TV channel in Bokakhat. These journalists were too much. They had their sources in the camps. Nobody knew who those sources were. Within minutes of such an incident, they would get to know.

The mobile kept ringing. Hridayananda did not pick up. Taking the call would only lead to a sticky situation. The news channels must have already carried a breaking news ticker under the headline, 'One more rhino killed in Kaziranga'. Hridayananda felt a rush of hot flush through his body. This time his transfer was certain. That was the law of the land.

He tried calling the officer-in-charge, OC, of the Kohora Police Station. After quite a few rings, he picked up the phone. The OC said there was a shortage of staff. The second-in-command was out on a case. As soon as he was back, he would be sent there. But that would take time.

Explaining a few important points to Kalita, Hridayananda was ready to go back. Rather than waiting for the police to arrive, it would be better to take stock of all the posts. Kalita could handle the formalities. Hridayananda would have to report to the CCF too.

What was the time? Hridayananda looked at his watch. It was not yet eight in the evening. But the jungle was quiet, like a cremation ground. The strange sound of a few night birds added to the eeriness.

Kalita wanted to see him off till the jeep. But raising his hand, Hridayananda stopped him in his tracks. Without wasting another moment, flashing the torchlight, Hridayananda started walking back.

Hridayananda felt depressed. What would he do now? He was bogged down by so many worries. He wanted to run away. How many people was he going to answer to? The bosses, the journalists, the questioning looks of his colleagues? He longed to be alone. From tomorrow, he would have to behave like a defeated soldier who lost an important battle. Keeping the fire burning within, he would have to function like a robot. Even if he did not feel like, he would have to sit in his chair, move around in the jungle and give orders to his colleagues and guards.

His steps slowed down as he kept thinking about what lay ahead. He felt like a rhino himself. Holding onto his heart, he kept dragging his body. The way he could not provide protection to the helpless rhinos, the administration too could not provide him with any security. Though he was a bachelor, he dedicated a phase of his life, leaving behind his society, his family, to this national park. What did he get in return?

All of a sudden, something crept past his body. Instinctively, he stood still. He moved his torch all around him. What was it? Hridayananda asked himself.

It was something like a shadow—something hairy and tall. Animal or human? He pulled out his revolver. Something or someone was following him. Or, was he imagining things? There was nothing but nothingness all around him.

No, it could not be his mind playing tricks on him. He clearly saw something zoom past him, so closely and disappear into the dark sky. Could it be a monkey or a horse? But did horses fly?

He started again, this time with measured steps. He was almost there—close to his car. He knew this jungle like the back of his hand.

Once again, he revolved the torchlight 360 degree. No. Nothing was moving. Not even the trees or grasses. No flying horse, no chimpanzee or monkey. He must have hallucinated. It happens when the mind is too tensed.

The dust that got wet in the mist made a layer around his shoes. They felt heavy. The Gypsy was standing in the dark; a layer of mist covered its glass.

The moment he started the engine, the mobile rang again. Who could it be now?

It was a landline number—an unknown number. The STD code showed it to be from Lakhimpur. Without thinking much, he received the call.

His younger brother was on the line. Without exchanging pleasantries, he asked Hridayananda to come home, without a moment's delay.

When Hridayananda asked him several times, his brother replied in a broken voice that their father had fallen down near the well. Since then, he has been unconscious. They called a doctor home. The doctor said that their father was at his last stage. He wouldn't live long.

Hridayananda turned off the ignition.

What cruel game was destiny playing with him? Throwing the mobile onto the passenger seat, he held his head with both hands and leaned on the steering.

Hridayananda's father was an old man. But he had recently got him examined by private doctors at Lakhimpur. They did a thorough check-up. Everything was alright till yesterday. He could see his beloved father's face in his mind's eye. At 80 plus, his father, a well-known farmer in this region, had got a new lease of life when his elder son, Hridayananda, spent a few days, taking care of him. What went wrong suddenly? Would he not survive?

Without knowing, tears welled up—they started flowing.

Moments later, he fought hard to gain control of himself. He could not afford to get emotional in such a complex situation. Trouble from all directions had attacked him. But he had to find a way out. He had to carry out his responsibilities. Now, that his father's condition was such, he would have to take a call. His attraction for his job was gone. The way he gave himself to this job, Kaziranga did not reciprocate.

He made up his mind.

What is to happen will happen! Writing an application to the CCF, Hridayananda would leave immediately. His brother, though not too qualified, knew the responsibility that Hridayananda's post entailed. He would not have persisted if the situation was in control. His bosses would take it otherwise, but he had no choice.

Hridayananda called Kalita. Hurriedly, he explained his situation to him.

Kalita was a sensible and sensitive man. He understood what Hridayananda was going through. 'Sir, our religious texts have put Father as the religion, as the heaven. I will handle the situation here. You leave immediately. Otherwise, you might have to regret for the rest of your life. Your brother has not called you without a reason. Your father must be seriously ill. You leave, sir,' Kalita assured him over the phone.

Hridayananda sped his jeep towards his house. He needed to leave immediately. He wanted to intimate Amal.

Amal would have to tie a few loose ends here on his behalf. In fact, Hridayananda would hand over the leave application to Rishi—it that to be submitted to his office in the morning.

As Hridayananda maneuvered his jeep towards the highway, he saw a Luxury Sedan turned turtle in the middle of the road. He could make out that the accident had happened just minutes before. No one was around on both sides of the road. There was not a single car in sight.

Pulling over his jeep to the side, he rushed to the car. He saw an old foreigner trying to pull a woman through the window of the car. The white woman, who was on the verge of a collapse, was crying out for help in a voice which was fast fading.

Amal, Rishi and Arunabh—all three had gone for the *shradh* of Hridayananda's father. Hriday's father, after taking the fall near the well of his house in the remote village of Lakhimpur, left this world while still in coma.

The day proved to be a nightmare for Hridayananda. It took him quite a few hours to complete the office formalities before starting for Lakhimpur. Just before he reached home by midnight, his father had breathed his last.

After the cremation, followed by *shradh* and *matsya sprasha*, Hridayananda applied for another few days' leave. His application was turned down. Hridayananda became stubborn. He wanted freedom, freedom to be with himself for a few more days. He needed to do some soul-searching. Despite the fact that his leave was not sanctioned, he decided not to join. He stayed back at his own house at Sabek in Lakhimpur. Eventually, he was suspended. But that didn't bother him. He distanced himself completely. He stopped taking calls even.

Dropping Amal at the guest house, Rishi came to visit Lakhimi. She had been suffering from fever for quite a few days.

Even then, she was doing all the household chores. Finally, her body gave up. She was bedridden. The neighbours helped to some extent. But without any guardian, the household was in shambles. She did not even get proper medical attention.

Amal, along with Rishi, took her to the Bokakhat Government Hospital. The doctor who knew them both, scolded them, 'Why was she not given proper medicine till now?'

Rishi was sad and nervous.

Amal once again took charge of the situation. 'Tell us what to do now. Can she be treated here or do you suggest something else?' he asked the doctor in all sincerity.

'That can be done here. We need to run a few tests. Then only I can give you a clear picture,' the doctor said, in a straightforward tone.

Keeping Lakhimi in the hospital for a day and after running a battery of tests, the doctor finally discharged her. But she was asked to remain strictly in bed—no moving around. And of course, take regular medicine.

It was detected pneumonia. Though her treatment started late, with the right medicines, Lakhimi slowly picked up her strength.

The villagers offered help, right from nursing Lakhimi back to health to taking care of the cattle and goats to sending the boys, who were having their annual exams, to school. After their father's death, all three had grown up considerably. They knew their responsibilities. But they had also grown quiet. They just carried out their tasks in silence.

The cold was getting severe. Even during the day, the people needed to build a fire for warmth. Many elderly people, almost in each family, were suffering from cough and cold. In fact, many old people were dying of diseases common in that age.

One of the families was celebrating the harvesting of new crop a few days ago. When the feast was still on, the old man of the house, who was 80 plus, died. Throwing away the fish curry and duck meat, the members of the family and invitees had to march towards the cremation ground.

This was the time of the year when wild elephants raided the villages.

Most families completed harvesting the ripe paddy by this time. Still, the elephants roamed around the fields, and even, walked on the village road in the middle of the night. The leopards that sometimes sneaked in to have a go at the domestic goats often ran away seeing the elephants. During this time of Magh Bihu, the villages in and around Kaziranga witnessed many such untoward incidents.

There was complete silence in Lakhimi's house today. The village head was organising a feast and everybody was there to enjoy the newly harvested rice and other accompaniments. Lakhimi's brothers too had gone there. Lakhimi was feeling slightly better now.

Rishi offered to stay with her till her brothers came back. Later, Amal da would pick him up on his way back from the guest house.

The cold and fog spread a thick blanket, reducing visibility. There was an icy-cold breeze that lashed the area. It was a full moon night. But the foggy blanket didn't let it shine through. As if the icicles in the air were adamant not to allow the moonlight to reach the earth's surface.

Sensing the situation, Rishi started a fire with a bamboo pole and a few pieces of wood in an iron kadai, and placed it on the floor of the house.

Rishi cooked a delicious soup too. This season brought along an assortment of vegetables. Picking up a few healthy ones, he made a broth on the kerosene stove. He served it to her in a small bowl. Tasting the soup, Lakhimi was surprised. These city-bred people made so many different recipes out the same, familiar vegetables. She enjoyed it thoroughly.

What was the time? Rishi looked at his mobile. It was eight, but it looked like midnight. The day had been hectic for him. They finally finished decorating the guest house. He examined each room thoroughly. Right from examining the water taps to beds to towels, Rishi and Amal took note of everything. Rishi even tried to boost the morale of the cooks. The initial plan was to open the resort for tourists in the first week of January itself. But there were a lot many things that needed to be done. So, now the decision was to open it after Magh Bihu. Amal was feeling bad about it. But what was the alternative? He conceded to the demand of the situation.

Because of the smoke coming from the iron kadai, both Lakhimi and Rishi's eyes started burning. They tried to shut their eyes to block out the smoke. The wood was probably not dry. Taking the bamboo pole, Rishi started blowing hard at the fire. The fire kept eluding Rishi. It burnt for one moment, and then, extinguished in the next.

Suddenly, the electricity went off. Load shedding was the usual norm in these parts. The entire house plunged into darkness. Only the half-lit fire tried hard to veto the darkness.

Blowing hard into the bamboo pole, Rishi's face had turned red. Lakhimi was secretly admiring the look on his face.

Did she ever imagine in her wildest dreams that this city guy, who travelled to so many foreign countries; this thin, lanky, young man with a mop of unkempt hair, would one day occupy such a huge place in her life? She started recalling each and every moment she had spent with him, right from the day they met… It seemed just like yesterday. But in reality, two years had gone by. The scene that unfolded on that fateful night when her father was admitted in the Gauhati Medical College came to her mind every day, without fail.

Lakhimi savoured each and every moment as she recalled how in her hour of sadness, she had broken down and offered herself to the powerful arms which embraced her with tenderness. As if two stone-curved statues had come to life that night. It happened almost a year ago. But it was all fresh in her mind.

Suddenly, Lakhimi got up from the *muda* and started towards the kitchen. She was feeling alright now, all thanks to this young man who took such good care of her. The least she could do was to offer him a cup of tea.

'Where are you going, Lakhimi?' Rishi was taken by surprise with her sudden movement.

'You have not had a cup of tea. Let me make one for you.'

Rishi ran to her and stopped her there. 'Don't get up. If I feel like having a cup of tea, I will make one,' he said with a stern voice, as his strong arms stopped her.

Rishi's touch ignited her body. Her arms were in the grip of Rishi's fingers. She felt quite weak. She felt faint. Like a weak creeper, she clung onto Rishi's body. She started breathing heavily. Seeing her condition, Rishi inched closer and held her tightly, but tenderly.

The fire had turned into a red hot mass. In its light, Rishi started planting kisses all over Lakhimi's body—her eyes, her forehead, her neck, her breasts. He showered her with slow and tender kisses. Suddenly, he felt like the most powerful man on earth. Lakhimi was glued to his chest and was breathing in an erratic manner.

She was savouring his touch, each moment of it.

The barks of the stray dogs and the irritating sound made by the crickets were slowly fading away. Rishi felt that nature was playing a beautiful love song. Love was in the air…

As Rishi ran his fingers through Lakhimi's hair, he felt her grip over his body tightening. Without realising what he was about to say, words came out from the deep recess of his heart, 'You get well, Lakhimi. I want to make you my life partner soon.'

Disturbing this intimate moment, even before Lakhimi could say a thing, Amal's car announced its arrival with a shrill horn. For a moment, the embracing figures were shocked. But no one let the other go. In fact, they hugged each other more tightly.

Amal had not shut off the engine of the car. Even the headlights were on. The car started making an angry sound. Amal did not come down. Probably he was tired, or feeling cold or afraid of the leopards or some wild animals hiding nearby. Whatever his reasons might have been, he was waiting for Rishi anxiously.

Amal, Arunabh and Rishi too were invited to the village head's feast. But they decided not to go there, as it was a crowded affair. Arunabh had gone to Bokakhat. He would wait for them there. They would have dinner together. Or else, they could eat from the kitchen of their guest house. But after spending the entire day, Amal was in no mood to have dinner at the guest house.

The spell was broken—in the physical sense at least. Bringing back the emotional waves into its fold, Rishi, with a calm exterior went out to meet Amal.

'Amal da, if you want to come, come. Otherwise, wait for five minutes. I need to do a few things for Lakhimi,' Rishi said, as he went up to the car.

'Carry on. I am sitting in the car. Just hurry up!' Switching off the headlights, Amal switched on the parking lights. He then cut the engine off.

Lakhimi was not hungry. She was happy. She would eat the sticky rice with soup once her brothers were back. She explained that to Rishi. In a soft voice, she told Rishi, 'You go. Amal da is waiting. Sleep early and don't wander too far.'

Giving her the prescribed medicine for the night, Rishi joined Amal in exactly five minutes. Amal immediately turned his car towards Bokakhat.

The layer of fog was so thick that even the headlights could not pierce through it effectively. So, even if the road was deserted, Amal could not drive fast. At places, the fog started rising in rings, lending a horror-like touch to the surroundings.

A few days back, Rishi had gone to Guwahati for a day and he was surprised at the difference in weather between Kaziranga and Guwahati. How could one explain this aspect of environmental science in the context of global warming? Recently, the forest department's step to move a herd of swamp deers to Manas fell flat, as the group refused to leave Kaziranga in a mute protest. Could ecologists have an answer to that?

'Rishi, call Arunabh. Ask him where exactly he is waiting,' Amal ordered Rishi like an elder brother. The fresh glow on Rishi's face did not go unnoticed.

Rishi tried calling Arunabh the moment he sat in the car. But every time he called, the network said 'out of coverage area'. Without telling Amal da, he kept trying Arunabh's number. He was getting worried. Arunabh had not called the whole day. What was keeping him so busy?

They were getting close to Bokakhat. The road was deserted. Only a few trucks passed by.

The fog had practically covered the road. It was getting scary now. And where would they find Arunabh in such a condition without having a clue where he was? Rishi was getting restless. All kinds of thoughts crossed his mind—most of them negative. In the last few days, he had barely met Arunabh. Even when they did, Arunabh did not talk much about himself. He seemed to be floating in a world of his own. Was he also falling in love? Was it love or something else?

'Why can't this donkey call? Does he not have any common sense? What kind of reporting is he doing, Rishi?' Amal was anxious and irritated at the same time. Looking at Amal da's face, Rishi got alarmed. Amal, when angry, could do anything. Rishi had experienced quite a few samples of Amal da's ire.

Making a screeching sound, the car came to a halt. Amal applied the brake with full force. The huge car screeched for a distance. Rishi thrust his hands to stop himself from colliding with the dashboard.

What happened?

The fog was thick in front of them. The road was barely visible. But with the headlights on, Rishi could see a herd of wild elephants crossing the road. This was not an elephant corridor. But the elephants thought nothing of it—as if to challenge the humans. In a careless manner, they crossed it slowly. They seemed to be having all the time in the world. Without giving a damn to the cold or the fog, they playfully carried on their journey across the road.

Amal switched off the headlights.

Amal's guest house was inaugurated on the Shukla Panchami after Magh Bihu. Taking into account the heated situation at Kaziranga regarding rhino killings, he kept the launch ceremony a simple one. Only his friends and family, the villagers who lived close to the resort, a few forest officials and the journalists from the local newspapers and TV channels were invited. Looking at the people's resentment towards the forest minister, he had long ago aborted the plan.

When he had come from Guwahati, he brought Yashodhar along. The students of Rishi's school organised a musical programme. Yasho, too, sang a few folk songs, old filmi songs and *bauul.* Rishi played the violin.

They pitched a tent in front of the guest house. Bipul and company brought chairs from the nearby tent houses. Many youngsters, both boys and girls, were now employed at the guest house. That was the reason Pamua village was happy at the opening of the guest house. Everybody at Pamua was linked one way or the other with it. In that sense, everybody was benefited. People from Rangsina village, under the leadership of Mansingh Rongpi, too participated in the celebrations.

According to the plan, Rishi and Amal had already started the co-operative committee to supply thread and other paraphernalia to the women-weavers of the village. The outlet at the guest house premises had already stacked exquisitely woven clothes and tea leaves to attract customers. In fact, the shop called Hajon-Kachon had already started operating much before the guest house came into being. The business had picked up considerably. In fact, only last month, the sales figured showed a ₹5 lakh turnover. This month it was expected to go even higher.

There was a puja in the morning. Amal got the priest from Guwahati and he stayed at the resort for two days to invoke divine blessings. The ritual was followed by music and a hearty lunch—the inauguration was a success. Amal's wife, his parents, Arunabh's parents and other members of his extended family stayed at the resort for two days. They enjoyed jeep and elephant safaris, ate puri bhaji with chilli chutney at Bokakhat and also bought *peda* from there before returning home.

Hridayananda turned up at the resort the evening of the inauguration. He had changed beyond recognition. His face was now covered with salt-and-pepper beard and the hair, which had grown to his shoulders, was tied into a pony. He said he had stopped shaving and getting haircuts since his father's *shradh*. His clothes, too, were ill fitted. His eyes were puffy and had prominent dark circles.

'Hey, what have you done to yourself?' Amal was both sad and angry, as he hugged his friend.

Seeing Hridayananda there, a few people came forward to meet him. Everyone in Kaziranga knew about his suspension and subsequent transfer to Manas National Park after he spent months in his village following his father's death. Hridayananda had no enemy. Except for a couple of jealous colleagues, everyone loved him. He seemed to be popular among the animals, too. Every forest guard respected this bachelor, who gave himself completely to Kaziranga.

Hridayananda was a respectable figure among the villagers too. But even then, many a time, he was not spared by them when a rhino was killed. They insulted him, burnt his effigy. He was even attacked by the agitated young men in the area. But they knew and respected his efficiency. That was the reason, even the bosses at the department kept him in his range for the longest time possible. But things had changed as the minister came into the picture. The minister, who was facing severe criticism from the Opposition and the media, used Hridayananda as the fall guy to save his own skin. Hridayananda was transferred to Manas. He felt more insulted than sad at the turn of events.

At night, after the function was over, a group of former college friends met at Hridayananda's old quarter that he was about to vacate. The party was picking up.

'You have grown old within these few months, Hriday,' Amal commented, as he rested his arm on Hridayananda's shoulder.

'What to do? After Father's *shradh*, all I did was eat and sleep. There was no work. The whole day, I just ate and slept. In the evenings, I visited my school friends, played cards and drank. So, I have become fat,' Hridayananda laughed at his own joke.

'What do you plan to do now?'

'What's there to do? Cannot defy the government order. Will go to Barpeta and join Manas. I have to vacate this house,' Hridayananda replied, as he put a paan in his mouth.

Changing the topic, Hridayananda steered the conversation to those good old college days. It was a nostalgic trip down memory lane for all present.

Around 9 pm, Deputy Ranger Kalita came to his house. A long-time associate and compatriot in many missions, Hridayananda treated Kalita like his younger brother. Hridayananda had visited Kalita's house in Lower Assam many a time. Kalita's wife gave him the respect of a brother-in-law and the children called him 'Bordeuta'.

Kalita got emotional as he met Hridayananda. They were meeting after long. Never in their career were they separated for such a long period.

'What to do, Kalita? We are government servants. We have to obey orders from above. Even if I am feeling bad about it, there is no way out but to accept this transfer. Thank God they didn't take away my job. At least, I am happy about that.' Putting his hand on Kalita's shoulder, Hridayananda consoled him. The one who was to take Hridayananda's place was an old acquaintance of both Hridayananda and Kalita. He was earlier posted at the Guwahati Zoo.

Promising that he would have lunch at Kalita's place the next day, Hridayananda saw him off till the gate.

Amal and his friends got ready to return to the guest house. After having dinner, two of his friends would return to Hridayananda's place to spend the night. Hridayananda did not want to go the guest house again. His place, which was closed all this while, had gathered dust. He needed to clean it up to spend the night there. Amal said he would send food in a hotcase.

Once Amal and company left, the place plunged into complete silence. Hridayananda was overcome by fatigue. His sisters-in-law had packed rice and sabzi which were still lying in the jeep. He didn't feel like taking them out. Managing to open his suitcase in the dark, he felt for the bottle that was lying at the bottom of the luggage. Carrying the bag to the house, he threw it carelessly inside. Taking out a jug of water and a glass from the kitchen, he made himself comfortable in a chair in the verandah. After a long time, he was drinking alone. He needed to. He gulped down two pegs in a short time. He was feeling heady soon.

Training his ears, Hridayananda tried to catch some strange sound. He felt in the darkness, the jungle outside was sending out greetings to him. The chirping of the birds that have suddenly woken up and the sound made by crickets blended to make a strangely sad cacophony. He closed his eyes to absorb that music.

Unconsciously, Hridayananda started thinking about Kaziranga. Yes, this year in the month of January itself, poachers killed five rhinos. Two of the poachers also gave up their lives at the hands of the forest guards. But neither the rhinos nor their horns could be saved. What strategy would the forest department device now to save its rhino population? After he left, would the poachers leave the rhinos alone? May be. Some divine intervention would happen once he left this range.

Hridayananda once again filled his empty glass.

They needed to make extreme sacrifices to save the rhinos. Sometimes, not a single rhino would be killed for a long period. It did happen. When there was some sort of political turmoil, strangely, poachers chose that time to strike. How's that possible? He was sure the big bosses and ministers knew the answer to his question.

'I also know some secrets. I have also solved some mysteries. That's why I have been shunted out of Kaziranga. Is it not true?' Hridayananda spat out the words into the darkness.

Hridayananda was getting sentimental. Despite knowing many things, understanding many conspiracies, he could not do a thing. Till he was doing this job, his hands were tied. But he wanted to join hands with the public and fight against the corrupt system. He would chalk out a full-proof strategy and fight against rhino killings. He would like to bring together the many organisations that were working in this field onto a single platform and apprise them of the conspiracies and loopholes in the system.

A chilly wind lashed over Kaziranga. The cold days were not yet over. But the charm of Kaziranga, which once used to enchant Hridayananda, had diminished. There was a decrease in the number of tourist inflow. The Internet had painted a sorry state of Kaziranga in the far-flung corners of the world. After reading about the heinous rhino killings, many tourists have struck out Kaziranga from their destination list. And on top of it, while inaugurating the tourist season, the minister came quite late, causing inconvenience to the tourists. Many foreign tourists threw pointed questions at the minister that day.

Blocking those thoughts that kept troubling him, Hridayananda sought refuge in sleep. He woke up when the car that came to drop his friends, blared its horn.

Quickly, Hridayananda took away the bottle and glass to the kitchen and started making the beds for his friends, Sushil and Devdhar. He knew both were dead tired after travelling from Guwahati at six in the morning and spending the whole time at the function.

They brought food for him, but he did not feel like eating.

After making the beds, Hridayananda too decided to call it a day. He was mentally tired. The familiar Kaziranga looked strange to him. He felt like a guest in his own house.

Did he ever think that he would spend the rest of his life in this jungle? Why did he fall in love with it? What was the attraction?

Outside, Sushil and Devdhar were busy talking. Though they were tired, they could not resist the lure of this serene jungle at night, like so many other visitors. The beds were made. Let them sleep whenever they were ready. Hridayananda didn't feel like joining in their conversation. He would rather be alone—at least talk to himself.

Suddenly, he remembered Amal's resort. Amal, of course, had gone by the rule book while constructing it. He was not greedy. His resort was an asset for the local people.

There were resorts inside Kaziranga, but most of them could not survive. Actually, the way the world reacted when a rhino was killed within an area of 1,000 sq. km, similar kind of protests should have been done for many other issues. One example being illegally constructed resorts. They were destroying the ecosystem with the smoke and sound they generated, along with many other pollutants.

Some areas of Kaziranga were so thickly populated that the delicate balance of the ecosystem had gone for a toss. Nobody had the time or the inclination to think about those issues. The forest was meant for animals, not for people's greed. The main aim for reserving this forest area has undergone a sea change.

Huh! Those who were in charge of protecting the rhinos were seen sporting rings made of rhino horns. While submitting the rhino horns, which were recovered from the poachers' clutches, at the government storeroom often one or two went missing. Hridayananda knew all about that. He remembered an incident that took place the previous year. A forest team reached a spot immediately after some poachers fired a few shots. But the officer concerned reported that they couldn't recover the horn. Hridayananda knew those officers well. He was aware how much of the revenue generated from the stone and sand quarries were submitted at the government exchequer and who were the DFOs who managed them. In fact, the Assam Forest Protection Force Battalion, which was created in 2012, had many ex-poachers and smugglers in its roll. Hridayananda knew the long list of corrupt practices by heart. The irony was that he could not talk about it, could not complain even.

But then, there were also people like Lahan, who didn't think twice before dying for Kaziranga. They were the forest officers and guards. There were honest DFOs such as Rajkhowa, who having fought with poachers for many hours, had to be hospitalised or rangers such as Kakoti, who lost his limbs during such a battle. He himself was one of them. Did he ever think of anything other than protecting Kaziranga during his service life?

There was complete silence outside. Probably, Sushil and Devdhar had fallen asleep. Hridayananda didn't feel sleepy despite the tiredness. His chest was heavy. There was no value for his emotions. But then, how could he stop his emotions?

The trend of thoughts continued against his better judgement. As he drifted in and out of sleep after a while, Hridayananda kept hearing the sound of the jungle's music.

Rishi was getting his house repaired; it was in a dilapidated condition.

It was on Amal's insistence, the mason and the labourers left behind to complete the remaining construction work at the resort, were now deployed at Rishi's house for the renovation. Amal had realised that if he did not take the lead in repairing the old structure, Rishi would start his new life with Lakhimi in this pigsty. It was not that Rishi was irresponsible; he was plain detached. His needs were bare minimum.

That's why Amal fixed a monthly salary for Rishi for supervising the day-to-day activities in the resort. At least, once Rishi starts his life with Lakhimi, he won't have to worry about his daily needs. And that way, Amal would not have to worry about his resort. He knew Rishi could take care of the kitchen to the interiors, gardens to popular music or films to adventure, and cater to the modern tastes of the visitors.

The thatched roof of Rishi's house was replaced with tin. It was painted green. They added a new room, which was painted pink. Amal had already modernised the kitchen and the washrooms even before he had started his resort. There were now flower beds and trees in front and a kitchen garden at the back. The bamboo fencing was now replaced with concrete posts and wire fence.

'There was no need for all that, Amal da…I could have make do with the previous one,' Rishi protested mildly.

'You have no clue about domesticity. Once you have a family, you will need the boundary walls and a proper gate. You should be able to provide such basic necessities to your wife. You will get to know all about that soon,' he advised Rishi, like a guardian.

Listening to Amal's words of advice, Rishi kept quiet. He just thought…God only knows when the government would bulldoze such structures in the name of eviction. What would happen then? Nobody could guarantee that there would not be any anti-encroachment drive. There was no conclusion even after the big meeting that was organised to address the issue. What would happen to those 50-year-old villages that fell under the range of Kaziranga? The villages along the highway, which didn't fall in the range, also received frequent threats from government officials. But how did those villages set up overnight in the catchments have the courage to take part in the agitation carried out by the public in demand of legal documents on their land holdings? They say the forest department, too, helped those illegal settlers with money and assurance. Most people were demanding land *patta*. But those without it and those who were forced to settle there because of erosion by the Brahmaputra, said openly that if the government provided them with a better option, both for settlement and livelihood, they would not hesitate to leave. People who had no ownership over these plots of land, didn't mind leaving. Only they needed enough to live their lives. But neither the government nor the administration was willing to solve their problems.

They just stirred the hornet's nest before the Elections and managed to get votes by scaring them. Rishi had heard from people that more than 40 years had gone by like that. In fact, there were some other issues in entire Assam, which the government kept in doldrums because of vote bank politics.

The sun was shining bright. A dry wind that blew from the jungle lashed this area.

The winter gave way to Fagun. It signalled the onslaught of a totally dry season. The wind was full of dust. The leaves of the deciduous trees were turning yellow. Anyway, deforestation caused by the encroachers was reducing the area of the jungle. On top of that, the irresponsible behaviour of the forest department when it came to tree plantation…Even most of the villagers were least bothered about afforestation to save the ecosystem. They thought they would never be affected by the depletion of forest covers.

Rishi formed an intense bond with the trees. He was dead sure that the jungle also conversed. Whenever he played a symphony, the trees, too, were mesmerised. In the morning, he would find the trees and plants blooming in abundance. The new leaves became greener. Sometimes, he embraced the familiar trees and kissed them. They reciprocated by singing a lovely tune that reverberated in the air. Rishi recalled what he had read once about music therapy that originated in some foreign country.

Before meeting Lakhimi, Rishi had fallen in love with the jungle. He used to spend days, and sometimes, nights in the lap of nature playing the violin. In fact, sometimes, he would even forget to eat. Once, he had fallen asleep under a tree at the hillock close to the village boundary. He was woken up by a few naughty jackals tugging at his shirt. Dew drops from the leaves drenched his face.

There were not too many takers for Rishi's theory that trees too talked and enjoyed music. After a series of arguments, Amal and Arunabh agreed to what Rishi had to say on this topic. Lakhimi, too, listened to him. But her brothers laughed at the thought of trees responding to either conversation or music.

There were so many others things that Rishi believed in. He was a firm believer that nature would take revenge against those who destroyed flora and fauna for their greed. Nobody could escape the wrath of nature.

Rishi could never forget how he had once left Delhi for his love of nature. His student life was over before time. His parents gave up their lives for the love of nature. He wanted to block those memories, but sometimes, they troubled him in his lonely hours.

When he was studying in Delhi, had a gang of timber smugglers not brutally murdered his father, his life would have taken a different course. What was his father's fault? Rather than joining hands with the conspirators, his father decided to stop the gang from the felling of trees. He had sought help from his higher-ups. But that went against his favour. Maybe a few officials were even linked with the timber mafia.

One night, a few miscreants abducted Rishi's father right in front of their house. Later, giving it a terrorism angle, they tried to extract money using some outfit's name. They send their mother a ransom note for ₹10 lakhs. Not knowing what to do, Rishi's mother called him up. With the help of his uncles, a negotiation for reducing the amount was initiated. But on his way to Goalpara, Rishi got the devastating news…His father was shot dead while trying to escape.

A few days later, the decomposed body of his father was recovered from the jungle. After that, Rishi's family was shattered to pieces. As they cremated the remains of the body at Nabagraha, their house at Jyotinagar had turned quiet, like a cremation ground.

Rishi was exhausted taking care of his mother. His simple, housewife mother had known life only under her husband's protection. As he suddenly disappeared from her life, she lost interest in life itself. She didn't even bother about what would happen to the young boy. Very soon, within three months, she too left them on the pretext of depression and ill health.

Within a hundred days, Rishi's life took a complete u-turn. All the opportunities in life were robbed from him. His uncles and aunts, though tried their best to heal his wounds, failed. He put an end to his student life. He went back to Delhi, packed his luggage and sent them to his uncle's address. He looked hard to find a job in the music field. His aim was not to earn money, but to forget his pain. He found a job in Mumbai. That's how he travelled around the world playing violin with many bands. The house was being taken cared of by his uncle. Once he was back, he was given the keys along with an advice to start afresh. The effort to start afresh was still continuing—Delhi, Mumbai, Guwahati, and now, Kaziranga. He was still not sure if Kaziranga was his final address. Wherever time took him, he would be happy to go. Nature and time were inseparable. That's the only norm Rishi, who had not much faith in rules and regulations, obeyed…

What was the time? Looking at the mobile phone which was lying on the bed, Rishi realised it was almost 11 in the morning. The repair work was almost over. There were no workers in his house any more.

Getting out of the bed, Rishi sat on the wooden bench which was erected under a tree inside the boundary of his house. He was not attached to anything—not family, not place, not house. The Guwahati house was locked and left neglected. Though this uncle at Pamua was only a distant relative, it was his love for Rishi that compelled him to come and look after their property. The aunt had passed away a few years back. They had no children and his uncle was not particularly close to the house. He had left for Haridwar and did not come back. Probably, he never would. Though initially, he called Rishi a few times to know how he was doing, the frequency of those calls decreased with each passing day. It was quite evident that his uncle was no longer interested in this materialistic world.

Yes, in all likelihood his uncle was not coming back. But if he did, Rishi would have no problem leaving this renovated house and going back to his Guwahati house.

Rishi was not materialistic either. He started becoming one when he was studying in Delhi. But after his father's murder, all it took him was patience to sever all ties. Many years had passed by. Many temptations came his way. But he overcame everything with detachment.

But life changed once again after coming to Pamua. Rishi, who was used to living in souless, concrete jungles, found the true meaning of life. In the bosom of this generous nature, he discovered himself, he discovered his emotions. He once again had the courage to sail in the river called life with Lakhimi by his side.

His mobile started ringing. Hearing the ringtone, four sparrows which were busy in a conversation, stopped chirping. Surprised, they turned their gaze at Rishi. They looked at one another in surprise as they saw him talking to himself.

'Where are you, Rishi?' Arunabh's voice was cracking. Probably, network problem.

'Home. Will leave for the resort in an hour,' Rishi replied.

Arunabh was in Dibrugarh to work on some story. His magazine was planning a special issue on the tea industry in India. Arunabh was asked to cover the North-east. Arunabh was enjoying his job. The laid-back Arunabh had become active. Rishi was close to Arunabh. He could do anything for him. Not only Amal da, but Lakhimi knew it too.

Arunabh told him that he had been trying to get in touch with Amal da, but he was not picking up his phone. There was some problem at Amal da's house in Guwahati. Amal da's father, not being able to talk to his son, called Arunabh. So, as soon as he could, Rishi should give Amal da this message. Even before Arunabh could complete the sentence, the phone got disconnected. Network problem…

Rishi got up.

Where was Amal da? Why was he not receiving calls? He was planning to go back to Guwahati in a day or two. The resort was almost ready. Amal da would not come to Kaziranga for a long time. Rishi was to oversee the operation. Amal da was supposed to go to Delhi and spend a month there. His wife wanted to come to Guwahati. So, Amal da had to be with his sons in Delhi.

Amal da had left for the resort early in the morning. Probably, he was there. But why was he not taking calls? Rishi tried calling him. No, his call was not getting through.

Giving up his hope of contacting Amal over the phone, Rishi got dressed in a hurry. He kick-started the old scooter. Rishi's house was in one corner and the entire road was covered with dust. As he rode the scooter, a whirlpool of dust came chasing it. It took him less than five minutes to reach the guest house.

Where was Amal da?

Heading inside, Rishi looked for Amal da in the kitchen and the pond area, but could not find him there. Finally, he asked Bipul, who told him that Amal had gone to visit Jiaur and had left his mobile behind. Rishi didn't have Jiaur's number. Should he go to Jiaur's tea estate? It was a few kilometres away.

But there was no time to think. According to Arunabh, there was some problem at Amal's house. His father was trying to get in touch with him desperately.

Rishi asked Bipul to get Amal da's mobile. Keeping it in his pocket, he started his scooter and rode towards Jiaur's tea estate. Towards Bokakhat, he would have to travel for a few kilometres before reaching there. It was near the highway. Rishi had never gone there.

Amal da's mobile kept ringing. There were several calls. Rishi did not receive any. They were Amal da's personal calls.

After taking a sharp turn, Rishi saw a procession—a long procession. But nobody raised any slogans. Covering their faces with a black cloth, and carrying posters and banners, the procession was approaching towards him in silence. They were demanding security measures for Kaziranga and protection for rhinos. The procession was being led by an old lady and an old man who were carrying a banner. It read that the silent procession was being organised by an NGO forum.

As the procession inched closer to him, Rishi stopped the engine of the scooter and respectfully allowed it to pass.

Pindrop silence. But the venue was packed.

They had arranged chairs, benches and tables in the courtyard of the *namghar* for the people to sit. A faint light that came from the *namghar*, fell on the courtyard.

The function that was taking place at twilight was actually to bid farewell to Hridayananda. The people of Pamua had organised it.

Many forest officials had come and gone. Never in the history of Pamua had they organised a farewell meeting for a government official. But the news of Hridayananda's transfer from Kaziranga to Manas made everyone, not just the residents of Pamua, but other villages too, very sad.

Hridayananda had become one of them. He had educated them about so many things. He motivated them to take up positive steps in life. Thanks to him, many of them were engaged in some sort of economic activities other than farming, after attending vocational trainings. Even women were coming out of their shells and getting educated. A life which they could only dream of was now a reality because of the effort this man had made. The best gifts he gave the villagers were self-sufficiency and self-respect.

The village head was presiding over the meeting. There were no loudspeakers. Even the person who was speaking was doing so softly. But because of the silence, everybody could hear him.

Everybody, one after another, stood up to speak. Like one recites the holy mantras, they recited the virtues of Hridayananda. Some became sentimental as they spoke. Their voice trailed off and they used their *gamosa*s to wipe the tears that threatened to flow. Seeing one shedding tears, the others got emotional, too. In the end, many men and almost all the women present there had red eyes, as if the place was in the grip of conjunctivitis.

A few of Hridayananda's colleagues were also invited. Deputy Ranger Kalita was seated in the front row. A few forest jawans were also present at the farewell function.

The meeting was a long one.

Everybody wanted to speak. But the moment they started, they broke down. The village head did not stop anyone. They all wanted to express their love and gratitude for this great person.

Rishi and Arunabh were sitting in the dark. They were surprised to see how much the people loved and respected Hridayananda. They were aware that Hridayananda was a popular figure in the area, but that he shared such a deep connect with the villagers was beyond their imagination.

Rish and Arunabh absorbed everything that was happening around. After sometime, the courtyard of the *namghar* got filled to its maximum capacity.

Hridayananda was sitting next to the village head with his face resting on his elbow. He sat in the same position, never lifting his head. As if the praises that the people showered on him and the tears they shed in separation pain, made his head heavy.

At the far end, Lakhimi was standing, listening in rapt attention. Her beautiful face also wore a sad expression. Even her friends had the same expression. Nobody ever imagined that Hridayananda would go away. The thought of his transfer never crossed their minds. Someone would take Saikia sir's position. But what good would that do? They would never get to know the person who would replace Saikia sir, as most officials preferred to stay aloof.

The jeep safari boys had organised tea. They served black tea and biscuits. Many refused to accept. It was a sad occasion. Tea and biscuit didn't fit in.

The village head requested Hridayananda's colleagues to speak a few words. Many tried, but as soon as they started, they too broke down. Only Kalita, with a firm control over his emotions, managed to paint a picture of Hridayananda's achievements as an officer, his dedication to his job, his humility and his affectionate behaviour towards his colleagues with his words.

'Dear people, Kaziranga has given us many things—primarily, the job that takes care of the needs of our families, but Saikia sir has given his life to Kaziranga. He assumed the role of our guardian and guided us with love and affection. We will never find an officer like him…we can never be like him…' Kalita's voice, too, trailed off towards the end. He tried to say something else, but words failed him. Trying to control himself, like a mute person, he just looked here and there, and then sat down.

Nobody said a word. Only the rustling of the dry leaves moving along the wind was audible. Far away, a dry leaf of a betel nut tree fell on the roof, making a rude sound.

The village head, who was presiding over the meeting, was getting mighty uncomfortable. He did not know the event would turn out to be such a tragic affair. The next step was to honour Hridayananda. As soon as he announced that, the Jeep Safari Association boys took the lead. Each family of Pamua wanted to offer him a *gamosa*. The village head gave everyone an opportunity to do so. Hridayananda's neck drooped under the weight of so many *gamosa*s. Kalita came to his rescue. As a collective gift, they offered him a silk kurta, a pair of gumboots, a traditional *xorai*, books, the Holy Kirtan and a decorative first-aid box. A few people got together and presented the items one by one to Hridayananda.

It was Hridayananda's turn to speak. After it was announced by the village head, Hridayananda got up and pushed his chair away. Wiping his face with a *gamosa*, he drank from the glass of water kept in front of him.

Clearing his throat, Hridayananda started in his baritone voice. 'Respected people of the village...'

His throat went dry. Probably, the last betel nut he had gulped down did not go down well. He stopped.

He did not bother to hide the teardrops that came out like two streams.

'Dear friends. I am going to leave you all and Kaziranga soon. I don't know where I went wrong! But I am forced to leave my beloved Kaziranga and you all. I have spent so many years in Kaziranga. I saw many births and deaths, so many ups and downs here. I dreamt that I would pass the rest of my working years amidst you all, in this beautiful jungle. But…' he could not speak any more.

The sound of sobs, especially from the womenfolk, filled the air. A few sighed.

Taking control over his emotions, Hridayananda started again, 'But I…'

He could not complete the sentence. His words were drowned in the sound of gunshots that came from inside Kaziranga—huge explosive sounds. It must have been fired from some powerful weapon.

Everybody heard that. The sound was too loud for a venue so quiet.

Hridayananda shivered. Without even knowing, his body straightened up, like a soldier going to the battlefield. The sadness on his face was soon replaced with deep furrows.

'Kalita, leave this place. Go to work. Don't leave them today. Must be the poachers. If you can catch them alive then great, if not, just shoot them…they are close by…move, move,' said Hridayananda, authoritatively.

Hridayananda removed the *gamosa* which was hanging loosely around his neck earlier and tied it around his waist as he thundered.

The village head was at a loss as to what to do. The people, who were seated everywhere, were now getting up one by one. When the chief guest himself was up and giving orders to move, how could they keep sitting?

'People, these poachers are the culprits. Because of them, we have no peace. They have wiped out the rhinos. Because of them, our Saikia sir got transferred. Let's move! Let's not leave them today…' The speech came from the tall, lanky guy named

Meghen, who was shouting at the top of his voice, standing on a bench.

Meghen could not even finish his speech. About 40 young people, armed with knives, axes and sticks, got ready to fight the poachers. The village head announced the end of the meeting and requested the people to maintain peace.

But nobody listened to him. Everybody was shouting, no one listened to anyone. It was an utter chaos. Adding to the chaos, the people starting using their mobile phones to mobilise the force against the poachers.

Hridayananda didn't imagine that the situation would take such a turn. Not knowing what to do, an agitated Hridayananda went up to the youngsters and requested them not take the law in their hands. But the boys were too angry to listen to Hridayananda. With an attitude of 'do or die', they decided to teach the poachers a lesson. The public had had enough. Let the forest guards do their duty. The public will act on its own.

Kalita and the forest guards had left long ago. Hridayananda tried his best to convince the mob not to act. But today, nobody was in the mood to listen to Hridayananda. Emotions were running high. Everyone was discussing about Hridayananda. Ever since he had joined, he worked in the interest of the national park. He caught many poachers, killed a few too. But what happened? Why was he transferred? So, no…no preachy talks any more! Even now, the poachers disrupted Hridayananda's farewell function. The public was ready to take those poachers on!

Within minutes, a team of more than 40 young boys started running towards the jungle, shouting, 'Catch them, catch them!' There were other groups too who would be coming from all directions to gherao the poachers.

Soon, the *namghar* courtyard was empty. A nervous Hridayananda, not knowing what to do, pulled his long hair and sat on the bench with a thud. Rishi and Arunabh stood close to him. Rishi placed his hand over Hridayananda's shoulder.

'They did not listen to me. They have gone mad. They will take the law in their hands and get into trouble,' Rishi's touch could not soothe Hridayananda's agitated soul.

'They were beyond control, Hriday da. Let's all go there. Maybe, we can try to stop them at the spot. If the poachers start shooting, God only knows how many of them will fall prey to their bullets,' analysing the situation quickly, Arunabh found this solution.

Hridayananda agreed. Shaking his shoulders, he tried to think rationally. Arunabh was right. There was no other way.

'Let's go then!' Hridayananda got up from the bench. Ready to spring into action, he looked at Rishi and Arunabh.

'But Hriday da, how do know for sure that the three rounds of shots were fired by poachers?' Rishi asked in a calm voice, as he started to walk.

Hridayananda lost his cool. Shaking Rishi's hand off his shoulder, he said rudely, 'Are you going to teach me the ways of the jungle, Rishi? What did I learn from my many years of experience here? I know the poachers inside out, the arms they use, the way they operate and the way they behave.'

'Are you just guessing or are you sure of it? If they were really poachers, they could have used silencers?' Rishi insisted, despite Hridayananda's rudeness.

'Rishi…' Hridayananda thundered now. He stopped. Was Rishi not talking more than was necessary? What did he mean?

Arunabh gestured Rishi to stop. Angry, Hridayananda started walking again, in a faster pace. Arunabh and Rishi, without saying a word, started running after him like two obedient dogs.

Soon, the three covered quite a distance.

Crossing the main road, they saw hundreds of people in the forest land, adjacent to the road. How did all those people gather at such a short notice? As if they were ready for such an incident. Not only the forest land, the nearby fields were also filled with people. A score of torchlights was chasing the darkness away.

Arunabh wondered how these naive villagers, without any training or a proper strategy, were planning to catch the poachers. After killing the rhino, they must have run away to safety. In fact, was any rhino killed in the first place?

The people were looking for the poachers with just the torchlights.

'People, please come back. Those poachers are carrying firearms. Listen to me.' Hridayananda, using every ounce of his energy, screamed. He stood at the point where the jungle ended and the fields started. His voice got faintly echoed. But nobody responded. The pent-up anger had spread like an epidemic. It finally found an expression.

Hridayananda understood the emotion. It was useless to tell them to keep quiet.

Ok, let them tire themselves looking for those poachers. They themselves would return. The poacher's gang must have, by now, sensing the situation, set sail in the Brahmaputra.

But no…suddenly, there was a huge commotion towards the other end of the field. The people scattered all over started looking towards the same direction. They tried to catch the words coming from that side.

'People...got him...got him...We caught one,' someone shouted.

Hridayananda heard that too.

Without wasting a second, he ran towards the point. With him were Rishi and Arunabh. Because of the excitement and tiredness, they were breathing heavily.

The group had already tied the man to a tree. Whoever was carrying a torch was placing it on the figure tied to the tree.

After receiving a volley of punches and kicks, the chin of the man was almost touching his chest. They could easily make out that he was a Naga. There was a thin beard on his chin. He was wearing a pair of jeans and a leather jacket. His eyes were closed. Everybody was hitting him aggressively.

'These people attack our villages in the border, they set our houses on fire, they kill our people. Now, they are eyeing our animals and trees,' one of the people spat the words into the darkness.

'He is saying he is just a hired poacher. The kingpin is someone else. Maybe an Assamese fellow,' someone else said.

'These poachers have no religious or cultural boundaries. These poisonous fruits come from the same tree—be it a Naga or an Assamese. Where are his companions?'

'True. And where is the dead rhino? Probably, they could not cut the horn?'

Excited, inflammatory talks filled the air.

By then, mediated by a few wise ones, they had stopped bashing up the poacher. How will they otherwise extract information?

By the time Hridayananda reached the spot, the other people too had come down. Maneuvering himself in the crowd, he reached the tree. Many people, seeing him, made way for him. Standing close to the tied-up man, Hridayananda tried breathing long and hard, just to steady his nerves.

Focusing the torch on the man's face, Hridayananda tried to lift his head up. The head fell down again. The man could not stay up.

Placing his right hand close to the man's nose, Hridayananda tried to find out if he was still breathing.

Seeing what Hridayananda was doing, the people became quiet. They understood what was going on in his mind. Next, with his right hand, Hridayananda tried to check the pulse, while with his left, he tried to lift the man's head again.

A stream of blood came out of his mouth.

The mute Kaziranga couldn't resist the charm of the spring. It spread its magical tentacles over the forest, making it shed its sad veneer. Green became the dominating colour. Cuckoo, keteki and a variety of birds gave the peppy background music and wild flowers added a sweet scent to the whole atmosphere. The naked trees sprouted new leaves once the first shower of the season lashed the region.

The sound of *dhol* and *pepa* reverberated through the villages, both inside and outside Kaziranga. Bihu songs were still being played. The number of tourists was, however, on the downslide. The summer would soon make its presence felt. The mosquitoes and other insects were already singing the summer tune. Because of the rain, the inside roads in Kaziranga were filled with puddles.

In such an atmosphere, spreading terror in the heart of Kaziranga, an armed convoy reached Kohora. It brought the central minister for forest and environment. The news of his arrival spread like wildfire. He had visited two years back too, but it was different then. This visit was the result of a hue and cry at the international level against rhino killings. In a seminar organised in a foreign country, Prime Minister Modi had to face questions regarding the protection of one-horn rhinos, which are found only in Kaziranga. After returning to India, he gave a strict order—stop rhino killings. If need be, let the CBI investigate the matter and deploy the army.

Hence, the surprise visit of the minister. Dispur was aware of this, but they kept the news from the forest administration. As soon as the top officers got to know about the visit from their own sources, they did not have much time to prepare. The minister had landed shortly after. It was not the protocol. But who would question the minister? The state forest minister and the central minister came in the same car. The state minister, who had recently taken charge of the forest affairs, was already angry with the department for not being able to stop poaching. The ministry was serving its last term. So, he also made a last ditch effort to impress the central minister. Casually, he mentioned that poaching got out of control during the tenure of the previous minister. He did not forget to add that he had taken charge only two months back.

The large cavalcade, complete with an ambulance, stopped at Kohora for a while. That April afternoon in Kaziranga looked fresh and unexploited. Though shops that dotted the greenery on both sides of the road were open, not too many people were around. Looking at the convoy, people couldn't guess it was a central minister, for even when the state minister or some higher officials came, he usually came with the same number of cars and other paraphernalia. So, they thought some minister had come seeking solitude in the lap of nature.

The pilot car in front of the convoy turned south from the Kohora Chowk, and immediately, the other cars followed. Travelling a short distance, they reached the centenary bungalow which stood next to Aranya and Banani guest houses.

By that time, everyone in the forest office had understood that the ministers who arrived without following the protocol, were not there for entertainment. Something was terribly wrong. That was enough for them to be on their toes. Even the forest guards in the interiors of Kaziranga got the message. They were already bearing the brunt of rhino killings, and now, these ministers! The poachers would not know that the central minister was around. If they killed a rhino tonight, then they had it. God knows how many of them would lose their jobs. So, the forest guards, the rangers and every single person in the field remained alert…their walkie-talkies and mobile phones ringing constantly. The frequency of messages was at an all-time high. The control room was buzzing with activities. There was no time to even breathe. The forest guards were patrolling every inch of Kaziranga.

By the time the ministers stepped down on the lawn of the government guest house, the sun had already set in the horizon. The weather was clear. This moment captured just the time before the darkness descended. The birds were chirping in gay abandon. A soothing breeze blew from the south.

The state minister now assumed the role of the host. All the top officials had gathered close to the minister. He started giving directions. He spoke non-stop.

The central minister had already left for the centenary bungalow, the oldest building in Kaziranga. He walked from the guest house. Following him were his assistant, his secretary and a few top officials who had come from the Delhi forest department.

After half an hour of rest, the Assam forest and environment minister had a heart-to-heart with the central minister. Despite the long journey, both of them were active. There was no time to rest. The aim with which they had travelled to Kaziranga had to be given priority. They needed to formulate a full-proof plan.

They chalked out a plan of action for the next day and the following days as well. First of all, a meeting had to be planned with the forest officials. The Director General of Police, Assam; CBI officials; the GOC 4 Corps; and the chief secretary and the forest secretaries from Dispur were also to participate in that meeting.

The topic of discussions in these meetings included rhino killings and other subjects, including the short-term and long-term government developmental schemes. They wanted to assess whether those schemes had touched the topics of protection, sustenance and the overall development of Kaziranga or not. They also wanted to gauge whether funds from the government and other sources had been utilised properly or not. Was the number of forest guards employed by the government enough or not? Were they being trained properly? Were the steps taken to stop poaching by the department in this critical junction effective? What was being done to compensate the families of those 83 forest guards who lost their lives while fighting poachers? What was the infrastructure in the forest camps in and around Kaziranga? How much area of the reserved forest was under encroachment? Why didn't the forest authority curb this? All these questions would infuse a sense of seriousness into the meeting. Looking at the alertness of the central minister, the state minister and the officials were in no doubt that the minister meant business. This might herald a good phase for Kaziranga...probably, this would also mean the end for the poachers.

The chirping of the crickets had added an eeriness to the night, which was at the same time oddly alluring. Adding to it were random cries of birds and the rustling sound of the wind. The sudden spell of drizzle came with a new promise for Kaziranga. Tomorrow will bring a new beginning...probably, all those things which seemed impossible would become a reality at last.

Almost all the guest houses were packed with the visiting officials.

One by one, the lights in the guest house went off. It was just 10 o'clock at night. But in anticipation of the impending meeting, the tired guests sought refuge in sleep, with the hope of a better tomorrow.

The next three days had turned Kaziranga into a battle ground.

The morning welcomed the top government officials and the big shots in the army. The employees of the guest house did not even have breathing space till midnight. The ministers ordered for tea, snacks and meals. The meeting was expected to go on till the evening.

The meeting started exactly at 10 in the morning. Right from the top brass to the ground level, employees spoke about their experiences and the problems they had to face. The central minister had asked for representation from each level. Those who could not speak Hindi and English, expressed their views in Assamese and a translator would immediately translate for them into English for everyone's benefit.

The old employees were also given a chance to share their experiences. The minister was listening to every sentence very seriously. Sometimes, he frowned as he looked intently at a certain speaker. Till mid-day, they listened to the field workers.

After lunch and a half-an-hour break, the top-level officials met. It was the turn for the administrators to talk about their grievances—those officers who were directly connected to the government schemes and plans. The DGP, the GOC 4 Corps and a CBI official who was already investigating a few cases in Kaziranga were listening to the discussions. This time, it was not a speech format. Pointed questions were thrown at the speaker from various quarters. The central minister himself was taking down notes and asking questions. Sometimes, they bombarded the speaker with questions. A few of them, not being able to answer satisfactorily, drank water, one glass after another. They had to face certain questions which they had never even asked themselves. Yes, nobody had an idea that it could get so tough.

That's how the day one passed. Once the meeting was over, the central minister quickly disappeared into his room. After that, the forest officials sat with the state minister. That meeting, too, lasted for about an hour.

Two employees, who were given the duty to clean up the venue for the next day, were looking at the proceedings and whispered to each other. 'Have you noticed, Jatin? This time they had it. The central minister is going to do something. The entire top officers are here. Even the army, the police and the CBI. Maybe, the good old days are coming back.'

'You are right, Brother. Forget about the killing of rhinos, the government officers themselves will now become extinct.

Some changes are bound to happen. Otherwise, why would everybody be here?'

The next day, the host minister supervised the day's proceedings. He was dead tired. On top of that, the non-stop calls from Dispur, even from the chief minister's office. The CM wanted to know what was happening.

He called back the CM's office. In a nutshell, he explained what was being discussed and what was going to be discussed. It came out in the open that the yearly central grant was sanctioned to Kaziranga quite late. Whose fault was it, the central minister wanted to know from the state minister. The Centre or Dispur?

The next day started with a trip to all the ranges in Kaziranga. They started soon after breakfast. By the time they took stock of the conditions of the forest posts, the arms and ammunitions, and the facilities meant for the forest guards, the sun had already disappeared. They also inquired about the veterinary hospital for the animals, about the elephants and the boats, about the mahuts and boatmen. The water bodies and the issue of soil erosion also were not left out.

The forest minister himself apprised of the efficiency of both the battalions of the Assam Forest Protection Battalion Force, which comprised 425 jawans. However, he had to concede that between 1980 and 1990, 340 rhinos were killed by poachers, the highest casualty ever. In order to stop poaching and other such illegal activities, Kaziranga needed a 3,000-member staff and the present strength was way below that mark.

The Burapahar Range had an area of 82 sq. kilometres, which was being protected by 19 forest posts. Still, this range was the easy target of poachers.

Inside the jungle, when Deputy Ranger Kalita managed to stand next to the minister, he, in his broken English, explained that everybody blamed a ranger when a rhino was killed, but nobody paid any attention when the same ranger approached the higher authorities for stuff necessary to protect his range. Sometimes, they were not even paid for the fuel needed for patrolling. Even the guards were not being trained to use those old firearms. Why was a ranger not paid any allowance to develop his sources? As he spoke, he remembered Hridayananda. 'Sir, can rhino poaching be stopped merely by transferring an officer? Has it ever stopped?'

By the time the team came back from the field inspection, the meeting ground was filled with people from NGOs, Civil Society organisations, Kaziranga Sangram Samiti, Jeep Safari Sanstha, village committees, Joint Forest Management Committee, village panchayats, student's organisations, and environmentalists and nature lovers. Almost every organisation brought their referendum. Submitting their referendum, they also gave a speech. The minister was not the type to turn down anybody. Even after an eventful trip, he was at his attentive best. He did not just listen, he even put up relevant questions and took down notes. He was hell-bent on finding out a solution to all those problems.

The meeting went on and on. The people stayed on till 9:00 pm. After which, the secretary made an announcement that since it was late, they would continue the meeting the next day. Those who could not talk to the minister would get a chance to do so at the morning meeting.

All the villages were informed about the public meeting which was to be held at the Kohora field. After being apprised of the public life in Kaziranga from the Nagaon and Golaghat deputy commissioners, the minister addressed the local people. With conviction, he told them about the government's willingness to develop Kaziranga overall and stop rhino poaching. But the government alone could not achieve that. It was proved in the past again and again. He assured them that the older plans which had loopholes would soon be replaced with well-coordinated and well-thought-of plans to win this mission of protecting Kaziranga. The conclusions which were drawn during the last three days of interactive sessions would be placed in front of an expert committee to chalk out a plan of action. However, only full public participation would ensure in checking those poachers who were creating havoc. The public alone had the strength to stop them.

The sound of applauses, along with cheering and hooting, rocked the venue. The thundering sound which escaped into the jungle got echoed.

The minister announced that the first step would be to make a special protection force to stop poaching. Once those commando jawans completed their training in the Dergaon Police Training College, they would be trained inside Kaziranga for three months in various traditional and foreign combat modes. This team of 100 jawans would be armed with sophisticated weapons and other facilities. They would be operating under the special direction of the army. However, the high-level committee would have to complete the task of eviction of those illegal colonies in Kaziranga, issue legal documents for land holdings, etc. within three months. The government would empower the Kaziranga Sangram Samiti to facilitate those tasks.

The old system of administration would be reorganised in consultation with foreign as well as Indian wildlife experts.

But before getting into those long-term plans, the Centre, in association with the state government, would execute the short-term plans within two months. While executing those plans, the minister asserted again and again that the suggestions put forward by the environment-related NGOs, civil society, Jeep Safari Association, panchayats, village protection force and youth associations, etc. would be considered. He concluded by assuring them that the plans would be made in the stipulated time and action would be taken accordingly.

Before evening, the convoy that spent 72 busy hours in Kaziranga, hit the same highway. They would spend the night in Guwahati and then fly to Delhi the next morning.

As a sign of respect for the well-wishers of Kaziranga, nature started showering its affection since the evening. As if it wanted to wash away all the negativity that had plagued Kaziranga so far.

The people of Pamua were informed about the new strategies. Like the people of the other villages, they, too, welcomed them with a sigh of relief. As the sound of the drums started coming from the *namghar*, lighting up a diya, Lakhimi kneeled down and prayed, 'Oh God, please bless my mother's soul, bless Kaziranga, bless us all…'

After her prayer, Lakhimi sat on the floor of the *namghar*. In a meditative posture, she thought of God and looked at the sanctum sanctorum.

Except for the pitter-patter sound of the rain, it was quiet. Stepping out on the rain-soaked grass of the *namghar* courtyard, Lakhimi started towards her home.

There was a thunderstorm just before dawn. And along with it, torrential rains. Probably, the spring was bidding adieu to Bordoisila. The storm left a trail of destruction not only in the jungle, but in the villages, too. Huge trees were uprooted. It blew away a few loose rooftops, too. Many betel nut and coconut trees fell onto the roof of a few homes. The occupants of those houses managed somehow to protect themselves by huddling together under their beds. In one of the houses, a huge jari tree fell on the cattle shed, squeezing the animals. By the time the owner could get there and remove the tree, one of the cows died of suffocation.

Everybody was fast asleep when it all started. Before they could realise what to do, the damage was already done. The focus was on saving their lives rather than property. So, everyone suffered loss in someway or the other.

After doing the *tandava* dance for about half an hour, nature got tired. Just before the first sunrays touched the earth, nature once again turned into its serene self. But the broken branches and the spinelessly lying trees, the anchorless leaves and the twigs, and the roofless houses bore the testimony as to how angry and rude nature had become only a little while ago.

Though a creation of nature, human beings do not want to bow down to nature's whims and fancies. They refuse to give up. As soon as the storm subsided, they came out to inspect the scale of destruction. First, they took stock of their own losses—the cattle sheds, the chickens and the ducks, the stray dog on the verandah. After they were reassured about their possessions, they went out to find out about others. What about the *namghar*? Was it still in place? Did the storm blow away its roof, too?

Rishi looked around his campus. The storm could not cause much damage to his newly constructed home. Amal da had replaced the bamboo poles with concrete ones. The bamboo door was also replaced with a wooden one. Only his garden looked devastated. The abused flowers and petals were lying all over the place. The chilli and ladyfingers plants, and the green leafy vegetables were destroyed completely. A big branch came off the mango tree in the southern side. Since Rishi's house was at the far end of the village, he could not make out how much damage the other villagers had suffered.

Rishi started getting dressed. He needed to find out. What about Lakhimi's house? And the guest house?

Paying a visit to Lakhimi's place first, he started inspecting around the house along with her brothers. Quite a few trees were uprooted. A betel nut tree that had fallen onto the roof flattened the tin over the verandah. The roof over the cattle shed was still intact, but it was badly battered. Looking at the intensity of the storm, such damages were only to be expected.

Within half an hour, Rishi helped them clean up the mess to a certain extent. Having a cup of tea which Lakhimi prepared, Rishi went out to find out about the rest of the village. In between, he tried calling Bipul at the guest house. But no. He could get through. He tried calling Arunabh who was also staying at the guest house. No response there, too. Probably, the storm had disabled the mobile towers. There was no signal.

The guest house was sturdy enough to stand up to such calamities. But then, one can never tell. Rishi planned to go to the guest house once he was done with the villagers.

A few people had gathered at the *namghar* courtyard. Rishi walked towards them. Everyone was talking about the intensity of the storm. They compared it to a few previous ones that fell in this league.

'Don't tell me…this one has been the worst in the last few years. I am telling you,' the village head gave his final verdict. As he said this, he stomped the earth with his walking stick for extra emphasis.

Jiten Kakoti, the eldermost in Pamua, whose eyes and cheeks had sunken into deep craters, blinked and made a hissing sound to second the village head's opinion.

With two young men for company, Rishi went around the village. One day was not enough to repair those damages. Today, they would clean up the mess as far as possible.

Once Rishi completed inspecting the village, he went straight to the guest house. Arunabh was in the washroom. Asking Bipul to prepare breakfast, Rishi too used a washroom in the outhouse to take a bath.

On the breakfast table, Rishi noticed Arunabh's face. It looked like his beard had not seen the razor for quite sometime, and those untrimmed growth was making his visage shapeless.

'What's wrong with you? Are you still busy? What's keeping you so occupied day and night?' Rishi asked Arunabh, as he bit into a slice of bread.

'Listen, I, as a journalist working with a magazine, can enjoy many benefits. If I want to work day and night, I have the liberty to do so. If I want to slow down my pace and enjoy life, I can do that, too. Nobody is going to ask me what I am doing,' Arunabh explained.

'Then why are you working your ass off? Are you writing about Kaziranga or trying to find a plot for a novel or something?'

'Not a novel, yaar. I am investigating Kaziranga. There are many interesting news. Especially after the central minister's visit. I have unearthed a few irregularities. Just wait! You are aware of the fact the administration has slapped a ₹10 crore defamation case on our magazine. I will not leave them in peace.' Taking a long sip from his cup, Arunabh explained.

Rishi kept quiet. He kept looking at Arunabh's face, still not quite convinced. Yes, Arunabh was getting too serious about Kaziranga. He was taking it personally after the defamation case. Especially after he got the encouragement from his head office that he should not bother about such lawsuits, but should rather continue with his investigation. They wanted him to reveal the corruption and irregularities in the administration. Arunabh had told him that.

Rishi, however, did not understand everything. He had glanced through the CAG report. He knew that many of the complaints and suggestions listed in the report had not been published in the local newspapers.

The guest house today looked deserted. The storm managed to damage two big trees in the campus. Apart from that, everything was normal. Only, of course, the campus was filled with debris.

Two new guests had checked in. Both the visitors were Assamese. Apart from the two, there was a German artist who had occupied a room for the past 20 days. Amal had asked Rishi to give this man a room on concession rate, as he was going to stay there for a long time. The whole day, the man painted, sometimes inside the room, sometimes in the garden and sometimes near the pond. He put up a large canvas on a stand and drew nature-inspired paintings. He was a professor in some university in Germany. Painting was just his hobby.

Kaziranga was closed down for tourists. In the coming six or seven months, no tourists would be allowed inside. This time would be utilised by the administration to do all the repair work and also start the fresh programmes. This was the reason why the inflow of tourists in the resorts and lodges was also going down. But not Amal's guest house. People who travelled from Upper Assam to Lower Assam, often dropped by. And a large chunk of the guests were either from Amal's or Hriday's or Rishi's or Arunabh's friend circle. As the word of mouth spread, more and more people came by, even during the off season.

The location of the resort—it being close to the highway, its beautiful gardens, ponds and less-spicy food attracted the tourists. So, Rishi was mostly occupied with the guest house and his music school.

Still, Kaziranga looked somewhat depressed, dejected. Rishi could never imagine Kaziranga without Hridayananda. It was because of Hriday da, Rishi decided to settle down at Pamua. Because of Hriday da, the guest house became a reality. Rishi's lonely existence was lit up with the entry of Lakhimi. Hriday da had played a very important role in that, too.

But when everything was finally starting to fall in place for Rishi, Hriday da had to leave. He went off to Manas. Rishi was overwhelmed when he attended the farewell meeting organised by the village people. Everyone loved and respected Hridayananda.

This was the reason why Kaziranga was starting to feel strange for Rishi, despite everything being familiar. Rishi felt like an orphan again. Amal da had gone to Delhi, Arunabh was busy with his work.

Hriday da had called last night. He was not settled in his new place. He was for the time being putting up at the Manas Guest House. He didn't say anything, but Rishi could tell how heartbroken he was. After spending so many years in Kaziranga, even Hriday da had not imagined that one day he would be transferred from there. After Lakhimpur, Kaziranga had become home for this bachelor.

Rishi saw Arunabh, after finishing his breakfast, was getting ready to leave.

'Oye. Where are you going so early?' Rishi asked.

Giving him a secretive smile, Arunabh replied in a monosyllable, 'Work.'

Arunabh soon would be leaving for Arunachal. Before that, he wanted to do a story on Kaziranga. After the central minister had stepped in, he was in no mood to let the real culprits go scotfree.

Rishi thought, how would he survive alone in Kaziranga? Hriday da was gone, Amal da would now come only once in a while. Arunabh also appeared like a comet. Would he be able to settle down in Kaziranga?

He was still thinking when Arunabh walked out, looking smart in a pair of blue jeans, white tee and black shades.

It was not true that Rishi was totally unaware of what was going around. The news that excited Arunabh, some of it, Rishi was privy to.

Actually, the central minister had started a special team during his last visit. This special team that comprised a few trusted and medium-rank officials from Dispur was entrusted with the power to independently plan and execute any operation within Kaziranga.

After just two months of forming this special team, many secret operations had been carried out. The team had a few commando officers who were excellent sharp shooters. During those secret operations many poachers were nabbed. Rishi's sources had told him that many notorious poachers had been gunned down too. The rhinos that were killed by poachers were secretly buried, but along with the carcasses, poachers were buried too. Those were off-the-record missions.

The central minister was not aware of these facts. While managing this special team, the sharp, topmost forest officer was taken into the loop by the army's GOC 4 Corps through secret meetings. But the lobby in Kaziranga, which had been till then enjoying the benefits, was not happy with the functioning of the special team. Rather, it was getting cagey. The lobby had quite a few forest officials and a few corrupt forest guards as well. They never confronted directly. Maintaining a low profile, the members tried to enjoy as much benefits as they could. The bribe went to a few higher-ups, too.

Rishi was aware that the lobby was trying hard to stop the raids being carried out by the special team. Probably, Arunabh was not even aware that the lobby had put pressure on Dispur and without the knowledge of the state forest minister, they had managed to order the team to wrap up their work in Kaziranga and proceed to Dispur, as they were needed there, not in Kaziranga. The order, in fact, did not even mention what mission they were supposed to carry out in Dispur. A big conspiracy! But probably, this time the lobby would fail in its nefarious designs. It was at the prime minister's order that the special team was formed and who knows what else the central minister was doing without confiding in anyone?

Everyone in and around Kaziranga, who were aware of the special operations by this special team, was happy. Many agreed that this was the only way to stop those habitual criminals who would often get arrested on charges of poaching, but would eventually, get out of the legal clutch. Rishi heard that the villagers themselves had handed over one or two poachers living in their neighbourhood to the special team. The villagers felt insulted that such people were living amidst them. In fact, the family members of such a person tied him up when he was sleeping and then handed him over to the special team.

Thinking about all these, Rishi was getting a little agitated. Had he been a member of the CBI, the FBI or the erstwhile Scotland Yard or the KGB or the CIA, he would have put a full stop to this heinous practice. He would have been a strict officer.

Rishi entered the small room in the north-west wing of the guest house; a room used to deposit cash and keep other records.

Rishi had not checked the previous day's account. He sat down to do that now. They had appointed a retired person as an accountant and a cashier. He used to commute every day from

Bokakhat. A sincere man. But Rishi made it a point to check once in a while. Amal had given him the responsibility.

Rishi's mobile started ringing. Amal da's number flashed on the screen.

Thank God, the mobile had started working, Rishi thought to himself.

'Yes, Amal da. I am at the resort,' Rishi said.

Amal da was supposed to have returned from Delhi long back. But as his wife was still in Guwahati, Amal da was stuck there. He couldn't have left his two sons on their own. Though they were grown up, they did not know how to cook. In the last one and a half month, half the time Amal da did the cooking, and the other half, he made do with home deliveries.

The voice at the other end was feeble. Amal said he would be back in the coming week. After staying in Guwahati for a couple of days, he would visit Kaziranga.

Amal da told Rishi not to postpone his wedding date, yet again. 'If possible, in this month itself, marry Lakhimi,' he asserted.

Rishi felt shy. He could not believe that he was going to marry Lakhimi. Till the other day, Rishi and marriage were two opposites, like the North Pole and the South Pole. But life had taken a complete u-turn after he met Lakhimi.

Amal da, once again, gave Rishi a stern order—not to change his wedding date. After enquiring about the resort, he asked about Kaziranga, how much change the central minister's initiative had brought and so on.

Rishi replied…

There were, indeed, a number of visible changes. The killing of rhinos had reduced. The special team of the central minister, after initiating a multifaceted scheme, was openly challenging the opportunist lobby. Earlier, let alone challenge it, the forest department was actually scared of it. They did not admit it, but scared they were. The visit of the central minister two months ago had brought about overall changes to Kaziranga. Right from implementing laws that sounded the death knell for the illegally constructed resorts to initiating afforestation to facilitating the legalisation of those rightful land owners, there were a number of positive steps taken up by the team. Yes, perhaps, peace and harmony would finally prevail over Kaziranga.

Amal da asked many other questions. He said that he had talked to Hridayananda. There was no stopping for Amal da. But suddenly, the line snapped.

Rishi didn't try to call back. Enough had been said. There was nothing else to talk.

Keeping the phone down, Rishi felt a little heavy.

Yes, he had postponed his wedding date twice since last winter. He knew Lakhimi was hurt, even though she never said a thing. Whenever he suggested postponing, she just looked at him mutely. She agreed to whatever he said, even without as much as blinking. He did not even seek her permission to postpone the wedding. He felt guilty. He felt he was taking advantage of her emotions. Since he was going to get married to her, what was the point of delaying it? He made up his mind.

Devoting half an hour to the records and calculations, Rishi came out. Bipul could now take care of everything—right from shopping to the bookings. Rishi just supervised. Though the simplicity of the village people was sometimes a hurdle while running such a sophisticated resort, their honesty made up for their shortcomings. Bipul and his team had proved it.

Arunabh again had borrowed Rishi's scooter. God knows where he was running around.

Many working at the resort had cycles. Taking one, Rishi started towards his house. Pedaling slowly, he entered the point that led to Pamua. Whenever he reached this point, he felt butterflies in his tummy. That's where Lakhimi's house was.

Keeping the cycle on the stand near the gate, Rishi opened the bamboo poles and stepped inside. 'Lakhimi, where are you?' he shouted from the gate.

No reply. The whole house was in silence. God knows whether the boys had gone to school or not. The storm had changed everything.

Rishi stepped onto the verandah. Still no response. The door was open. The birds were chirping everywhere. But where were the people?

Dusk was gobbling up Pamua from end to end with an uneasy quietness. The birds and the bees had returned home long ago. So, there was no chirping anywhere. Only far away, some unknown bird kept bellowing from time to time. It touched one's heart.

The people, too, were returning home after the day's work. Only those who had to shop for grocery were still out.

Fanning the smoke in the cowshed, Lakhimi remembered there was no salt in the house. It got over in the day. She had planned to go out and buy in the afternoon, but there was no time. Later, she forgot about it altogether.

God, what would she do now? How could she cook without salt? Her brothers would throw a fuss. They were getting too sensitive. They started wearing a sad look since the day her wedding date was fixed. There were often tears in their eyes.

It was as if she was leaving the house and going away! Rishi's house was a stone's throw away. She would run both the homes. She would raise her brothers. She had talked it out with Rishi. She had discussed this topic with her brothers at length. She was sure that Rishi would not interfere. He had given her total freedom.

It was a good thing for her brothers. They would have two homes. Whenever they felt like, they could stay in either of those.

Lakhimi's brothers had grown up. After losing their mother six years ago and recently their father, they had matured beyond their age. Though they mixed up with the other boys of their age, they behaved differently. Lakhimi had noticed that. They remained quiet even in school. Once they were back, they refused to leave her side. Their young minds were filled with an unknown fear. Like their parents, if their sister too… They wanted her to get married to Rishi, but at the same time, silently endured the pangs of separation.

Lakhimi understood everything. She was not educated, but she had the sensitivity to understand human emotions. That was the reason, as the wedding date approached, she started feeling sad herself.

Sometimes, Lakhimi felt scared too. As she was going to step into a new life, there was no one by her side—neither her father nor her mother. At the initial stage of her relationship with Rishi, her father passed away. Those talks which a daughter could only share with her mother, she was deprived of it early in life. There were relatives, but they too could not fill the void left by her parents. Everybody in the village was taking active participation in the preparations for her wedding. She was aware of the fact that many young women had dreamt of Rishi, but once their marriage was fixed, they came with an open heart to be by her side. Many of them had made it clear that she was the right woman for Rishi.

Since the last two months, they all had been there for her, at every step. They were all so simple, so generous. Yet, the emptiness in her heart persisted.

This evening, too, they had gathered at the *namghar*. They all were excited about the wedding. This was a unique one. Both the bride and the groom belonged to the same village. The distance between the two houses was also only a few steps. That's why Rishi's friends had been insisting that the barat came from Bokakhat. Just two years in Kaziranga, Rishi was already a popular figure, not just in Pamua, but also in Bokakhat.

Rishi's students at the music school and their guardians were ready to make the pandal inside the school campus. His journalist-friends promised to be in the reception committee. All Rishi had to do was be there at the wedding.

With each passing day, the talk of the marriage took centre stage. Lakhimi had heard so much gossip. Every day, her friends would bring her some new gossip. Though Rishi himself never said anything when they met. She used to laugh at those gossip and news. She felt shy at times. Even though, she did not want to think about all that, she couldn't help herself.

At the gate, the dog started barking.

When their father was unwell, Lakhimi's younger brother brought home this tiny pup that was out on the street, shivering from cold and hunger. He brought this spotted pup home, fed him milk and made a bed for him to sleep on. From that day, it became a part of the family. The pup kept them busy from dawn to dusk. Before going to school, her brothers would tie Spotty with a chain and would tell her time and again to take care of it. Spotty soon became her companion to carry out her imaginary conversation with till her brothers came back from school.

The half-yearly exams of her brothers were on. Lakhimi was very strict with their studies during the tests. She could not study herself, but she was determined to educate them.

At times, Rishi taught them English and Maths. Both of them were sharp. If something was explained to them, they could catch on fast. That enthused Rishi to teach them often.

Lighting up the diya and incense sticks at the *thapona*, Lakhimi started pacing up and down inside the house. This was something her mother had initiated her into. Moving the burning incense sticks around the study tables of her brothers, she placed them in front of her parents' photo in the main hall. She had kept the photos on a small table close to the wall on the east side.

A couple of days ago, Rishi had given her a huge painting of her parents. There was a foreigner staying at the guest house. He was an artist. On Rishi's request, he painted both her parents in the same frame. Lakhimi kept looking at the painting. She did not tire of looking at it. Her brothers, too, kept staring at the painting the day it arrived. Before going to school, they bowed their heads in respect in front of the painting. She did not have to teach them that. They did it themselves. This painting had become central to their existence now.

Last evening, too, she was standing in front of it. She kept murmuring, as if she was trying to infuse life into the lifeless sketch. Rishi, who was shouting for her from the gate, had a fright when he got no response.

Lakhimi actually did not hear him calling. Suddenly, when she became aware, she came out and stood in front of him. Rishi was really scared. He hugged her tight when he saw her. He didn't let her go till her brothers, who were studying inside, came out to greet him. They all were afraid—for different reasons.

Lakhimi put the incense sticks into the holder and placed it in front of the painting. Yes, to overcome pain, one had to first embrace it. Then, they would have to push that pain out of their lives. If one wanted to enjoy the view from the peak of the mountain, first, he had to conquer the steep climb. Like pain, one had to face it first.

Rishi had once said, 'It is nature's law. Nobody can break it. What will happen, will happen.'

She stood there for a long time in a meditative posture. She started breathing long and easy. She started promising herself—she would be a good daughter, a good sister, a good wife. She would be the good Lakhimi for the village. She must. She kept thinking, with her hands still folded.

When her mind reached the state of calm, Lakhimi opened her eyes. She then turned towards the kitchen.

Pouring two glasses of milk for her brothers, she started making tea for herself. Putting the pan on the stove, she gave Spotty two biscuits. Spotty, chewing the biscuits noisily and happily, did a somersault at her feet.

Ever since Spotty had come into their lives, Lakhimi started thinking seriously about the wildlife. She had started noticing the problems the wild animals were facing inside Kaziranga. The forest cover was depleting. The mute animals were deprived of their habitats. It started only in the recent past. There was no security for the old settlers in Kaziranga. And on top of that, hundreds and hundreds of foreign migrants were making it their home. She had heard Arunabh talking about it, that the high court had issued a legal notice to evict the people who had settled along the elephant corridor. It was making Kaziranga tense. The local people were in the protest mode.

But after the visit of the minister from Delhi, things were looking up. She did not know all the details. But Arunabh had told her that one-fourth of the total area of India was covered with forest. There were 400 such national parks. It seemed too big a number to her. So, how come the wild animals were facing problems? In the past 40 years, 52 per cent animals, birds, insects and fishes had become extinct. He said 76 per cent of aquatic life had disappeared from the face of earth. Was it true?

Arunabh told her many such facts. Most of those, she could not grasp. Arunabh told her people played the key element in this destruction. With the enthusiasm that they cut trees, they never showed the same while replanting them. The earth was in grave danger. Whenever Rishi and Arunabh met, they discussed such topics. She would get scared. But still, she liked listening to them. She tried to understand the gravity of the situation and contribute something to this earth. But what could a semi-literate girl do?

It was time to cook. But salt?

She didn't see Rishi the whole day. Where was he? Rishi spoke very less. Probably from the music school, he went straight to the guest house.

She felt a little hurt. He could have at least called.

The house was in complete silence. Had it not been for the exams, her brothers would have teased Spotty and put the house on fire by now. Realising the situation, Spotty, too, remained quiet. Whenever the wind and the falling leaves made a rustling sound, he barked once or twice. Probably, he scolded the trees and asked the wind not to disturb them.

Right, Rishi said the trees had a soul. Rishi could talk to the trees. What does he tell them? Rishi's father was killed when he went to stop timber smugglers. His mother died soon after. Probably, that's why he spoke to the trees, to share his grief. He shared a deep bond with the jungle.

She had no answer. But she deeply believed that the destiny brought them, the two orphans, together.

There was very little kerosene in the stove. But she felt lazy to start a fire in the clay hearth. She had used wood to cook lunch.

She started the stove. Just then, the phone started ringing.

Running to the bed, she picked up the mobile.

'Lakhimi, how are you all?' Hridayananda's familiar voice came through the line.

'We are fine, sir. Are you alright?'

'Yes, I am okay. We are government servants. We have to carry on with our work in any jungle. But I do miss you all. I miss Kaziranga,' Hridayananda sounded sad.

Lakhimi did not know what to say next.

'Sir, take care of yourself. Everyone here talks about you,' she said in a calm voice.

'Yes, yes. I will, Lakhimi. I will come for your wedding. Ask Rishi to call me when he is free. I have been trying to call him, but could not get through. Now, I am going into the jungle.'

Lakhimi started saying something, but the phone got disconnected. She let out a sigh. Hridayananda's face came to her mind. Not just she, but everybody at Pamua missed him. The man, who loved Rishi so much, is now in another jungle called Manas. She hoped he was happy there.

Someone opened the gate.

Spotty, who was sleeping in the verandah, ran to the gate. Giving out a few loud barks, it started cooing. Must be someone it knew, Lakhimi gathered.

Must be Rishi.

A tide of happiness washed over her. Rearranging her *chaddar*, she picked up the lamp and opened the door. A while ago, the electricity went off. It was a regular affair. It's only recently a few families in the village got electricity connection. But it was of no use. It was as bad as not having electricity at all.

Rishi was carrying a few bags in both hands. There, Spotty in its happiness was jumping around, making it difficult for Rishi to walk.

'Hey, stop, stop. I will give you food,' Rishi tried to assure Spotty.

'Lakhimi, have you cooked? Bipul has sent meat curry and sabzi from the guest house. You just need to cook rice,' said Rishi, handing her the packets.

Lakhimi felt uncomfortable. She protested every time he brought food. But Rishi put the blame on Bipul.

Hesitantly, she accepted it. A meek protest escaped her lips.

Lakhimi looked at Rishi. His handsome face looked tired. He must have slogged the whole day.

'Come inside. Wash your face. I am making tea,' Lakhimi offered.

Rishi sat in a wooden chair.

Only then, he realised how tired he was. Lakhimi's pampering had reduced the tiredness to a certain extent. He remembered his mother. She was as loving as Lakhimi. Even their voices were somewhat similar.

Rishi had no clue that Lakhimi saw the reflection of her mother in his face. His face cut and complexion bore some similarities with her mother. She never told that to Rishi. Probably, she never would.

Placing water and a *gamosa* at the backyard for Rishi, she went to the kitchen to make tea. Her heart was singing. A sweet tune from a flute came floating around. She swayed to that tune…

It was drizzling.

It rained last night—rained cats and dogs. Climatic change. Usually, it didn't rain during this time of the year.

Amal's huge SUV was parked outside Rishi's house.

Amal was waiting at the guest house. He had the company of Arunabh and Yashodhar. As soon as Rishi was ready, they would head towards Guwahati.

It was the starting of a new chapter for Rishi—with his wife! He was married for six days. The bride had moved into his village house. But she was yet to see the family house in Guwahati.

The wedding that took place in Kaziranga was attended by Rishi's relatives and friends. But everybody couldn't come, especially the old and the busy ones. Taking everything into consideration, his uncles were planning to throw a welcome party for the newly-weds.

From Delhi, Amal had come to Kaziranga after resting for a couple of days in Guwahati. Arunabh, too, took a leave for Rishi's wedding. Amal da, as usual, assumed the role of a guardian. The villagers worked day and night for the wedding. The boys from the Jeep Safari Association had made a community kitchen in Lakhimi's backyard. They served khichidi to one and all, whoever visited the bride's house. Everybody enjoyed to the hilt.

As per the plan, the students of Rishi's music school and their guardians at Bokakhat came as baratis with the bridegroom. Rishi was clueless as to who was doing what.

Amal was the guardian for both. Arunabh was with Rishi like his shadow. He was Rishi's best man. He was the only childhood friend Rishi had.

The whole village transformed itself for this wedding. The roads were swept, many households pruned their gardens and cleaned their front yards. Two days before the wedding, the villagers took out their fineries and added to the festive mood. Lakhimi was tired greeting everyone, but she didn't have to worry about any of the arrangements.

Even with everyone around, Lakhimi shed tears remembering her parents. All three, Lakhimi and her brothers, huddled together and cried whenever they were alone.

Rishi, too, remembered his parents. Looking at the emotional upheaval these orphans were going through, Amal da and Arunabh, too, could not control their tears.

'Destiny, you see. Who knows what's written in one's destiny?' Amal consoled them like an elder member of the family.

Bipul started putting the luggage into the SUV. The boot of the car was full. But there were still a couple of bags to be loaded.

Lakhimi's friends helped her get ready—like a bride. With the *pat-muga-mixed* silk *mekhela-chaddar* and make-up, she looked enchanting. She was glowing. Her friends kept teasing her and that made her turn red. They all laughed out loud. One of them whispered something to her and Lakhimi ran away, the blood rushing to her face.

Till they were in Guwahati, a distant aunt of Lakhimi would stay there and take care of the house. Two of her friends from the neigbourhood would keep her aunt company. Bipul would stay at Rishi's house. Everything would be taken care of.

Rishi checked the luggage one last time. Bipul was an efficient boy. Keeping everything neatly, he was standing by the vehicle.

It was time to leave.

Taking the cue from Rishi, Lakhimi's friends formed a circle around her and slowly took her to the car. They all chanted the ritualistic *uruli*. They didn't let Lakhimi feel that she was an orphan. They followed every step of a traditional wedding.

Lakhimi sat in the car. Both the brothers, too, got up. Amal would sit next to the driver's seat. Rishi, Lakhimi and her youngest brother occupied the front row of the back seats. The other brother, Yashodhar and Arunabh would sit at the back row.

Amal had brought along Yashodhar from Guwahati. Yasho was his lucky mascot. Amal had firmly believed that just because he got Yashodhar along when starting the resort, it was completed without any hiccups and was doing good business so far. And then, Rishi and Arunabh were also close to Yashodhar. So, Amal ordered Yasho to accompany him for the wedding. Yashodhar liked the attention. A great deal of the year was spent paying flute on the streets of Guwahati. Only Amal took him to different places. Thanks to Amal, Yashodhar was having quite a few admirers for his music.

The vehicle started moving.

Separated from her friends, Lakhimi started sobbing. A new life had started for her. Lakhimi knew that she would come back to this village, but who knows? What if Rishi changes his mind! Now, her life was connected to Rishi's.

The villagers came out of their houses to see them off. They waved at the newly-weds. With teary eyes and a slight smile, Lakhimi acknowledged their love and affection.

The driver turned the car towards the *namghar*. Lakhimi wanted to offer a small prayer before leaving. After that, the car moved towards the guest house.

Amal was talking to a few people in front of his guest house. The new, young ranger, who had replaced Hridayananda, was also a part of the group. Actually, the man had turned out to be a resident of Kharghuli in Guwahati. Amal didn't know him earlier, but once they were introduced, they hit it off. This young and energetic boy called Banajit Chaudhary had recently come back from Dehradun after a special training on how to employ technology effectively to protect the forest.

Hridayananda, who had known Banajit from before, was all praise for him. He told everyone how competent a forest officer Banajit was. Kaziranga was in good hands, he told everyone he met at the wedding.

The government, too, had realised that minus the full support of the public, those forest-protection plans were meaningless. That's why the central minister had sought active participation from the public. Banajit was also emphasising on that point. People said that Banajit was in direct contact with the central and state forest ministers. But nobody dared to ask him. Straightforward and aggressive, Banajit reminded them of a wrestler.

Rishi got down from the car. Bipul and the old accountant were given the charge of running the resort. That should not be a problem. As it was off season, there were not many guests.

Checking out the important things and giving suggestions to the young employees, Rishi, too, joined the group.

'Are you ready, Rishi? We are already late. Let's not delay any more. We would reach by mid-day,' Amal rushed.

Arunabh led Yashodhar to his seat. The people who were standing there, congratulated Rishi. All the employees came out to see them off.

As the clock struck 11:00 am, the driver started the vehicle. It sped off within seconds.

Lakhimi had covered her head with her *chaddar*. Rishi asked her not to, but she did not listen. Her friends taught her what to do. She valued tradition.

The road was empty.

'I am hungry, Arunabh. I had my breakfast a long time back. After all that talking I had to do, it's natural to feel hungry,' Amal said lightly, but he meant it.

'Oh, God. Alright! We will travel some distance, then eat whatever you want to. Let us at least cross Kaziranga,' Arunabh retorted. But then Amal's hunger pangs were legendary.

Yes, they were leaving Kaziranga. Rishi realised then that in the last two and a half years, all three had never left Kaziranga together. At any point of time, at least one of them was around. This journey was, indeed, different. Rishi felt uneasy. Would Kaziranga mind if they all left her behind?

Arunabh was trying to click photographs from the moving car. He was not a pro. But photography had been a hobby since his college days. Recently, he had brought a powerful camera from abroad. With that now, he was capturing various moods of the forest. He has been clicking thousands of pictures. But still, he could not have enough of it. Today, he clicked the bride and the groom too, taking a detour from nature photography. Sometimes, Rishi would just turn his face and that would invite Arunabh's scolding.

Amal tried to ignore it, humming a song by Dr Bhupen Hazarika that was about Kaziranga. Yashodhar sometimes laughed out loud as he listened to Arunabh's and Rishi's banter. Only Lakhimi and her two brothers remained quiet.

The vehicle was a big one. But Amal asked the driver not to speed.

Arunabh's mobile started ringing. He did not feel like picking it up. He looked at the caller id. It was an unknown number. He received it reluctantly.

It was from his lawyer in Guwahati. His case would have a hearing next week. His lawyer had assured him that the forest department, which had filed the defamation case against his magazine, would lose the case hands down.

In fact, the inefficiency of the forest department would be exposed.

'The forest department is nothing but a toothless entity. God knows what would happen to the honest officers, but those corrupt ones would fall into a trap now.' Thinking of that, Arunabh felt self-assured.

Arunabh recalled how Kaziranga's forest department had involved the residents of 110 local villages to form 30 EDCs, eco-development committees. It started somewhere around 2002. The aim was to protect the jungle, and at the same time, induce economic development of the villagers. But those remained only on papers. The forest department did not allow these EDCs to function, because they threatened to upset the power equations for many corrupt officials. Like Banajit Chaudhary had put it, only if these committees were made active, can many crimes in Kaziranga be stopped.

When Arunabh had asked this intelligent officer about the case against his magazine, Banajit just gave him a strange smile. Arunabh could not fathom the hidden meaning the smile concealed.

This particular patch of the road was dotted with potholes. The vehicle was moving at a slow speed. All the occupants inside the car could feel the jerking. The constant jerks put a stop to Arunabh's trend of thoughts. How the mind wanders…

'There are so many jungles in Assam, but what makes Kaziranga so attractive, Arunabh?' Amal looked back to ask, as the car slowed down.

Arunabh was just about to freeze a particular scene into his camera, but stopped as he heard the question.

'Kaziranga is the most beautiful because of its diversity, Amal da. Perhaps because this is the place where the idea of forest preservation germinated. It goes through so many problems—right from rhino killings to legalisation of land holdings, but still it has not lost its charm,' Arunabh replied in a matter-of-fact tone.

Then, on second thought, Arunabh asked Amal, 'Amal da, how many jungles have you seen in Assam? Each one has its own charm. But maybe because you have a resort here which is getting you a good profit, you are biased towards Kaziranga.'

'Shut up! Do you call mine a resort? In comparison to those big ones, mine is like a fly in front of an elephant. And did I open it to earn money? I am actually doing social service by opening the guest house. In my old days, I will settle down here and meditate,' Amal was irritated.

The situation became serious. Rishi, without a rhyme or reason, started combing his beard with his fingers. Yashodhar, not knowing what to do, started looking here and there.

'Yasho, you could sing a song,' Rishi proposed in his calm voice.

Yashodhar opened his mouth to say something, but before he could do it, the driver pressed the horn with all his strength and applied the brake. After screeching for about two metres, the SUV stopped.

The suddenness of the incident took everyone by surprise. Everyone looked in front of them.

A wild buffalo had crossed the road at a lightening speed. It probably got separated from the herd. Or, probably, it got scared for some reason and just bolted. Usually, no wild animal crossed the road during the daytime. They had crossed Bagori long back. There were no other animals in sight. So what could have happened to this one?

The driver was a young fellow. He has been with Amal for a long time. He was an expert driver. But this incident unnerved him. Especially as the engine shut down.

'Here, drink this. It's nothing. You saved that buffalo,' said Amal, offering the bottle of water which he was holding.

The vehicle started again.

The trees and bushes on both sides were running in the opposite direction.

Though Lakhimi and her brothers lived in Kaziranga, they had never seen it from the outside. Lakhimi had once gone to

Guwahati for her father's treatment, but her brothers had never gone out.

The three pairs of eyes looked mesmerised as they drank from the beauty of their beloved Kaziranga. They could not have enough of it.

They soon approached the Mahi Miri Peak. It lay on the left side of the road. Long ago, an aware young man, Mahi Chandra Miri had started a mission to save the forest. He had many dreams for its flora and fauna.

'Who named this peak Mahi Miri, Arunabh?' Amal asked in a mellow voice.

Arunabh knew about it. He had learnt the history of Kaziranga by heart.

'Way back in 1939, this man in khaki shorts and a shirt thought of preserving Kaziranga. He devised a strategy of saving humans and animals from the flood. Because of people like him, Kaziranga exists on the world map. When Mahendra Mohan Choudhury was the chief minister, he dedicated that peak to Mahi Chandra Miri.' Arunabh narrated the history of the place with the precision of a professional tourist guide.

'Huh! What happened? The government thought it had done enough by putting the Mahi Miri signboard. Now, look there is a resort coming along just under the peak,' Amal retorted, even before Arunabh's narration could be completed.

The car crossed the peak. Everyone looked at it. It was devoid of any green cover. A symbol of utter neglect. The people who ought to see it in this condition, probably close their eyes when they cross this area.

The boundary of Kaziranga was drawing closer. After covering some distance, they would cross it and enter the populated areas—probably, in about half an hour.

This patch of road had a few houses on both sides. Leaving behind the tea gardens, they noticed the big trees on both sides. There were many elephant corridors. The speed limit was fixed for the traffic.

Yasho had not forgotten Rishi's request. As soon as the speed of the car was reduced and the sound of the engine subsided, he started singing—

> The inside of the earth would become home one day…
> Oh, my mind, why make a house?
> The life would leave the body
> Oh, my mind…
> No bother, sister, family would be around
> The only companion would be the sin and virtue…
> Why make a house?
> Oh, my mind…

Though the lyrics had no support from the tunes of a *dotara*, each word managed to touch the listener's heart. It was such a sad tune, everybody started feeling empty. Lakhimi and her brothers started missing their parents. The realisation of how temporary life was, hung heavy inside the car.

These days, Yasho sang mostly *baaul*. He said the underlying philosophy of it was as good as religious texts. He sang the last few lines again and again. As if he wanted to tell them the truth of life.

The song was finally over. But the heaviness persisted for a long time.

'Hey, Yasho. Why do you sing such sad songs? It hurts. It's depressing. Don't sing such heavy songs,' after a long time, Amal opened his mouth, expressing his helplessness.

Yashodhar, whose eyes were filled with only darkness, smiled like an idiot. He said in a soft voice, 'I sang because Rishi babu asked me to. And this is the biggest truth of life…no, the ultimate truth of life.'

Amal turned back to say something in retort, but after looking at Yashodhar, said nothing. He turned his face away.

As they reached Kanchanjuri, a spot for tourists to watch wild animals, Rishi asked the driver to halt.

Rishi was taking the lead.

'Lakhimi, get down. This is where people watch the wild animals roaming inside Kaziranga. Come and watch.' Saying this, Rishi got down from the car and held the door open for the others. Lakhimi and her brothers got down too.

Amal welcomed this break. He was craving for a cigarette. He and Arunabh went far and standing under a tree, Amal lit up a stick. Yasho didn't want to get down.

Lakhimi and her brothers had never seen the park from a tourist's angle. She did not even know how many varieties of animals lived in Kaziranga. She admired those stray animals that entered the village once in a while, but was scared of them too. She could not stand the sight of a tiger after her father was attacked by one. Even the name was enough to remind her of the ugly sight of the wound on her father's shoulder.

But today, the new avatar of Kaziranga held her captive. She knew what a tourist saw in this wilderness. Rishi kept explaining everything like an expert guide. It was a new experience for her.

Immediately from the highway, spread a green grass cover which extended as far as her eyes could see. In the sunlit vastness, roamed several rhinos, an elephant, a wild boar and a herd of spotted deers. As a flock of birds flew away, another flock came down to claim the earth. There was a small rhino trying to match steps with the mother. It must have been only a few days old. Lakhimi and her brothers loved the scene. Rishi, on a side glance, noticed their happiness. He had seen them smiling after a long time. He removed the strap of his binocular and handed it over to them. All three got busy with it. They chatted merrily about their beloved Kaziranga.

Rishi let out a sigh of relief. This is what he wanted. He had learnt to love the forest because of his parents. He did fall in love with it eventually. Lakhimi and her brothers were born amidst the richness of nature. But the hardship of life had never allowed them to understand or appreciate their surroundings. They never had this opportunity to go deep into it. Whatever little they saw and experienced, they knew it to be the truth.

Rishi walked a little ahead. From the direction they had come from, a few metres behind them, just at the foothills, was an area of tall segun trees. From far, it looked like a lush green painting by some artist. Step by step, he walked towards the tall trees. The shadow of the trees soothed his tired body.

Leaning onto a big tree, Rishi stood there. The mild breeze rejuvenated his body and soul. Time stopped. Everything became quiet, serene.

'Are you leaving, Rishi? You are leaving us for good?' somebody whispered. A deep voice, full of love.

He got a shock. He moved his half-closed eyes to find the source of the voice. Who could it be?

A wind blew away the dry leaves. He heard a soft giggle.

'Don't forget us, Rishi. Come back soon. Congratulations and best wishes for your new life.' It was the same loving voice, barely audible.

Just above Rishi's head, a heteluka bird sang a strange song. The cacophony of the flock which flew over him, conveyed so much.

But Rishi was still thinking about the deep, caring voice. He stopped breathing and closed his eyes. Now he was sure. Yes… it was his friend's voice, with who he conversed day and night, played with; whose song took away his pain, in whose whistles he could feel his parents' love. Yes, it's her…his Kaziranga. His loving friend, his soulmate.

Rishi's face got a golden glow at this realisation.

He embraced the tree he was leaning onto. Rubbing his bearded cheeks to it, Rishi said, 'No, how could I ever forget you all? You are a part of my existence, my entity. For all eternity, I love you. I will come back to you soon…'

The whispers continued…

Oblivious to the rest of the world, Rishi kept talking softly as he held onto the tree, tightly. In his heart, a symphony started playing. A ballad or a simple, happy song, he could not tell. He was like a child, half-asleep, holding onto the tree.

In a trembling voice, Rishi continued, 'We are here…So will you…You will live forever, Kaziranga…so long…'

After sometime, everyone got back to their respective seats in the SUV. Making a light roaring sound, the car started its onward journey. Within seconds, it picked up its speed.

Nobody uttered a single word.

Everyone, looking out of the window, was lost in their own thoughts. They had crossed the boundary of Kaziranga. The love for the forest seeped into every inch of their being. As they moved forward, Kaziranga moved further and further behind. The sun overhead showered all its light and energy to illuminate Mother Earth.

The end

Glossary

Bargeet: devotional song associated with the Vaishnavite sect of Assam

Bauul: a form of Bengali folksong

Bhogali Bihu: the harvest festival which involves feasting and merry-making. It is also called Magh Bihu

Bordeuta: the Assamese kinship term for father's elder brother

Bordoisila: high-speed wind accompanied by hailstorm, usually occurs in February–March

Bota: a traditional paan thali

Chaddar: a garment to cover the upper half of the body

Chang ghar: a house, which is usually made of bamboo and hay, built on a raised platform of poles, for protection from flood and wild animals

Dhol: a traditional drum

Dogar: a musical instrument

Dotara: a musical instrument with two strings

Durri: carpet

Ektara: a musical instrument with one string

Endi chaddar: a shawl, mostly worn by men

Fagun: month in Indian calendar, mid February–mid March; a very dry season

Gamosa: a piece of woven cloth with floral designs used as a towel

Ghila pitha: a delicacy made with rice flour and jaggery, usually prepared and relished during Bihu

Ghungroo: anklet worn on the feet by classical Indian dancers

Jugalbandi: a duet of sorts

Kahudi: pungent mustard sauce

Kati Bihu: one of the three Bihu festivals celebrated in Assam, observed in mid-October. People light a diya and pray for a good harvest in front of the Holy Basil/Tulsi plant

Khar: curry made with alkali or soda

Khartal: a musical instrument played with devotional songs

Kirtan: Holy Scripture

Magh Bihu: the harvest festival, which involves feasting and merry-making. It is also called Bhogali Bihu

Matsya Sprasha: the ceremonial eating of fish to break the fast after one's death

Mekhela-chaddar: traditional Assamese two-piece attire worn by women

Mezi: a tower made of hay and firewood which is set fire to on Magh Bihu

Muda: a cane stool

Naam: prayer

Namghar: a community prayer hall

Patal: a summer vegetable

Patta: legal record of land holdings

Pat-muga: an exotic yarn extracted from silkworm pupae raised on mulberry leaves, and used to make traditional attire

Peda: a variety of sweet

Pepa: hornpipe musical instrument, usually made with the horn of a buffalo

Pitha: a delicacy made from rice powder

Riha mekhela: chador made of muga silk, popular during the old times

Saunf: fennel seeds

Shradh: a ceremony held on one's passing away

Shukla Panchami: fifth day of the Full Moon; an auspicious day

Taal: a two-piece musical instrument made of brass metal

Tadka: the frying of spices in hot oil, which makes a sizzling sound

Taka: a musical instrument made of bamboo, played mostly as a part of Bihu festivities

Tandava: dance associated with the wrath of Lord Shiva

Tenga: a sour dish made of tomatoes or green leafy vegetables, along with fish

Thapona: an altar

Til: sesame seeds

Tirpal: a tent

Uruli: a ritualistic sound made with the tongue, usually during weddings

Xorai: a tray on stands, made of brass or bell-metal, used for offerings in worship

Synopsis

A bored, rich, middle-aged businessman planning to open a resort; a journalist trying to break a few sensational stories; a vagabond musician finally finding his love and muse, Kaziranga provides the perfect background for ideas to collide, tears to roll and happiness to soar…

As Amal Duara shifts his focus from the concrete jungle of Guwahati to the pristine environs of Kaziranga, where he plans to build an eco-sensitive, culture-friendly resort, he involves three people in his core team—his cousin, Arunabh, who is the correspondent of a Bengaluru-based newsmagazine; Arunabh's childhood friend Rishi, a musician who makes Pamua, a village that touches the boundary of the national park, his temporary home and Hridayananda, Amal's friend from his college days who is now a range officer with the forest department.

What follows is a riveting story with unpredictable twists and turns. As Amal Duara constructs the foundation of his resort, brick by brick, Kaziranga reveals itself, layer by layer.

This is not the Kaziranga National Park that is shown to tourists as they go around in a jeep or on an elephant safari. It is very different. This is a battleground where fierce fights between forest guards and poachers break out at the drop of a hat, and not always resulting in the victory of the righteous. It is a political arena where nobody can be trusted. It is an ecosystem where people and animals do not always live in harmony. It is also a place where human settlers are not just fighting against poverty and the constant threat of eviction, but also encroachments of their so-called 'land' by illegal migrants.

Amidst the nail-biting suspense of midnight raids on poachers, devastation caused by flood and attacks by wild animals, a beautiful love story germinates—the confirmed bachelor, Rishi, falls in love with Lakhimi and marries her to make the village of Pamua his home. Amal Duara manages to build his resort, thus allowing modernity to enter Pamua, which had until then been frozen in time.

About the author

Dileep Chandan is a senior journalist working in Assam for the last 30 years. A student of English Literature (MA from Gauhati University), he started his journalistic career with *Ajir Somoy* magazine and later moved to *The Sunday* (now defunct), a publication from the ABP Group, Kolkata.

He has been editing *Asam Bani*, a 61-year-old newspaper published by the Assam Tribune Group, from 1997 onwards. Dileep Chandan has been awarded the Sarojini Naidu Prize for Best Reporting on Women and Panchayati Raj (Delhi), Harivansh Rai Bachchan Award for Journalism (Mumbai), The Sentinel Rural Reporting Award, K.K. Birla Foundation Fellowship (Delhi *Hindustan Times*), National Foundation for India fellowship (Delhi), among others. He is also a member of several national and regional organisations and a guest lecturer in journalism at several universities.

He is also a popular novelist and writer in Assamese language with some 18 books on various facets of society and the North-East to his credit. Among them are biographies, essays and novels. His new novel, *Kazirangar Ballad*, has been awarded the prestigious Sayed Abdul Malik Literary Award in Assam. His first novel, *Majulit Etiya Godhuli*, was based on the Majuli river-island., The novel is now in its third edition with several thousand copies sold. This book deals with the problems faced by the biggest river-island in the world, Majuli. His other novels are based on various issues such as insurgency that have been plaguing the region for a long time. He is currently involved in research work for his next novel.

About the translator

Parbina Rashid hails from Guwahati and grew up during the turbulent times of the Assam Agitation of the '80s, which was fought against the problem of illegal migration from Bangladesh, and later, the rise of terrorism, which still continues to plague the state. After her schooling in Guwahati, Parbina left for Aligarh Muslim University (AMU), from where she completed her graduation. She later joined Jamia Millia Islamia (JMI) for her masters.

She started her career as a Project Fellow under the Women's Studies Research Centre at the Gauhati University and contributed two research papers titled 'Dowry Deaths in Assam: A Few Case Studies from Guwahati Municipal Area' and 'Women as Decision Maker', which were published in a complied volume titled *Status of Women & Social Change* by the Gauhati University.

At present, she is working with *The Tribune* and is based in Chandigarh. She writes a column called Beyond Chicken Neck, reviews books, writes opinion pieces and middles for *The Tribune*.

One of her translated short stories, 'No Man's Land', has appeared in *The Little Magazine*, edited by Antara Dev Sen.

Parbina has also translated stories for *The Sentinel* (Assam) and Nezine.com, an online magazine. She has translated and compiled a book, *Echoes from the Valley*, which is an anthology of short stories by 11 Assamese writers. Her second translated book, *If a River and Other Stories*, is a collection of short stories by Sahitya Akademi-awardee Dr Kula Saikia, DGP, Assam. While *Echoes from the Valley* was published in 2017, *If a River and Other Stories* was launched in February 2018 at the Brahmaputra Literary Festival, Assam.